THE STARS IN THEIR EYES

KRISTY GARDNER

THE STARS IN THEIR EYES

KRISTY GARDNER

City Owl
Press

This book is a work of fiction. Names, characters, places, and incidents either are products of the author's imagination or are used fictitiously. Any resemblance to actual events or locales or persons, living or dead, is entirely coincidental and not intended by the author.

THE STARS IN THEIR EYES
The Broken Stars, Book 1

CITY OWL PRESS
www.cityowlpress.com

All Rights reserved. Except as permitted under the U.S. Copyright Act of 1976, no part of this publication may be reproduced, distributed, or transmitted in any form or by any means, or stored in a database or retrieval system, without the prior consent and permission of the publisher.

Copyright © 2022 by Kristy Gardner.

Cover Design by MiblArt. All stock photos licensed appropriately.

Edited by Danielle DeVor.

For information on subsidiary rights, please contact the publisher at info@cityowlpress.com.

Print Edition ISBN: 978-1-64898-194-4

Digital Edition ISBN: 978-1-64898-192-0

Printed in the United States of America

PRAISE FOR KRISTY GARDNER

"*The Stars in Their Eyes* is chilling, thrilling, and full of emotional depth that will leave you on the edge of your seat and questioning your own reality." — *Madison Lawson, author of The Registration*

"Visceral, creepy, and disturbing. Dark horror fans will love this startling debut." — *Chana Porter, author of The Seep*

"A juicily twisted path through what it means to be human, what it means to be alien, and, above all, when our world is lost, what it means to find home in each other." — *Ann Fraistat, author of What We Harvest*

"At once exhilarating and philosophical, this debut dark sci-fi is a tour de force of twists and turns." — *Sarina Dahlan, author of Reset*

"A gripping tale of survival. The Stars in their Eyes shows us the dark, violent side of humanity, but also the promise—however out of reach it may seem—of something brighter." — *N.C. Scrimgeour, author of The Waystations Series*

"A pacy, visceral and action-packed romp through a vividly depicted broken future. Resident Evil meets War of the Worlds in this compelling debut." — *Kate Murray, author of We Who Hunt The Hollow*

"Heartbreaking and heartwarming, this book has great chaos and all the feels. It's sci-fi and adventure and romance and a must-read!" — *K.C. Harper, author of Marked For Grace*

For the universe.
And all the star-blazing adventures it holds.

CHAPTER ONE

Calay was shattered.

She felt it. Everywhere. Deep within her heart. Her mind. Her spirit.

Her left tibia.

Something wasn't right.

Every time she moved, a raw grinding forged its way through her leg. Bone against bone. And enough pain to make her wince long enough to contemplate...nothing. Nothing at all. It hurt. Everywhere.

Between stabbing torrents of full body agony, the cold of the concrete penetrated her soul. She pressed herself against the floor. The hardness of it a welcome retreat—and somewhat alien feeling—from the heat searing through every inch of her being. The recalescence of her broken body a brutal admonition of the misery that came with living. Of living, itself.

It was all that ever was. All that ever would be.

Breathe in. Breathe out. Just breathe. Do. Not. Panic.

With every inhale, small particles assaulted the back of her throat. She coughed. Each shudder sent ripples of pain through her chest. Her fingertips grazed the floor, coming to rest in a powdery substance. Granular and smelling sweetly of pine.

"Sawdust," she gasped and it gathered in the back of her throat. She coughed again.

"Sit up," she gasped.

Fighting against slowly choking to death on the dust, Calay pushed her body upright. She leaned back and surveyed her surroundings.

It was dark.

Her head ached.

Her eyes too.

It was like she'd downed three too many gin and sodas and was trying to make sense of her surroundings through the bottom of a shot glass.

Hell, it wasn't like she hadn't done that before; she could do this.

"Hello..." she called into the murky blur in front of her.

Nothing.

"Tess?" She waited. "Tess! Is anybody there?"

Silence.

She was alone.

A nondescript stickiness welded her eyes half-shut. Calay brought her hand to her head and felt a puffiness where her right temple should have been. Her hand traced the sticky substance across her forehead, down the flesh of her cheek, past the ridge of her collarbone, and into the large, dark puddle below. It was like she was sitting in a black hole brimming with sawdust, stars.

I'm lost in space.

Between labored gasps, she tried to focus her eyes. The black hole she was sitting in wasn't a black hole. It wasn't black at all. It was red.

Really red.

Only one thing was that shade of red. She'd seen enough of it over the last four years, that was for sure. Since The Change began.

Blood.

A funny thought occurred to her that it was her blood.

And then she had a more serious realization that wasn't funny at all.

It was everywhere.

Furiously, she wiped at herself, madly clearing the coagulated liquid from her face and eyes as best she could. It clung to her eyelashes, stained her lips, and matted her hair to her ear. Dried bits flaked off in chunks, creating a spectacle of falling paint chips.

If painting was self-discovery and every good artist paints what he is, Calay had painted a mess of her internal workings all over the damn place. That is, if twentieth-century Abstract Impressionist art meant anything anymore. But it didn't.

Don't think about that now. There's nothing you can do about that. No choices to be made. Focus on what you can control.

"So what *can* I control?"

She tried to open her eyes again. Clearer. An improvement.

Spots of red still garnished her vision, but she could see more now. Aside from the darkness, small rectangular windows splayed light across the floor in tidy, broken cross sections. Dust danced midair like woodland fairies lost—or trapped—in a maze. Through a thin door, she spied stacks of large crates littering a far wall and beside them, a plastic sheet dividing the doorway to what she assumed was another room. Before The Change, the wooden rafters in the ceiling would have been home to cooing pigeons and families of sweet mice. Now they were cold and barren, littered with abandoned cobwebs and dark shadows. Who knew what roosted up there? When The Change started, even rodents knew enough to get the hell out of Dodge. Or they were dead. Like everyone else.

And the room–it was big. Bigger than big. *It's fucking huge.*

A warehouse.

"Where am I?" She coughed. She recounted her last steps, trying to remember something. Anything. It seemed she'd spent half her life trying to recount why she was in the situations she found herself in. She was no angel, but she wasn't worse than anyone else, was she? In the small town where she'd spent most of her childhood, kids got into trouble all the time; there wasn't much else to do. A little too much to drink on a Friday night. Driving a little too fast on the backroads. Enjoying a little too many rendezvous in her twenties. And thirties. But she'd always found her way back, hadn't she? She'd always made it home. To her apartment. To herself. And eventually, to Tess.

Tess.

Calay's heart fluttered at the thought of her. She was happy and in love with Tess the morning of The Change. She'd had no idea the world was about to literally come crashing down around her. It had been a morning like any other Sunday morning—an ocean of cozy sheets and not nearly enough kisses. There were never enough kisses. Their breath had pooled on each other's necks while the sun wrapped their naked bodies in the warmth of a late Spring sunrise. The skin on Tess's thighs was warm. Tender. Familiar.

Tess released a gravelly moan as Calay's tongue plunged deeper. Her fingers, too. She took her time. There was no rush; she wanted to explore every inch of Tess. Every morning. For the rest of their lives.

The world would wait.

Calay looked up at Tess, her eyes shining. Tess took Calay's face in her hands.

"Come here, Cay," Tess smiled, bringing Calay up to meet her mouth. Their hair intertwined as they kissed in the sparkling morning light, their soft bellies pressed flat together.

The feeling of Tess wasn't new to Calay. When they had got together five years ago, Tess immediately felt like home. But her body had been foreign. It was the first time Calay had taken a woman to bed. Or rather, they'd taken each other to bed. Calay was nervous and awkward; Tess was confident and gentle. Until she wasn't. It didn't take long for their passion to rise and consume them that first night. And through every first since.

"You get all my remaining firsts." Calay beamed between kisses.

They were made to love each other, if you believed in that kind of thing. To save each other. From the obligations of life, and the expectations they'd never live up to. From their own vices–and Calay had many. She wasn't in denial that she tended to drink too much or that she'd faltered in her relationship with her parents.

Poor decision making was a habit for her, and she often relied on Tess's stability. She was impulsive, and Tess accepted that–Tess accepted *her*. They were two halves of a whole, a team, and had been for much of their adult lives. Once they'd left the rural community in which they'd grown up, they'd found a six-story walk-up in the city at the end of a tree-lined street with cobblestone sidewalks. It was new and exciting and quaint and absolutely charming.

It was a place to call their own.

It was also small and old. The cupboards were chipped and often bare, but their hearts were full. Over the years the linoleum floor peeled, and the curtains they'd foraged at the local thrift-store faded with sun, while their relationship fastened and grew into something less than perfect. Tess could be hard at times and Calay, stubborn. Their fights–loud and sometimes lasting for days–embedded themselves in the foundation of the apartment. A chipped doorframe that had been slammed too strongly and a shattered mirror tucked behind the water heater were evidence of their passion. Once, the proof made its way out of the fridge, past Calay, and through their fourth-story window, landing at the feet of a neighbor below. That was the last time the freezer ever saw a container of Chunky Monkey.

But they always made up. Their love for each other pulled them back together as much as it drove them to argue. They were strong women and stronger together.

They liked their neighborhood. Here no one furrowed their brow at two women holding hands. Folks didn't gossip as they passed through the supermarket. Neighbors occasionally even invited them over for dinner parties, which they almost always attended, grateful for the company and a hot meal. Eventually, the dated apartment with the tattered orange sofa and clunky TV became not just a respite but a home. As much a home to them as they were to each other. It was all theirs.

"Make love to me," Calay gasped between breaths.

Tess rolled Calay onto her back and gathered her full breasts in her hands. Her teeth gently teased her nipples which rose to attention. Calay giggled breathlessly.

"I need you, T..."

Tess moaned back in response as her mouth made its way down Calay's stomach, her hands cupping her mound, fingers dancing over her clit.

"Yes, please," Calay moaned.

"Tell me you love me."

"I love you."

"Do you love me?" Tess grinned and cocked an eyebrow.

"I fucking love you!" Calay laughed.

Tess's fingers plunged inside Calay at the very moment the city exploded around them.

It sounded like a jet engine crashed through the wall of their apartment. It felt like it too. The room shook violently. Both women screamed, jerking backward, severing the physical connection between them. Their eyes widened in fear. Calay clamped her hands down over her ears. The entire building vibrated under the weight of the noise. Neither one of them knew what to do, so they crouched, cowering with the sheets tangled around them.

The noise stopped.

Tess looked at Calay, her eyes wide, "What the fuck was that?"

"I...I don't know," Calay stammered.

Moments passed. Then minutes. Neither one of them willing—or able—to move.

"It had to be...was it an earthquake?" Tess pressed.

Calay shook her head. Her legs trembled too.

"Calay, what the hell just happened?"

"I don't know Tess! I know as much as you do. Maybe we should turn on the televisi—"

The noise started again.

It was metal grating against metal and some kind of deep whirring like they were inside a car compactor. Only louder. So much louder. The building shook more violently this time, and the room seemed to tilt on its axis before righting itself, only to shift at an even more severe angle the other way.

Then it fell.

Calay shuddered. Shook off the memory. As she peered across the warehouse a chill wound its way around her spine. The cold, hard truth was unmistakable: she was no longer in her apartment; she never would be again. Still, Tess should be there with her. Where one went, the other followed. So why wasn't she? After The Change the stakes became clear:

survive together or die. Calay couldn't bring herself to think about what their separation might mean. For her. For Tess.

* * *

CALAY DIDN'T THINK SHE'D BE HERE. IN THIS WAREHOUSE. AT thirty-two. Broken, bloodied, and begging for her life. She didn't think she'd wake up one morning and have her entire life turned upside down. Or her apartment. But that was exactly what happened four years ago. She didn't think everything they'd built together would burn up in the Dumpster fire they had once called Seattle. Or Earth. She didn't think she'd lose everything—and everyone—she'd ever loved.

She didn't think, at thirty-two, she'd be utterly alone.

She had to find Tess.

Calay slowly–painfully–dragged her body to the far end of the warehouse and through the thin door. Every push and pull sent lightening rods of pain through her leg, threatening to overcome her consciousness. She looked at the mountain of crates in front of her. Getting up was going to be a fight, and fight she would. Like she'd always done.

She reached up from the hard floor and placed her hands on top of a box. It creaked beneath her palms. She leaned on the surface, taking some time to steady herself. It bent under her weight.

"Just breathe."

Her throat released a yelp of desperation as she rose. Her balance waivered on her good leg. She tensed her stomach muscles and pulled herself up. *You are strong. Steady, now.* There. Good. She was standing. Calay looked at the boxes. *Maybe there's something in one of these that will help me get out of here. Or mend my leg. Or both.* She tried to lift the lid off a crate. It wouldn't budge. She pressed her lips together and her body forward and tried another. It was locked tight. The same thing with the next five. No matter how she pried her fingers between the cracks, all she had to show for her effort was bloodied knuckles and scraped fingertips.

Eying the crates at the other end of the room, she knew she had to somehow make it over there and try them too. She leaned carefully on the injured leg and found the floor rising to meet her. Or rather, she was falling to meet it.

"Fuck!" she howled as she fell forward into another box. *Oh no.* If hell existed, this was it. Her ass hit the concrete with a loud *crack*. Whether it was the wood or her leg, she wasn't sure. Calay winced; this was a disaster. Her leg couldn't be broken. It just couldn't. If it was fractured, she was as good as dead. If it was sprained or the muscle or ligament was torn...well, she could work with that. She examined her body, running her hands over her joints. Her puffy eye. Her shivering limbs. Toes to tailbone to the top of her head, she was intact. *Mostly.*

"What the...?"

The box. The force of her body collapsing into the wooden crate knocked the lid

clean off. Inside, amongst the packing material and wrapping were bottles of water and bags of dehydrated food. She spied cans of beans, cellared potatoes, even some sacks of dried fruit.

"Small miracles..." She exhaled. She tore the top off a bag of dried mango and savored the explosion of sugar on her tongue. It railed into her bloodstream, giving her a burst of energy. Of hope. She cracked the top of a bottle of water and gulped down half of it. Took a breath, then drank the rest.

Rolled the dice on that one. But then again, she'd always made her own luck. When The Change happened, it was her resourcefulness that kept her and Tess alive as they made their way out of the city. It was also what made her such a pain in the ass to love. She'd never been one to compromise, let alone fail. Except for maybe where her family was concerned. Her mother always told her stubborn was her middle name. And she'd always replied she'd gotten it from someone.

Maybe that was part and parcel why their exchange had been so explosive when she'd come out. Her parents were stuck in their ways and she was stuck in hers. Stuck. Stuck in that town. In a life she didn't want. In relationships that didn't make her happy. How many years had she fought who she was in order to be who *they* needed her to be? All she'd ever wanted was to belong. To them. To Tess. To the truth of her identity. If they couldn't handle it, that was their issue. Not hers. Or so she told herself. And yet, her heart ached at the memory of her mother and father. She shook off the mental image. She'd survived then, and she would survive now.

Despite her resolve, the strain of the effort washed over her body. Her eyes grew heavy and her torso slouched against the wood. Time didn't pass. It merely faded between bouts of consciousness. Sometimes light shone through the fractured glass windows, sometimes it didn't. In those dark moments, a chill wound its way through Calay's mind and refused to let go. It threatened to steal the breath from her lungs. The life from her veins. The world–hope–ceased to exist. She did, too. As the light turned over, rising brighter and then fading to black, Calay would try to rise again. And again. And again. And then, one day, as the sun crept across the windows high above, she pushed herself from the bottle and plastic littered floor. And this time, she stayed up. She pressed her heel down and put a little weight on her injured leg, hobbling around the enclosed space. The pain was excruciating, but she could move. *Thank Christ, it wasn't broken.* The gratitude that flooded her body almost sent her off kilter, but she held her own. She had to. For herself. And for Tess.

On the morning of The Change, Calay had taken care of Tess. As books piled off shelves, and the meager amount of dishes they owned smashed onto the kitchen floor, sending shards of razor-sharp glass throughout the apartment, Calay had grasped for her. The bed rolled on its side, sending the two lovers onto the floor, clinging to each other with their eyes sealed tight. Furniture tumbled around them. They screamed, but beneath the noise of bursting pipes, breaking gas lines, and layers upon layers of crumbling drywall, their cries went unheard.

"Tess?" Calay choked out, her hands feeling their way through the chaos, "Tess!"

No reply. Panic rose in her throat once again.

"TESS!"

She slid from beneath fragments of their splintered dresser and pulled herself up on the plasterboard that used to be their bedroom wall.

"What the fuck is happening?"

Surveying the apartment that was no longer an apartment, she coughed and choked back a sob. Beams of morning light fought through the wreckage, casting shadows over what was left of their home and deep within her mind. *If anything has happened to Tess*—she pushed the thoughts out of her mind and blinked back tears. Tess had to be there somewhere. She didn't know much, but she knew at least the room had stopped moving.

"Tess!" she tried again. Silence. A whimper crawled up her throat.

"Cay...Cal...Calay," Tess stuttered from somewhere in the dust, "I...I'm stuck."

"Tess, where are you?" Calay's hands flew over the debris, desperate for any sign of movement. "Tess! Say something!"

"I'm over here." The sound of Tess's labored breathing filled Calay's ears, but she saw nothing.

"Where? I can't tell where you are. Keep talking!"

"I think...there's something on top of me. I think I'm under the mattress."

Her head dizzy from the fall, Calay spied the mattress across the room. She gripped what she could to keep herself upright—jagged pieces of the snapped bedframe, the edge of her sanity—and stumbled toward it.

"Tess! Tess, I'm here." Calay bent to find Tess pinned beneath what was left of their bed.

"You'll have to lift it, Cay. I can't."

"It won't budge!" Calay looked around, confused. "Why is it so fucking heavy?"

Then she realized the television and the rest of the dresser were on top of it.

"Um, hang on Tess, I gotta move this shit off to get ya out." Calay hesitated, swallowed hard. She was desperate to know but terrified to find out the answer, still, she asked, "Are you okay?"

"I think so. My arm hurts. I think I banged it."

"Is it broken?"

"No, I don't think it's broken."

"Are you bleeding?"

"No, no I don't think so. Are you okay?" Tess's voice raised several octaves. She reached for Calay's face, her fingers marred and covered with dirt. Calay grasped her fingers and held them to her cheek.

"Yeah. I hit my head, but I think I'm fine. It's a good thing the mattress is on you." She stopped short of what she was about to say as she peered at the sharp, splintered wood. She didn't want to think what would have happened to Tess if the mattress hadn't landed on her first.

Slowly, Calay pried enough of the weight off the mattress and Tess wiggled free.

They fell into each other's arms.

"My darling, are you alright?" Tess cooed.

"I'm fine. I'm fine. Are you?"

Tess's hands shot to Calay's face again, brushing her hair out of her eyes, examining her head.

"Seriously, I'm fine. Just a little concussed. I'm sure the hospital will fix me right up."

Tess's eyes pleaded with Calay, but Calay shook her head and forced a smile.

"What the hell just happened?" Calay asked, redirecting Tess's attention to the disaster in front of them.

"I don't know. I think…I think the building collapsed."

"We have to get out of here." Calay reached into the dresser, pulled out a couple t-shirts, and handed them to Tess.

"Here?"

Calay shrugged. "Where else?"

Tess nodded; her blue eyes sunken behind a curtain of shock. Calay knew the look well—she was feeling the same way herself.

"Right," she replied.

"Right," Calay agreed.

There, in the ruins of what had been their home, Calay and Tess got dressed together in their bedroom for the last time.

"You ready?"

Tess nodded, still shaking as she tried to tie the laces on her sneakers.

"Let me help you." Calay bent, finishing the loops for her. "There. Like new."

She looked up from Tess's feet, their gazes meeting. Calay tried to hide the fear behind her eyes but failed. They both did. Seeing Tess this way made Calay's heart ache. But there wasn't much she could do about it now. All she could do was try to get them to safety.

"Which way?" Tess asked.

Calay looked around, her lips pressed firmly together. She took Tess's trembling hand. They both swallowed hard. And began to make their way toward the light.

✴

THE WARMTH OF THE SUNLIGHT CRAWLED ACROSS CALAY'S eyelids as it inched across the warehouse floor. She pulled herself from her reverie and the questions tumbled through her mind. *Where is Tess? Is she looking for me? Is she safe?* There was only one way she was going to get her questions answered. She had to move.

Calay sized up the plastic sheet leading to the other room. Before now, she'd been immobile. Trapped. But now the notion of freedom tugged at her limbs. She hadn't seen a doorway yet, and there had to be an exit somewhere. The contents of the boxes had kept her alive, but they wouldn't last forever. Now she'd have to save herself.

She limped toward the door, one unsteady step at a time. As she reached the opening, the plastic sheet rippled. *The wind?* The air was stale with the scent of old blood and sawdust. *What fucking wind?* A halo of light encompassed the frame and a loud bang echoed through the room. No—someone was there, just beyond the curtain of plastic.

Calay wasn't sure if she should duck and run, stand and fight, or hug whoever was on the other side.

"Look, if we're going to use this space for the mission, we need to dispose of the body. We can't have a corpse rotting in the middle of an operation."

Okay, no hugs.

Calay flailed more than ducked behind the closest crate. She squatted, pressing herself against the cold brick wall, hoping to God the trail she'd left in the sawdust and blood wouldn't lead them right to her. *Maybe they'll think I'm already gone.*

Two figures in military-green and black brushed through the slab of plastic only feet from where she crouched. They marched into the next room.

This is it. Now or not ever.

Calay mustered her strength and pushed through the plastic in the opposite direction. On the other side was pitch blackness. Nothing but an abyss of shadows. She stood, paralyzed by indecision and fear. Those men had come from somewhere; if she could just find a light. Shaking, she reached her hands forward, following the wall. Small nails and pointed edges poked the tips of her fingers. The weight of the darkness swam around her, threatening to pull her down. She had to keep moving. She placed one foot in front of the other, careful not to bump into anything and give away her location. As her eyes adjusted to the lack of light, ahead, something glinted. Something huge. Sharp metal glimmered through the darkness, nearly twice her height. It towered before her. Her breath caught in her throat; her hands flew to her mouth. She stifled a scream. *There's no such thing as monsters.* Except, there was. And they'd ended civilization as the world knew it. Calay edged closer to whatever it was in front of her, ignoring the feeling in her legs to flee the other way. She took a break, steeled herself, and placed a palm on the silver surface. *Do or do not.* A large steel door. This was the chance she was looking for. She threw herself against it, leaning on the metal for support. She turned the handle and pushed as hard as she could. It didn't grant her so much as a courteous nudge. She knew if she didn't move now, she never would. The body dumpers would see to that.

"Where the fuck did she go?" one voice boomed across the warehouse.

"She should be right here," said the other.

"Where could she go? She's dead."

"Well, she's supposed to be dead."

"What do you mean 'she's supposed to be dead?' Of course she's dead! I saw to it with my own hands."

"Dead people don't move."

Rapid footsteps circulated beyond the plastic sheet. It'd be moments before they were on her. And in this world, that could mean any number of things, even in her state. She'd seen enough to know a little blood and a few cracked ribs didn't stop the unthinkable from becoming doable.

Calay's vision swam and her mind drifted. The morning of The Change, she and Tess had learned that grim truth the hard way. Society—humanity—had crumbled like sheets of ice in spring. Swift, jagged, and without warning. Smoke stung their eyes and billowed from piles of bricks that had once been buildings. Electricity poles dangled over sidewalks. Electrical boxes shot sparks up into the dusty sky like birthday cake sparklers. And the smell—shit and piss flowed freely down gutters and into drain ducts.

"Don't look at it." Calay gagged, turning away from the street, resting her hands on Tess's shoulders. They faced what was left of their apartment building only to find that view not much better.

"We should have stayed inside." Tess had mourned as they stepped out of their apartment and into the street. "What the fuck happened?"

No words came to mind. Calay stared in disbelief.

The apartment complex didn't just collapse, it was literally flipped on its side. What was six stories was now less than one, stretching the length of the entire city block. The remains of other buildings were spread beneath it, shattering the lives of the people they'd called their neighbors. It was a cemetery of broken bricks and concrete. Calay squinted, fighting to see through the dense cloud of ash. Human limbs protruded through the wreckage, pale and at odd angels. Survivors clawed forward from beneath it all. Tortured sounds of pain and panic bled into the air.

"But...how?" Calay's eyes teared up, swollen with confusion and fear. *It's like a scene out of a war movie.* She pushed down the urge to cry. "We have to remain calm."

Tess's arm brushed against hers and she jumped despite herself.

"What's happening, Cay?" Tess begged.

"This wasn't an earthquake," she said, "was it...do you think it was terrorism?"

They looked at each other, their mouths agape. Calay's went dry. Since 9/11, and the Berlin and Paris attacks, terrorism was something you saw on the news or in movies. It was something that happened over "there," never to anyone you actually knew. Not in your own backyard. Not here, not now. That was the belief, anyhow. The false truth they all told themselves so they could sleep at night; so they could feel safe. The idea someone may have bombed their building turned Calay's stomach. Her legs began to give way. Her vision turned woozy. *I have to remain strong, for Tess.*

"Hey!" A large man barrelled into them; two small children tucked under his arms. Calay hit the ground with enough force to rattle her teeth as he pushed past. The children were crying, their faces marked with soot and their clothes mangled and torn. Calay recognized the kids from down the street. She'd hopped their hopscotch only a week earlier.

"Look out!" the man growled.

Blood pooled in his dark beard, dripping in a steady stream onto his chest as he careened down the road. His eyes were dark, wide, and manic. The kid's frail arms waved in the air, jostling side to side as the man ran, his breath labored and heavy.

"Are you guys okay?" she called to them, dusting herself off, starting to rise, "hey wait—are you alright?"

"Help us!" the one child pleaded. Her dark curls waved to Calay from the motion as she bounced in the strange man's arms.

"Help us!" the small boy parroted. His body shook violently with each step the man took.

Calay spun to Tess. "Are they asking us?"

Tess stood, her mouth hanging open, at a loss. *Who is that man?* Calay turned back to the trio, bounding further away. *I have to do something.* The kids seemed to be asking for her help. *I have to do something.* Seconds later and they'd be gone. *I have to do something, now!*

"Stop! Hey you, stop!" She took several steps after them, only to watch all three disappear in a plume of red twenty feet in front of her. Calay's feet planted themselves firm where she stood.

"What...where did they...?"

"Oh my God." Tess's skin went pale.

"Where did they go?"

Tess looked at Calay, her eyes wild, desperate, and afraid.

"They were right here!"

"I feel nauseous."

"This is impossible, T! People don't just disappear."

Tess doubled over. Calay rushed to her side, crouched, and wrapped her arms around her shaking body as she heaved what was left of last night's dinner into the street.

"Where did they go?" Calay muttered to herself, more than anyone else.

Tess said nothing.

"People don't just disappear. Where did they…?"

Calay's eyes returned to where the threesome had been only moments before. Gone.

※

JUST LIKE TESS. FOUR YEARS AFTER THAT AWFUL DAY, CALAY now knew what happened to people when the blue lights hit them. Still, her mind couldn't reconcile the idea someone existed and then they didn't. Tess was gone, but she was out there somewhere. *She has to be.* So Calay firmed her resolve, focused on the door in front of her and decided: she, too, had to exist. She had to survive. She had to get out of that warehouse.

"Open! Please dear God, open!" She pulled, she pushed, she pleaded, she begged. The panic rose like a tsunami in her chest. Tears began to roll down her cheeks as she fought with the door handle.

And then she saw it: the pin. Like the walk-in freezers in the bar where she used to work. Before The Change. Before everything went to shit. *Pull the pin, you idiot! Pull the damn pin! Pull it now!*

She wrenched the pin out of the hole and the door popped open with a gentle click. She burst through it into fresh sunshine. It was warm, full of life, and best of all, not in that damned warehouse.

She looked around—and her heart sank.

The light shone through a skylight above her, stairs on either side.

Up or down? Her heart thumped in her chest. *Up or down, damnit?* Down certainly meant out, right? But wouldn't that be the logical–and expected–thing to do? She leaned over the railing and peered over. There were a lot of flights below, more than she could count. The sun felt closer than the Earth. Calay considered her leg and wondered if her knee could handle the impact of all those stairs, one after the other. Would she just collapse in a heap at the first landing? *Oh please,* she prayed to a God she'd long since stopped believing in, *don't make me out to be the woman in a bad horror movie.*

"Up it is." She decided.

She climbed as fast as her leg would allow, hoping against hope the decision would buy her time to figure out a plan. A plan—the idea was laughable. *Plans are what fall apart when you're busy running for your life.*

Calay shook her head. The morning of The Change, all their plans went out the window when theirs exploded under the weight of their falling building. She could still smell the smoke and burning bodies that day. It was seared into her memory. Particulate matter hung in the air around them, settling to the ground in a fine dust. Voices floated amongst the ash.

"Place them in the street! Keep them clear of anything that might fall!" Someone shouted.

Calay watched her neighbors move the injured from the remains of buildings to the center of the road, gently placing them on the fractured concrete as to not exacerbate their pain.

"Wrap them up!" someone else ordered, "keep them warm!"

A woman was dragging sheets and blankets from wherever she could find to wrap them with until help could arrive. Another was wrestling water from a gushing fire hydrant into buckets and bowls. The initial shock seemed to be subsiding. People were rallying.

Whatever happened—whatever it was—seemed to be over.

"I got you." Calay pulled Tess closer. "It's okay. It's going to be okay. Help will be here soon."

"Shouldn't there be sirens?" Tess became rigid in Calay's arms.

Calay's breath caught in her throat. Tess was right. Where were the emergency responders? Surely, they'd hear them coming. Aside from the sounds of people shouting and crying, it was quiet. Too quiet. Something wasn't right. As the air cleared, every hair on Calay's body stood on end. A prickle curled down her spine; dread flooded her body.

"I was wrong," she gasped.

"What?"

"Something's off," she whispered to Tess.

"What's off?"

"I don't know." Calay's pulse quickened, her breathing shortened. "Something's wrong."

"What do you mean, Cay?"

"I don't think this is it."

"Why?" Tess pressed, "what are you talking about? Do you hear something?"

Calay shivered as she looked up.

"Oh my God!"

A hundred feet above them, something hovered.

It was large, round, smooth, and white. Bigger than the city block, it hung in the air like a balloon, weighing nothing, and at the same time, carried the weight of a planet. With the city buildings in rubble on the ground, it was the only thing in the sky, blocking out the sun, and emanating a pale blue aura. The glow filtered down through the smoke, illuminating an eerie glow through the street.

"What is that?" Calay gasped. She inhaled sharply but none of the air reached her lungs. She couldn't breathe. She couldn't move.

Tess raised her head from Calay's chest.

"Oh my God—Calay, what *is* it?" Tess echoed, scrambling away from Calay's embrace and against what was left of a wall. What was just moments before, their wall.

Calay shook her head, stunned with fear.

A flicker of movement pulled Calay's gaze from the floating orb. *What...?* As she tried to make sense of what she was seeing, people laying in the middle of the street started to disappear into clouds of red mist. The words evaporated from her tongue as pale dots littered the ground where their bodies had been. In some places, it oozed, thick and red down the broken pavement, seeping into the cracks and pooling far beneath their feet. Beneath what was left of the street, the city's sewers were slowly being paved in blood.

The realization of what was happening cascaded over Calay like an avalanche.

People—her neighbors—were being murdered and vaporized in front of her eyes.

"We have to go," Calay said too quietly for anyone to hear, "we have to *go* Tess!"

The strange silence that just moments before echoed through the city, ended abruptly as blood-curdling screams of terror washed over Calay. People cowered and ran, glass shattering underfoot. They trampled one another, young and old, in their flight to escape the danger. Many of them burst into fogs of red themselves.

Calay turned to Tess, who was standing behind her throwing up on her own shoes. Calay kneeled before her.

"I don't know what's happening, but we have to get out of here! Right now, okay?"

"I don't know if I can, Cay."

"You have to Tess." Calay dared a glance up and saw a woman trip over the curb and explode into red just before her head hit the ground. "Right fucking now! Or you're going to die. Like them."

Tess nodded, her eyes glazed and red from the smoke. Calay held Tess's face in her hands, forcing her to meet her gaze. She needed some kind of agreement from Tess. An acknowledgment of what she was saying.

"Got it? We run. We run now."

Calay grabbed Tess's hand, unsure if her lover had the wherewithal to follow her, and they ran. People poured out of cars and into streets. Around them, city blocks burst into chaotic nightmares of death. And red. So much red. New trails of smoke decorated the morning sky as cars were lit ablaze. Buildings crashed into each other, sending the people within them into a hailstorm of concrete and glass.

"Run!" they called to people frozen in the street, "you have to run!"

Those that did, followed close behind. They raced across the street, narrowly avoiding getting hit by a city bus. The people behind them were not so lucky, getting caught in the wheels and dragged along the undercarriage. Calay turned to look, regrettably. Their insides were smeared onto the pavement before her. The bus's horn blared.

Calay felt herself scream more than she heard it. Her voice rattled inside her chest like a freight train. She felt herself moving toward the mess of people that no longer were.

"Calay!" Tess called after her.

"Oh no, oh no!" Calay stammered, "I told them, I..."

"It's not your fault," Tess told her. She put her hand around Calay's arm and pulled her along, away from the carnage.

"I told them to run!" Calay wailed. Tess answered her, but Calay didn't hear her words. Instead, a deep whirring and grating sound filled the air, chasing away her reply. The screams and wails of people afraid to die or mourning the loss of someone who *did*, momentarily drowned out. As she stared at the mess in front of her, Calay caught fragments of Tess's words.

"Calay!" Tess snapped, herding Calay's attention.

"Huh?" Calay replied.

"We keep moving."

Calay nodded, her mouth twisted from shock.

"Stay with me," Tess urged. She leaned in, pressing her forehead against Calay's. Tess caressed Calay's face with one hand while lifting a gold pendant from around her neck with the other. Subtle gold ridges glinted in the shape of a crescent moon at the end of a delicate chain. "To the moon and back, remember?" Tess's eyes went to Calay's throat. Calay fingered the same shape around her own neck. It was the first gift they'd ever given each other. A reminder that no matter what happened or where they went, they'd belong to each other. It was destined in the stars. The feel of it between Calay's fingers brought her back from the darkness that threatened to overtake her.

"You and me, right?" Calay whispered.

"You and me." Tess nodded.

※

So that's how it was, until now. Tess was somewhere and Calay was going to find her, if she could just make it out of that damned building. As with that first morning, Calay put one foot in front of the other. *One flight at a time. Just take it one flight at a time. Don't think about how many there are. If you make it through this one...*she stopped short. She'd what—make it? She wasn't so sure. She wanted to tell herself it would all be alright, but she'd stopped believing in fairy tales long ago. Before The Change, fairy tales gave humanity hope. But now, fairy tales got you killed.

Calay reached the top of the staircase; there was another door. She reached for the handle and it opened rather easily; too easily. She stepped outside and found herself on the roof. Several smokestacks towered to her left; a shed sat to her right. And it was a long way down to the ground on either side. She was surprised to see other buildings on the block, spaced within only a few feet of each other. She'd assumed —wrongfully—they'd have dumped her somewhere more remote. This wasn't remote at all. She squinted at the busted skyline. She knew this area. It was in the core of the city.

I could scream. Maybe someone will hear me.

"Right," she scolded herself, shaking her head, "like the thugs who are trying to find and dispose of your corpse."

She ran her hand over the back of her neck, working out a kink while she worked out a plan. Shouting would be a stupid idea, at least in that moment. *Give them time to give up and get lost; hide. Then you can take your time making your way down the stairs.* But before Calay had the chance to move, the door to the roof swung open with a clang.

The two men regarded her, and she them. Their eyes a dangerous combination of confusion and anger. Hers were overflowing with fear. She was in no condition to defend herself and they knew it. What were they waiting for? Her eyes shifted between them and the door. She'd never get past them. She felt like a wounded bird being eyed up by a pair of foxes.

She looked around the cavernous expanse of sky and air and sunshine. She had nowhere to go. Never before had being free felt more like a prison.

The bigger one smirked. This was not going to end well for her.

Facing the consequences of her impetuous decision to climb rather than descend, she knew she had to make another quick decision. There was no way they were going to let her walk out of there. She was either going to be killed or would have to risk killing herself in her attempt to escape. She knew what she had to do. *I have to jump.* She wished she could fly. *Wingless little bird.*

She steeled herself against the pain she knew was to come and sprinted for the closest side of the building. The gravel crunched behind her under their heavy boots while every step she took felt like someone was wailing a sledgehammer against her knee —an incessant throbbing drummed along her bones, culminating as a monstrous symphony in the back of her head. Her knee may not be broken but it certainly wasn't in any kind of shape to run. Her vision wobbled; her lungs refused to cooperate.

She couldn't stop. She wouldn't stop.

Keep moving.

As she approached the ledge, a long, desperate, frenzied howl escaped Calay's mouth and she leapt into the abyss. Into the unknown. Into a total and complete chasm of air.

It was all that ever was. All that ever would be.

CHAPTER TWO

Human garbage. That's how Calay felt.

If it weren't for the stench of rotting waste and excrement, she'd think she was dead. But she wasn't, that much was clear. She was in a dumpster, not unlike the ones behind the restaurant she used to work at. Before The Change, Calay used to take out the trash. Now she was the trash.

She was unsure how much time had passed, but judging by the swelling and soreness of her leg, she was pretty sure it'd been a while. The sun was getting low in the sky. It skirted buildings and cast long shadows on the ground.

She struggled to sit up, her breath catching in her throat. The ache nestled so deeply in her knee was the kind of pulsing that needed time to grow. To radiate from within. To take over everything. *Did I hurt it worse by jumping?* It didn't matter. She was alive. She was free. And given the time that had passed, the men pursing her probably presumed her dead and moved on; no one should have survived that fall. If she'd have landed on the ground below, rather than in a container full of garbage bags to cushion her landing, she wouldn't have.

She almost lamented that she did.

The tall edge of the dumpster towered before her, daring her to brave the ascent out. It felt like an insurmountable climb, but climb she must.

"No time like the present..."

Reaching for the lip of the container, her fingers gripped the edge, wrapping painfully over it. Chips of blue metal flaked off and buried themselves under her nails. She dug in, knowing her leg could bear the weight if it had to—her escape proved that. It didn't mean she wanted it to. Plastic crinkled under her feet. With every ounce of strength she had, she leveraged herself up, bottles and bags cracking beneath her and tumbled out the side.

She landed flat on her back on the cold asphalt below, the breath she was holding knocked clean out of her.

As she struggled upright, she examined the damage. Her knee was where it belonged, just badly bruised. The gash in her forearm was worse. Shards of blue metal poked through her skin and into swollen flesh. That didn't look good; they'd have to come out. She pinched each one by her thumb and forefinger, bracing herself each time for the sting she knew was inevitable. She'd have to rinse the wounds with alcohol when she got back to camp. Infection was not something she wanted to risk.

Hunger ached through her body—toes to tits. No longer in fight or flight mode, she realized she hadn't had a half-decent meal in...she didn't even know how long. She imagined thick cheeseburgers and mountains of French fries. What she wouldn't give for a slice of cheesecake or a batch of her mother's chocolate chip cookies; a peanut butter and honey sandwich on white bread; a big tall glass of ice-cold coke with a bottle of rum for good measure. How she could think about food with the smell of garbage and sewage thick in the air, she wasn't sure. She didn't seem to know much these days, but she knew one thing—she needed to eat.

Old brick buildings climbed out of the darkness, casting shadows at odd, violent angles. More than once she jumped at her own reflection in the broken glass that littered the concrete. Fear was something she'd learned to live with since The Change, albeit not very well. She used to consider herself rather brave, but the last several years had shattered that confidence. She was scared all the time. Scared of those men.

Scared of all men. Scared of other people. Of herself. Of the unknown. The known. All she wanted was to feel safe. To feel like she had a home. Somewhere to belong. But those things were all gone and in their place, fear. Loneliness. Waste.

It had all been a waste.

Their plans. Society. Humanity. The morning of The Change reset everything to zero. Decades of progress and social niceties were reduced to rubble. As she and Tess had ran, they kept tight to buildings—or what was left of them. They were careful to avoid being in the open, as they witnessed human after human become nothing but red mist. It clung to their clothes and their hair, fighting oxygen for space in their lungs. They gagged as they made their way block after block, the giant white orb still hanging above them.

Tess pulled Calay under the protection of a hanging doorway. They tucked themselves as far back against the brick building as they could, obscured by deep shadows.

"Do you think we're safe here?" Tess asked.

"I don't know. I...I don't think so."

"Well, what *do* you know?" Tess demanded, catching Calay off-guard, "we need a plan, Calay."

Confusion, panic, and their love for each other boiled between them.

"The plan is to not die," Calay said.

"Very funny. I'm serious right now Calay."

"I am too. You're right. I don't know what the hell is happening, but you're right," Calay confessed as she peered at the carnage within arm's reach, "we have to come up with something. Or..."

She didn't need to finish that sentence. They both knew where she was going with that statement. If they didn't do something soon, they'd both die in the maze of ruin that had just this morning been Seattle.

"Okay, we need a plan," Calay continued, swallowing hard.

Glass shattered as looters crusaded through the front doors of whatever designer department store was beside them.

"They're losing their damn minds. We can't stay here."

"We can't," Calay agreed. Those who weren't running for their lives were rioting; smashing shop windows. Underneath the noise, Calay swore she heard a woman scream, followed by a chorus of men laughing. She shivered. Things were starting to get ugly.

"What do you want to do?" Tess pressed.

That was a good question. What *did* she want to do? Calay was at a loss. What did one do when the city was under attack by terrorists, or the government, or alien space crafts, anyhow? She looked at the devastation and death around them, her mind in shock both at what was happening, and the fact that they'd managed to make it this far together.

"We have to get out of the city," she concluded.

"Out of the city? Where?"

"Our luck won't hold. We aren't going to last much longer. Everything is falling apart." The cement holding the bricks above their heads sifted down around them with the rumble of a nearby blast, the shadows threatened to swallow them where they stood.

"But where will we go, Calay?"

"We could go to my parent's place."

"We haven't talked to your parents in years Cay." Tess shook her head, her hands rested on Calay's face. "Would they even let us in?"

"They'll let us in. They'll have to. I'm their daughter for Christ's sake." The words felt raw on her tongue, foreign, even.

"After the way they treated you, I don't know if that's the best place. For you or for us."

Calay felt the pain of their abandonment as strongly today as she did five years ago.

"Tess, we have nowhere else to go. The city is gone. All of our friends, fucking gone," she choked on the words as she said them. She swallowed a mouthful of dust.

"And if they turn us away?" Tess's eyes filled with tears. She leaned against Calay; her fists balled up by her sides. "If they turn me away?"

"I won't let them."

"You can't change them Cay, any more than they can change you."

Calay looked into her lover's eyes, the fear and pain as real for Tess as it was for her. She reached for her face and held it in her hands. Soft and familiar, her love, and her life.

"I go where you go, T. Always."

Tess's eyes shone with tears.

"Please Tess, it's the only place we have. I won't drop you. Ever. We're in this together."

"Together?"

"Together."

✸

THEY WEREN'T TOGETHER NOW. CALAY FELT TESS'S ABSENCE like molten metal in her chest. It weighed on her, slowed her down. She leaned on a rusted fire escape and let the feeling of loss flow through her. Grief was like that now—a surging tide. If you resisted, it would overtake you and you'd drown in it. But if you rolled with it, let it bring you to the deep, dark places it wanted you to go, you'd come out the other side whole. Or at least, not any more broken. The fire escape creaked under her weight. She pushed off it and kept moving, though her gaze lingered on the staircase. It climbed four stories, pausing by darkened windows. Balconies housed moss-covered terra cotta planters lined with long-dead foliage and clotheslines with laundry that would never be put away.

The apartment building was not unlike her own; their own. Calay wondered if the apartments that belonged to those balconies had been picked over yet. It didn't matter, she avoided buildings when she foraged for food. You never knew who was inside. Who might be looking at her now? At first, she'd counted on markets, gas stations, and convenience stores for their rations. Then, abandoned homes. But as supplies dwindled, people began to turn on each other. Hell- they'd started to turn that very first day. Limb from limb, as the saying went. The shelves were bare within a couple months, and the return simply wasn't worth the risk. Besides, The Others knew humans needed food. It was common knowledge that to enter a high-level food zone you were taking a risk of being found. And extinguished.

Now it was safer to keep to the shadows. To brave the nightmares in the darkness. To limp down the alleys in search of something edible; places you could easily escape from. Four walls once a respite, were now a death sentence. So she focused her efforts on rummaging through dumpsters and sorting through bags and boxes she found on the street like a feral dog. She'd often wondered about them–the bags and boxes. Especially when they delivered a particularly good yield. Who'd left them there? Or rather, who'd lost them? And what had happened to those people? Surely someone wouldn't have left food behind of their own free will. Not anymore. Especially now, with fall on the way again, it was getting more and more difficult to find something edible at all. *How long will it take for humans to start eating our own kind?* She shivered at the thought.

Her stomach growled.

"Yes! Score!"

Rolled in a bag, at the bottom of a garbage can, at the end of the world were a handful of cracker and jam packets and an old can of green beans. There were *always* green beans. She weighed the can in her hand. *They're the cockroaches of vegetables.* Regardless, it was food. And food was always a bright moment in an otherwise dark day; the bottom of the barrel was good enough for her.

She resisted the urge to rip into her prized-winnings immediately and tucked them safely inside her pack for when she got back to camp. There would be supper tonight.

Tonight.

Calay blinked as she looked up—she was chasing more shadows than light. It would be dark soon and this was the last place she wanted to be when night fell. She pulled herself away from her search, her body screaming for rest, and made her way out of the alley. She'd been down this one before, so retracing her steps home wouldn't prove too difficult. *I hope.*

Their impulse to leave the city had been right. Cities weren't places you stayed if you wanted to survive. Instead, they became fortresses of violence, disease, and decay. So Calay built their camp on the outskirts of town. Close enough to make day trips when needed, far enough to avoid the horrors of humanity. *It's incredible, the things we're capable of doing to one another. The pain we're willing to cause if it means an extra can of food, the ability to squat in a particular building, or to preserve a belief. Fuck, sometimes it's for no reason at all*. As far as she was concerned, she'd stay away from the cities unless absolutely necessary.

The morning of The Change, cities became borderlands. Lawless. Ruthless. Inhumane. They'd broken down only a few hours after the initial attack. It didn't matter if you were on the business end of brutality or a bystander—no one had escaped with clean hands. *We tried.* As they ran, that truth chased them like a rabid dog. Death was an inevitability and it was only a matter of time before it sunk its teeth into you one way or another. It was relentless.

"We aren't going to get anywhere on foot. We need a car." Calay looked around, sized up their options. As she said it, a small vehicle turned in their direction, making its way around blockages at a steady pace.

"There!" She pointed.

Most vehicles had already crashed or were jammed in bumper-to-bumper traffic—basically sitting ducks waiting to be obliterated into mist. Red mist. Calay shuddered at the thought. This could be their one chance at a ride out of here. It would be on them in moments!

"Come with me." Calay took off across the street toward the car. Tess followed, her gait a few paces behind Calay.

"Stop!" Calay called, waving at the driver, "hey! Stop!"

The car wasn't slowing down. Calay stood in the middle of the road. The car was getting closer. *Is it speeding up?* She had to stop this car. She had to get herself and Tess to safety.

"Please! Please stop! We need a ride!"

The driver is definitely speeding up.

"Stop!" Tess yelled, "Calay - move out of th..."

"You have room! Please let us come with you!" Calay waved harder.

As the car sped in their direction, Calay saw the driver was waving back. And missing half his face. His jaw clung to a stew of cartilage and torn flesh. The cheekbone protruded grotesquely beneath what was left of his right eye.

"Oh, my God," she gagged. Calay ducked out of the way just as the car lurched past. She rolled on the ground, scraping her knees on the churned-up cobblestone. Tess rushed to her side.

"You okay?"

"I think so. Did you see?"

"Did I see what?" Tess pushed.

Calay couldn't bring herself to say it out loud, his butchered face seared into her memory. Instead, she asked, "why didn't he stop?"

Tess looked at Calay and blinked. "Would you?"

Calay considered it. She liked to think she would have. But maybe Tess was right. The way people were looting and forsaking each other to save themselves and the ones they loved, it was possible no one would stop for them. They'd do what they needed to survive. Just as she'd do for Tess.

"How are we going to get out of here?" Calay wondered aloud.

"The train." Tess's face lit up. She took hold of Calay's arm, pulling her forward. "The train! We'll take the subway out of here. It's underground. It's possible it hasn't been affected."

"I don't know, T." Calay planted her feet on the pavement. "Public transit is usually the first to get hit in a terrorist attack. Do you think it's safe?"

"I don't know. We don't even know if this is terrorism, Calay. But it's only a couple blocks from here. Let's check it out. Unless you have another idea."

Calay pursed her lips and racked her brain; she had nothing.

The deep whirring and grating of metal grew louder above them as people continued to rush past. Far in the distance, beyond the expanse of the orb above, fire and smoke trailed behind a plane dropping like dead weight from the sky.

Calay, at a loss, nodded. "Okay, let's do it."

"Really?"

"Give 'em hell, kid." Calay took Tess's hand and they pulled as far back out of the street as they could, dashing for the subway station.

"It's right around this corner," Tess gasped, choking on the smoke hanging in the air. They plunged down the stairs and over the turnstiles. White tiles panelled the walls and big yellow lines marked the gap. All the lights were on. The place was deserted.

"Where is everyone?"

"Maybe they know something we don't."

"Maybe the trains aren't running?"

"Maybe..."

The rumble of an approaching train shook the platform.

"Ha! Yes!" Tess smiled at Calay, rubbing some of the red and dirt off her face. "They are running! We're going to get out of here."

Calay pulled Tess to her and kissed her hard.

"I love you. So fucking hard." Calay swallowed. "I'm scared, Tess."

"I love you, Cay. I'm scared too. I don't know what's going on, but we're going to make it through this, just like we've made it through everything else. We're a team."

"The dream team."

"Damn right." Tess smiled, kissing her again. Their eyes met as the lights flickered.

And then Calay screamed.

The train blasted past the platform, engulfed in flames. Screeching at full speed, it dared to jump the track, shaking violently as it passed. Passengers, many of them still flailing inside the cabin, burned alive. Ash and the smell of seared flesh danced in the air above them, catching in their hair and nostrils.

And then it was gone.

Until another passed.

And a third.

And on it went. Calay and Tess sank against the platform wall, their hands locked as tears streamed down their faces. The cold floor rose to meet them as they huddled together, taking in one horror after another.

"Every one..." one of them choked out.

"Hell on wheels..." the other replied.

"Maybe this will be the last one." They hoped.

It wasn't.

Unable to tear themselves away, they waited. But the trains didn't stop. Not for them. Not for the passengers inside, now turned to charcoal. This was it. An endless inferno of death.

Rural good, city bad.

※

CALAY SKIRTED THE CITY LIMITS. BEFORE THE CHANGE, THIS area was home to some of the most derelict and forgotten buildings in the area. Windows busted out, bricks on the ground. No one lived in them for years. As kids they used to venture out there on their bikes and make up ghost stories. No one ever braved going inside. But from the safety of the woods and their ten-speeds, it was exciting. Now it was an amassment of ash, brick, and stone ensconced by spruce trees. Rising out of the rubble, a pod someone managed to take down provided shelter from the elements. And The Others. Pockets of grass and moss that dared to grow frayed at the edges. Now, it was home. Or as close to a home Calay imagined she'd ever see again.

As she approached her camp, she felt less anxious. It wasn't home, but it was hers. *Out of ruin comes life. Out of life comes ruin.*

It was a sick joke.

Like her campfire. Calay's face fell as she poked at the ashes with her toe. It was completely out. Not even a waft of smoke or the glow of a patient ember.

"Damn it."

She limped to the forest edge. The tree's leaves danced in the darkness. Bushes and ferns crouched beyond sight. The hair raised on her neck. She paused, listened. Her eyes scanned the blackness within the canopy for signs of anyone else. Anything else. *The damn fire isn't going to make itself.* She tensed, forced her feet to move forward. The sound of the rustling leaves haunted her steps as she gathered a handful of small twigs. Branches. Bark shavings. Dried grass. She chanced a glance over her shoulder, bracing herself to find a pair of glowing eyes at her back. There was nothing. Nothing but what lurked in the shadows. Calay took a deep breath. *Lurk if you must, I have things to do.* She made her way to the bucket she'd placed under a tree to gather pine pitch. She'd learned in Scouts as a kid that sap was a natural fire starter. It was a lesson she'd practiced when she went camping with her dad on their father daughter weekend trips. Before all of this. Before he'd kicked her out. Before everything went horribly awry. They'd pack up the truck for the weekend, her mother staying home to indulge herself in a little alone time and to take care of the farm. Her and her dad—off they'd go on their little adventure. Establishing camp was always her favorite part. Getting the tarps strung, setting up the tent, unrolling the sleeping bags. They all had the pleasant smell of a responsibility-free childhood. Of happier times. Of love. It was a place she'd felt safe and cherished with her dad. It was just them, together.

A sudden gust of wind pulled her out of her reverie, rocking the bucket in her hand and tossing new twigs at her feet. The trees groaned as if calling to The Others. *Here she is, come and get her.* It was silly to think such thoughts. To have those fears. But that was the way of the world now. Fear bubbled inside her veins. Clawed at her mind. Threatened to spoil her sanity. She had to stay focused. Stay calm. It was difficult without Tess there to tether her to reality. To safety. *Get it together, Cay,* that's what Tess would say. She always was the more practical one. The level-headed one. *The* one.

The cool air dampened as cold droplets of rain started to land on her hands. Sensing the change in weather, she had to hurry. She dropped the supplies next to the dirt pit at the center of her camp and got to work, starting with a construction out of the kindling. She dug a match out of her pack, stroked to light it. It failed her.

"C'mon..."

She tried another.

"Motherf..."

One more.

The weather was getting worse, the wind picking up. Every time she lit a match, it was extinguished by wind, or rain, or the Gods. *The Gods,* she scoffed, *abandoned us.* Not for the first time that day, panic started to set in. This was the last thing she needed after the—week? she'd had. She still wasn't sure how long she'd been out—long enough for the fire to die. At least she hadn't died. Not yet. *Not today,* her thoughts echoed the words she'd promised Tess as they fled during The Change. A bit of warmth would have gone a long way to provide comfort. But it looked like that wouldn't be happening tonight.

Again.

Defeated, tears formed in her eyes and she yearned for the kind of campfires her dad would build on their trips. Or the rolling fire in the mantel at home. Or the warm embrace of Tess. What she wouldn't give for all three. She sighed.

Accepting failure, Calay crawled into her tent. It was hardly perfect. A log positioned against the downed white pod, draped with a tarp and secured with some old rope, fishing line, and loose bricks. But it shielded her from the elements. And prying eyes. She twisted the top off an old bottle of vodka she kept on hand for just such emergencies and tended to her arm. She gritted her teeth against the sting. It wasn't a permanent solution, but it would stem the infection and get her through until morning.

She took a swig for herself too.

Fumbling despite the pain, she tore into the packet of crackers and jam, careful not to lose a single crumb to the ground. Not that it would matter—she wasn't above scrounging. It wasn't exactly a gourmet meal. Not like the one her and Tess shared the night before The Change.

Warm toasted bread, gluttonously covered in decadent fresh cheese, topped with a sweet balsamic drizzle, and fat slices of heirloom tomatoes. Goblets of wine, bowls of fresh pasta, caverns of tiramisu. Food was constantly on her mind then and even more now. *I'd give my right arm for that meal again.* But as grandiose as the food was, it was nothing compared to what followed. The dancing. The kissing. The passionate sex they still had after several years together. But it wasn't about the sex. It was about them being together. They fit in every way. Since she'd met Tess, Calay had never felt alone or wanted for anything. They were inseparable and totally in love. With each other. And everything that was real between them. Tess was home.

Where was Tess? What had they done to her? And how would they find each other again?

Looking around the makeshift tent, Calay's heart rumbled. And her stomach, despite the crackers she'd just eaten. She crinkled the wrappers, shoving them into her bag, and pulled out what was now a rusted half-moon at the end of a tarnished gold chain. The gift that tethered she and Tess together. It always would. She held it close to her chest like it was her last breath and began to cry.

I'm so alone.

Her tears washed away the dirt from the day and sent her off into a fitful sleep of nightmarish memories.

SHE AWOKE EARLY THE NEXT MORNING WITH A START. Delicate streams of light made their way through the trees and onto her face. Her lips tasted of salt with a lingering sweetness of jam. *Jam.* She and Tess used to wake up on Sunday mornings just like this, sharing spoonfuls of jam over pancakes and drinking coffee that was always far too strong. After, they shared their bodies with each other. Their hearts. Their lives.

Again, Calay's body ached. For a hot meal—for Tess.

The rain stopped at some point in the night. The steam rose off the ground in the warm morning sun. Her clothes were damp, and she wasn't sure if it was from the rainwater or her tears. It was a new day. She pulled herself up to a sit and took a deep breath, unwinding the necklace from her fist. She gently placed it in her bag. Safe.

From outside the shelter, there was a loud crack. Calay's spine snapped to attention. She froze. Her heart started to race, sending bursts of blood through her ears as she strained to listen. *Swoosh swoosh swoosh.* One crack after the another like thunder, the breaking of twigs and branches was unmistakable.

Someone was in her camp.

CHAPTER THREE

It was only a matter of time before someone found her camp. Until someone found her. She knew that.

She'd done a pretty good job of concealing her location with overhang and brush, going so far as to paint the tarp they used for their shelter. Rather than a gray patch in the middle of the forest, it now blended in with the surrounding area. Shades of green, black, and brown became invisible as the sun rose. Someone would have to look hard to see it against the natural surroundings. They'd moved to the city, away from the small town she grew up in, to fit in more with the environment. It was a form of survival. And comfort. But now more than ever, it was literally the difference between life and death. Calay recounted her steps from the day before. She'd covered her tracks in town and was careful to keep to the shadows and tight against walls when she could. But that was the thing about society—you were never really far from another person. And yet, you could still be totally alone.

Humanity had a way of seeing you, and seeing right through you, at the same time.

Calay hated what The Others had done to them, but she hated what humans had done to each other even more. As she shivered under the fucking tarp, she knew if she was going to find Tess, she'd have to make a move. She released a shaky exhale. She was bone tired of feeling conflicted. Hungry. Afraid. She paused just long enough to consider possible scenarios.

It could be the men who chased her off the roof; they'd followed her home and were there to finish her off. She was a fool to think she'd escaped. Maybe it was a gang of vapid sex-addicts, coming to violate her in the worst possible ways. When society fell, it didn't take long for the evil to bubble up. Or worse yet, it was The Others and she was about to be obliterated into a haze of blood and plasma. Extinguished. The word glowed in her mind like a neon sign.

Whoever it was, she had to do something.

She could duck and run, try to make a break for it. Just go. Since The Change, that was usually the safest option. *When in doubt, run.* That's what Tess always told her. You never knew someone's strength or their intentions. Running was the option that kept you alive. *But this is my camp, God damn it! Our camp.* She'd scouted it. Set it up. Knew it inside and out. This was hers! It might be the last thing in the world that was hers. And she had a constitutional right to defend her property. Like the constitution meant anything anymore, but that was beside the point. This was principle. And principle could very well be all she'd ever have again.

This is it. Make or break time. Do or do not. Do or die.

She'd stand and fight.

She pulled a large stick close to her chest, poised, ready for attack. Then, hurled herself out of the tent toward the noise.

And saw no one.

What the hell?

The yard was empty. Just the constant hum of nature. And loneliness. A contradiction of sounds, making the silence even more conspicuous. A light breeze danced across her face in the warm morning sunlight.

She was alone.

And then something out of the corner of her vision. A flash of movement, quick and low. She whipped around to face the intruder, prepared to smash the silence with the breaking of their skull.

Golden eyes gazed at her from behind a bush. A dog. Just a dog.

A big dog.

The black pit bull skirted the edge of the trees surrounding her camp. It was skinny. Too skinny. Its short hair wiry and dull. It looked how she felt. Broken. Calay's breathing began to slow and she noticed how fearful it was as it eyed her up. Its strong legs crouched low and ears back.

It doesn't seem rabid or dangerous, just scared. And hungry. She knew that empty, wanting glaze in its eyes all too well.

Calay didn't dare turn her back to the beast. Instead, she inched inside her makeshift tent and grabbed her pack. She pulled out the can of green beans. These days a regular supply of food was tenuous at best, but the idea of having a companion defrosted her mood. She'd share her breakfast with this mangey animal. It was the least she could do. Even in the fall of humanity, Calay refused to lose hers. She pried open the can with a knife, careful not to gouge her hands, stealing curt glances to see if the dog was still watching.

It was.

With the scent of something edible wafting from the container, she had its full attention. It licked its jowls, ears low, eyes pleading and anxious.

She poured half the beans onto a nearby rock and garnished them with the remaining crackers. Bowls weren't a luxury she had the privilege of extending.

"Come on buddy, this is for you. Come eat."

She stepped back and retreated to the other side of the pit to give the animal space. She averted her gaze and busied herself building the fire she'd so epically failed at the night before. Twigs. Branches. Bark shavings. Dried grass. Pine pitch. Lather, rinse, repeat; it was a formula. And this time it only took three matches for the tinder to catch. A small plume of smoke rose into the early morning air. She built the fire one branch at a time, careful to choose larger pieces of wood that weren't soaked from the night before.

"This is how we do it.," She coaxed herself, "it's how we've always done it."

She chucked the other half of the beans into a warped frying pan and placed it over the flame to cook. It wasn't fancy, but it was breakfast. *And it'll be warm.* She wished she had a side of bacon or even an onion to make the beans less...beany. The idea of growing their own vegetables and maybe raising some chickens was something they'd talked about in the beginning. After seeing the devastation in the cities and the precariousness of food supplies, Tess was adamant they become self-sufficient. Skulking around old restaurant kitchens and abandoned garbage dumps for leftover cans of food wasn't sustainable. Or safe. She knew that. They discussed it on multiple occasions. But every time they planted seeds or started to feel like a garden was something that could actually work, they were run off by groups eager for their land, their bodies, their lives.

Everything had gone to shit in a matter of weeks. *A matter of days.* Once The Others arrived, it didn't take long for society to break down. For food to stop being produced. For humans to lose their humanness. She wished she could stop thinking about it, even for a few minutes. But then she remembered the desperate screams as humanity sacrificed itself for the individual good. The smell of smoke in the air. The eerie silence that followed. As they ran through the city that first day, and the days that followed, she'd been terrified. It was like witnessing every horror movie ever made, in real time. At night, it was the stuff of nightmares. The worst was hearing what was happening—the voices, the explosions, the deep whirring of alien pods—without being able to see it. More than once, she woke in the night in a cold sweat or to Tess's screams. Their dream of a quiet life in the city were replaced by night terrors, both awake and asleep.

She yearned for how it was before. Even though she was estranged from her family, it was good—really good—just the two of them. It was a small life and a happy one.

The sound of slurping pulled Calay out of her trance. She looked up from the dancing flame in front of her and was pleased to see the dog had emerged from the treeline and was sharing breakfast with her.

She spooned her green beans into her mouth and smiled despite herself. She and Tess talked about getting a pet more than once. A dog to add to their family. They had plans to visit the pound to adopt one the weekend everything fell apart. When they lost their home. When they lost their city. When humanity lost everything. *I'm not much better than this mutt. Humans really are just animals.*

"Good boy," she said.

Calay finished her beans and set the pan aside, checked her leg. It was still painful, but she could almost put her full weight on it now. She marvelled at how well it was healing. The open wounds in her arm seemed to be recovering quickly, too. *The vodka must have flushed it out well.* She wasn't sure if all the marks on her body were from the fall she took or from injuries she'd sustained at the hands of the men in the warehouse. Or even from sometime before. She couldn't remember what happened to cause her wounds, but in that moment, she was glad she was alive to examine them.

The dog braved a sniff of the empty pan beside her and licked it clean, then settled beside her leg.

"Well, that didn't take long…Max."

Calay released a breath she hadn't realized she'd been holding and slumped back against the dog. She knew she wasn't in good shape, physically or emotionally. Luckily the emotional stuff was easier to ignore. Until it wasn't. But right now, her body needed tending. She examined the supplies in her pack. A couple Band-Aids, a bit of gauze. Low, too low. *Idiot, you should have checked this before.* Granted, she hadn't been expecting these kinds of injuries upon her return. But like Tess would say, *always expect the unexpected.*

She needed to go back into town. Stock up. Gather what she needed while the sun was still high, and she had plenty of daylight to get home again.

She knew where to go.

Wasting no time, she stuffed everything back in her bag, kissed the necklace for luck, and threw an extra log on the fire. *I'll be damned if the thing goes out again.*

✳

CALAY LEANED ON THE WALKING STICK SHE PICKED UP ON her way back into the city, facing the clinic. It had been twenty minutes. The place looked desolate; it seemed abandoned. But that was irrelevant. Whether there was anyone holed up in there or not, she had to go inside. She needed supplies. And she needed them now before something else happened.

She crossed the street, gaze transfixed on the glass double doors ahead. She remembered protesting there for women's rights before The Change. She and Tess were strong supporters of reproductive rights, canvasing politicians and marching in parades. Once a month she even volunteered there, refilling free-condom baskets and folding information pamphlets. They didn't plan to have kids of their own, but she believed every woman had the right to control her body. Every human did. It all seemed so superfluous now. How naive they had been. *Our right to choose went right to the dogs.*

"No offense," she said to Max, "come on."

Calay carefully opened the door and slipped inside. The dog tucked its tail between its legs and followed her, unsure just what it was getting itself into, but seemingly unwilling to let her brave the derelict building alone. She glanced around, Max close at her heels. She gazed down at him and a warmth spread through her chest–she wasn't the only one in need of a pack. Of somewhere to belong. She reached down and patted Max's head, both for his comfort and hers. Broken sunlight illuminated the dark space. Ransacked and vandalized, graffiti adorned the glass partitions. Smears of red dotted the walls. Papers were strewn across the floor. Half-burnt plastic bottles and fast-food containers littered the corners. She made her way down the long corridor she was already familiar with—memories and ghosts of a past life fluttering through her mind.

It didn't matter now. None of it did. How could it?

A closed door blocked the end of the hallway, leading to a room she knew she needed to enter. She peered through the thin, double-paned window and located the cabinet. It looked intact as usual. *Too intact?* Calay looked back down the dark hallway, her nerves a knotted jumble of Christmas lights. Her hand reached for the doorknob, its latch easily giving way as she inched into the room.

The space was immaculate. She'd wondered more than once how this could be—every time, actually. The rest of the building was in shambles. It seemed impossible that this one room would remain standing while the rest of Rome burned.

"It doesn't matter," she chided herself. It was here, and it was what she needed.

She closed the door and quickly made for the cabinet—locked.

It was always locked.

"Of course."

She dug a screwdriver out of her backpack and began to jimmy the bolt. She hadn't known how to do this kind of thing before. If she was being honest, she didn't really know how to do it now. But desperate times called for desperate measures. She shoved the screwdriver between the top of the door and started to pry, using her full body weight as leverage.

Seconds later a loud bang thundered through the clinic. The cabinet doors flew open, the force sending Calay across the room onto the examination table. Several bottles of pills and boxes of gauze tumbled to the floor. The sound was a monsoon of rattling jars. Max cowered in the corner.

Calay's throat seized mid-breath. She froze. She listened. Waited. Eyes transfixed on the goldmine of first aid supplies rolling on the floor before her. And the pills. *To lose it all now...*but no one came running down the hall to investigate the noise, shoot her, or beam her up to their spaceship.

She frantically crawled forward; eyes wild. She gathered as many of the bottles and boxes as she could fit in her arms. *This* was the kind of break she needed. She wasn't sure what was in each bottle but there was no doubt in her mind it would all come in useful at some point. One of the first lessons she learned since The Change was the value of resources. And the importance of protecting them.

Max whined.

Calay stopped what she was doing.

Turning her head ever so slowly toward the dog, she saw his eyes trained near the door.

It was ajar.

Was it open before? Or was it shut? The perplexity bounced through her mind. First one, and then its opposite. Her bravery wavered as her stomach rose to greet the back of her throat. She pushed the panic down.

Not yet. Not yet.

She was alone. *There's no one there. If they were, they'd be on you already.* Nevertheless, Calay grabbed her stick and slung her pack over her shoulder, stuffing the remaining supplies inside.

This is what The Others did to us. This. They forced her to question what she thought. How she felt. Her own perceptions. They made her question herself. And everyone else. If the sole meaning of life was to serve humanity and humanity no longer existed, what purpose did her life now have? What purpose did any of it have?

She steeled herself and approached the door. Prepared for the worst —to run or to fight. She peered around the corner.

There was nothing; the hallway was as empty as it was when she arrived.

"You scared the shit out of me, Max. Let's go, come." She patted her leg and he followed her out of the room.

Calay broke through the main doors of the building. The sunshine was glorious. It was a beautiful late-Spring morning. There was still an early chill in the air and it was a welcome release after being inside that wasteland of a building. She inhaled a fresh breath. Feeling she'd come and conquered, Calay's limbs felt light for the first time in days. She had a full stash of medical rations and everything she'd need to treat any injury in the near future. Well, almost any injury. The physical ones, anyhow. That was progress.

Soaking up the warm sun, she had a jaunt to her step. The pain in her leg and arm even felt less fierce. She'd done well. She'd won this round and decided to follow the river back to camp, rather than take the quickest and most direct route. She deserved to treat herself to a little natural beauty. And then, she'd figure out how to get back to Tess. She was feeling damn confident, if even just a spark happy.

She took a deep breath and released it. For now, everything was okay. More than okay, it was good.

Calay turned the corner of the clinic and stopped dead in her tracks.

She'd walked smack into the line of sight of an alien pod, hovering not ten feet above her.

CHAPTER FOUR

Oh. Fuck.

The pods weren't huge. Not like Calay had seen in the movies. Or even the ship that had hovered above them so ominously the first day of The Change. But that didn't make them any less deadly. Spherical and blindingly white, they were about the size of a large SUV. There were no windows in the front. Well, she assumed it was the front. Where the driver must sit, looking at her. If they even had drivers. They almost looked like an accent piece out of a post-modern furnishings store. Before everything happened, she and Tess might have purchased a smaller, less murder-y version for their living room table. But these zapped people with laser beams into clouds of blood and plasma. *No thanks*. And the noise they made. That relentless whine and metal chomping on metal noise. But this one hadn't made a sound—she would have heard it.

Wouldn't she?

Questions slithered through her mind, wrapping themselves around her thoughts like a boa constrictor. Was it waiting for her to come out of the clinic all this time? Could it be in sleep mode? Was that even a thing? Did her presence wake it? Was it about to pulverize her into a million tiny pieces? Calay knew that either way, it didn't matter. All she had was this moment, and in this moment, it was definitely keen to her presence, bouncing in the air above her.

The pod glided forward. Beams of pale blue light appeared out of its hard shell, inching close to her toes. Calay took a long step back, retreating out of range. She'd seen what those lights do to people. The mess they created of the human form. A life, blown up and then evaporated into fine mist like they were never there. Humankind was so transfixed on leaving a legacy, but within a few months these machines had dwindled the human population so efficiently people could be classified on the endangered species list. If such a list even existed anymore.

What legacy?

Calay knew she couldn't outrun this thing. They were far faster and more agile than she'd ever be. She remembered how even when people began to evacuate the cities, the pods picked escapees off one by one in their cars, indiscriminately firing their lasers at people, regardless of age or gender. Entire ships sank deep below the ocean's surface as passengers were zapped into oblivion; many ran aground. Planes fell from the sky as beams fixated on pilots through the front windows of aircrafts. She shuddered at the memory of the trains and how they derailed and crashed into each other as everyone burned inside. That was how they terminated civilization en masse—travel technology. Hundreds of people tucked into annihilation vessels, just waiting to be demolished.

Stadiums were next. Then schools, churches, high rise apartment buildings. Anywhere humans gathered in groups. Catching them where we felt safe—where they congregated together—made the thinning easier. The Others used human's innate need to group and gather, against them.

Then after the initial assault, The Others didn't even have to do most of the work. Humans turned on each other. Which, on some level, was to be expected. For a while the good in humanity prevailed in pockets. Husbands protected their wives, parents nursed their children, strangers assisted the elderly. But having seen the television reports about people going apeshit over discounts in department stores before The Change, it shouldn't have come as a shock that when posed with the question of 'you or me,' the answer was always and unequivocally 'me.' Wives sacrificed their husbands, children abandoned their parents, the elderly became a liability.

As people began to pick themselves off, doing The Other's work for them, The Others sat back and watched. *They let us do the heavy lifting.* They were patient, in no rush. Until there weren't enough people left to do the picking. That's when they started targeting individuals. Weeding out the last vermin; the final purge.

Like this. Like now. Cornering Calay behind an abandoned, derelict building. Alone. Afraid. In seconds, she'd be gone, like she'd never been there at all. She wasn't sure if it was that idea or the actual incineration of her body that scared her more; both thoughts were about self-preservation. Both had meaning. Or they did, at one point.

Now? She wasn't so sure.

Still, evolution persevered.

Animals.

Calay spun on her heels and ran. Putting one foot in front of the other, she pounded the pavement with Max barking on her tail. Panic coursed through her body, her heart thundered in her chest, blood rushed through her veins. Rubble and the remnants of buildings created a maze of destruction. One she knew well, and yet, felt alien in the ever-growing and writhing shadows in the high afternoon sun. Bloated, dark shapes twisted beyond her vision. She turned one corner, then another, darting down alleys and side streets, not sure if she was doubling back or not. When she turned her head, the shapes would disappear, transforming into various shades of gray or black. They threatened to overwhelm her. To swallow her whole. She was becoming disoriented. Tears stung her eyes and her lungs roared for oxygen. Her knee threatened to give out—begged, even. With most of the defining characteristics blown to pieces at her feet, every building began to look the same, every block poured into the next. She was exhausted. Her reflection in what was left of the shattered windows dared her to stop. But the only thought she'd allow herself was, *escape!* The whirring and whining of the pod was relentless in its pursuit.

I will not die today! I can't. Not yet.

A tangle of vehicles blocked her path. Beyond it, a narrow alleyway. Beyond that, freedom.

"There!" She charged for the darkness.

She slid over a car and tumbled across the hood of a Jeep, sprawling on the other side. Her leg throbbed in pain and she muffled a scream. *No sense inviting anyone else to the party.* The stench of garbage and decay was palpable. Out of breath and her leg on fire, she knew she couldn't outrun the pod. It was incredible she hadn't been shot yet. It wasn't the first time she was grateful for the protection of the winding streets of the city. Weak from exhaustion, her body screamed for rest. She had to hide.

She grabbed Max by the scruff of his neck and pulled him close to her as she pushed her body flat against the pavement, gravel cutting into her skin as she spread herself underneath the Jeep. The concrete was cool in the shade, a brief respite from the burning in her lungs.

Then, she waited.

Moments later the sound of the pod grew louder. It was coming. Beams of blue light illuminated the dark alley, tracing the road and chasing shadows from behind dumpsters. Calay covered her mouth, swallowed a sob. That light was scarier than the darkness. The pod was scanning. Searching. Prodding.

It was going to find her.

The strange, throaty noises and whirs threatened to suffocate Calay; it was directly overhead. The Jeep rocked, its axle squeaked under the weight. The tires compressed. It was right above them. Darkness clouded her vision. She choked back the urge to vomit. There was nothing but a hunk of metal between her and certain death.

Yet the pod seemed unsure. Reluctant, even. She held her breath and prayed the dog wouldn't give them away. Yet despite her new-found spirituality, Max growled.

"Shhhhh..." she pleaded in a whisper, petting the dog's head. He fought against her arm, giving into his own need to flee. But she held tight and gently nuzzled his body, "stay. Please stay."

The glass popped out of the windows of the Jeep, exploding in a fire of shattered glass. Tiny shards fragmented the pavement, reflecting the pod above as it pressed down on the roof. *If I can see it, can it see me?* The Jeep tilted onto two tires, then dropped back down. It rocked back and forth, inching closer to one side of the alley and then the other. Calay pulled Max across the asphalt, careful not to be crushed by the vehicle. She was desperate to avoid being found. Cornered. Killed.

Is this it? Alone in a dark alley…?

And then the Jeep was still.

The noises started to fade; the blue light dimmed.

It was giving up. Leaving. They were safe! *As safe as one could be in a post-apocalyptic smorgasbord-of-what-the-fuck, anyhow.* Calay squeezed several tears from her clenched eyes. She sniffled and ran the back of her hand across her nose. Her breath rattled in her chest as she exhaled. She couldn't believe it.

Taking the most incremental of steps, she crawled out from under the Jeep and looked around, eyes wide. The Others had been obliterating the human race for the last two years and they were ferocious in their pursuit. As far as she knew, no one had actually seen their actual bodies. Just the pods. As society fell, the news broadcasts depicted them as Hollywood always had—humanoid, big head, long limbs, green. Before committing mass suicide to beat the End of Days, several prominent religious groups depicted them as pallid devils or insect-like in form. There was speculation amongst survivors that they were nothing like anything we could imagine. The likelihood they resembled anything human was small. The requirements for life to develop on Earth as it had, were very specific. It was much more likely they'd evolve to unique conditions on their home planet. Wherever that was. Calay shivered. She didn't know what they looked like and he didn't want to hang around and find out.

It was time to go.

"Max, come on," she commanded, reaching for her pack. It wasn't there.

Calay got down on her hands and knees and scoured the pavement. She looked left and right, underneath the cars. She retraced her steps as far as she dared without leaving the alley. She searched and found nothing.

"Oh no."

She'd lost it in her frantic state trying to get away. Slipped right off her shoulder. She hadn't even noticed it fall off.

"Oh no no no no no!"

Calay sunk against an old refrigerator marred by fire. She didn't notice the plushy toys stuffed in the freezer or the human arm sticking out of the half-open door. She was too busy lamenting her carelessness. The pack was gone. The supplies. The necklace. She considered going back to the clinic to search for it but couldn't risk being found again. It was pure luck the pod hadn't killed her already, and if it was still searching, it would find her again; that was inevitable. If it did find her again, she knew she would not get away a second time. She wasn't even sure which direction she'd come from. It was all a blur of footsteps, dark shadows, and tears. And that mechanical whining. Despite the silence that stalked her now, she covered her ears with her dirty palms, shook her head loose of the noise. Besides, the sun was starting to set, and she knew she needed to leave the city. Night would be coming soon, and there were theories that The Others detection technology worked even better in the dark.

She'd heard stories about their technology, but like their appearance, no one really knew for sure. There were rumors the pods were equipped with night vision. That they could see better in the dark because it was akin to their normal environment in space. They supposedly used thermal technology that allowed them to see the infrared heat of humans better at night. Even now, little was known about the small number that had been taken down. The pods seemed impervious. Yet, somehow, some of them fell. The details of how got lost along the way. The scientists who could have shed more light on how to best defend humankind were simply eradicated too quickly, then the media, and finally, the general population. Every time someone figured something out about The Others, they were killed just as fast, and the discovery became mere rumor. The truth became myth. *And now there are so few of us left....*

Calay glanced skyward. It would be dark soon. She shuddered. Where had the day gone? *Time flies when you're running for your life.* There would be more pods soon. There would be more people too. Despite the risks of running after dark, there always was.

"It's time to go." She repeated to herself.

Reluctant to leave without her pack, Calay pulled off her t-shirt and examined the fabric. Using what little strength remained, she tore the cuff off the shirt and tied it around her sore knee. Since she'd lost the bandages—*idiot*—it would have to do for now. She slipped the sleeveless shirt back on and wiped away some of the dirt from her face.

"Well…" She patted her leg, and Max replied with a whisper of a tail wag. He was now quite literally, the only thing she had in this world—in any world. They started out of the alley together, moving quickly for home.

They arrived just as the last light of day crept behind the trees. Grateful to be back alive, Calay stopped at the edge of her camp, breathing in the quiet. She escaped The Others but the whirring noise it made—the clamor of machinery—still haunted her. The stillness a respite from the churning and grinding of the pod. To think only twenty-four hours ago she'd found that silence deafening. She was glad for it now.

Today she was alone. Tomorrow she'd continue searching for Tess. But tonight, she was going to sleep.

Calay exhaled, smiled a moment, wished for a glass of whiskey. She walked back into her camp ready to collapse into a deep slumber.

Only sleep was the last thing she would enjoy that night. Because there, crouching by the roaring fire, was a man.

CHAPTER FIVE

A BEAUTIFUL MAN.

Right, like that was the thing to focus on. It didn't seem to matter what state the world was in or where she found herself, her old vices always came back to taunt her. Like self-medicating. Like impulsiveness. Like men.

Hot, sexy, manly men. Like the man sitting in front of her.

Calay's breath caught in her throat and she stopped dead in her tracks. Her feet grew heavy as she planted them in the moist ground. This was not okay. His being here was not okay. And his level of hotness—whether he'd maim her or not—was definitely not okay. No, this was very, very wrong. She had to get him out of there. But how?

"Hi there," he said. His head was tilted facing the fire. He wasn't looking at her and yet, Calay could feel his gaze. She could see the ripple in his broad shoulders as he shook the contents of a pan back and forth. Whatever it was smelled hearty and made her ache for food. He chanced a glance up at her from the furrow of his brow, his wavy dark hair spilling into his eyes. He had the audacity to let a smile scrape the corner of his full lips. Was he mocking her? Goading her? She couldn't decide.

When was the last time she'd been with a man? Felt the touch of one? The weight of one on top of her? Calay wasn't sure if she wanted to kill him or fuck him. Or both. The thought of sex made her think of Tess, and Calay felt a pang of guilt. And then loneliness. *What's wrong with me?* It wasn't that she didn't love Tess or that she even wanted other partners. To want to be close to this strange man meant she wouldn't be alone. To feel him inside her. Just to be in his company. She watched him closer as he tended to the pan, stoked the fire. He seemed friendly. But then again, everyone seemed friendly right before they took everything you owned—which, albeit wasn't much at this point—gutted you and left you for dead. Given she'd fought so hard to survive today, that would be an unfortunate outcome. One she'd rather avoid. Emotions coursed through her body as she fought one thought with another.

Calay stood silent. Still as a grave. As if the slightest movement would set him upon her. The wind rustled the canopy of leaves above, casting shadows that danced across the man's dark features. Max's hair raised on his back and he curled behind her legs and whined, equally suspicious of their new house guest.

"Heh, I guess this is your camp huh?"

She nodded, cautious and deliberate. 'Don't let them see your fear,' Tess had told her, 'they home in on it like wolves.' As if he could hear her thoughts, the man retrained his stare from the fire and focused on hers. *Stay calm.*

He coughed a little and cleared his throat. "Sorry to intrude like this. I've been on the road for a while now. Haven't seen anybody in a long time. Then I came across this…this set up. I thought it might belong to someone, so I waited a while before helping myself to your fire. Didn't want to press my luck, ya' know? I watched."

There was something about his turn of phrase that put Calay on knives and needles. *He watched?*

"Anyhow, no one came. I figured after a couple hours, no one would. Plus, it looked a little overgrown, might even have been abandoned. You know how people come and go these days," he paused. She gave nothing away. "I was getting pretty hungry—it's been days since I've had a proper meal. Longer since I've had anything hot."

"You want some rabbit?"

His attention was back to the pan. Calay deflated a little as he looked away. She didn't want his attention and yet, she craved connection. Something about him wasn't quite right though. He seemed too relaxed, too sure she wouldn't spill his intestines in the dirt or bury a knife in his skull. But then again, he had food. Hot food. Protein. And it smelled incredible. *We really are just products of biology.*

"Sit," he offered.

She didn't.

He raised his head, looked her square in the eye, and stood up. Damn he was tall. Probably had a good foot or so on her. His arms were wide. His stance sturdy. He'd be hard to take down if she needed to do something about this.

"Sit," he said more firmly.

Calay realized if she was going to take him out, she'd have to do it with the advantage of surprise. This guy was far too big for her to attack head on. She didn't stand a chance. Which got her thinking. The men from the warehouse were large, and she didn't get a good look at them. Her mind was too focused on getting the hell out of there. *Is this guy one of them?* Even if he wasn't, what was to stop him from taking anything he wanted? From taking her?

"Please," he said. His wide hand stretched to a log dusted in flickering shadows. The fire was warm and bright. It roared louder and higher than she'd managed to build on her own. She brushed past the log and made her way to a stump beside it. She was unsteady on her feet, her breath shallow. She sat. And gussied all the nerve she had inside her.

"Who the fuck are you?" she asked, hoping the shake in her voice didn't betray her bravado.

"My name's Jacob. It's nice to meet you." He handed her the pan. It did smell amazing. "Take it. It's good. Judging by the looks of you, I imagine it's been a while since you had a decently cooked meal too."

He was right. But Calay didn't want him to know that. She didn't want anything from this man. This stranger. Except for what she imagined to be his long, hard...he smiled. A full smile. All teeth and lips and his eyes lit up. Her mouth fell open. She clamped it shut, cleared her throat.

Jesus.

"Look, I know I startled you. I'm sorry for that. Please. Times are tough, take the rabbit. I promise it's not going to be the worst thing you've ever had." To demonstrate, he took a bite out of the remaining leg which he held like a chicken wing.

She looked at the pan, then the veins in his forearm. It all looked so good. She reached forward with caution, keeping her eyes on him. Not daring to look him directly in the eye. As she took the pan, he nodded and went back to the other side of the fire to finish his portion.

"So what's your name?" he asked.

She brought a piece of the rabbit up to her lips and smelled it. When was the last time she had real protein? Something—anything—besides warmed beans or the meat of a bird she'd found dead in the woods? It wasn't that she and Tess couldn't kill animals for food, it was that there just weren't many animals *to* kill. They'd thinned out considerably over the last year as humans stopped producing garbage. And as they hunted them. She'd have thought the animal population would have thrived without humans. Some had, deep in the forests. But in the cities, the landscape became concrete wastelands. Their borders, like this one, purgatory for animals and humans alike.

"I didn't know there were any more rabbits. Where did you catch it?" Calay asked as she pushed the meat around in the pan.

"I could show you," Jacob said.

She shook her head, bringing the meat to her mouth. It smelled delicious. She tore off a piece. Chewed. Then had another. It tasted delicious too. She was ravenous. She felt him watching her as she devoured the meal, unable to stop herself, conscious of his gaze on her. Within seconds, the pan was empty.

Max lapped up the pieces she dropped in her voraciousness. She tossed him one of the larger bones. The dog tucked behind the log to enjoy his reward. When she was finished licking her fingers, Jacob spoke.

"I still didn't catch your name," he said.

"Calay," she murmured.

"Like I said, it's nice to meet you, Calay. Guess I got pretty lucky running into you here. It's nice to talk to someone. And by the way you just devoured that rabbit, I'd say you got pretty lucky running into me too."

She looked at him, blinked, folded her hands in her lap. "You have no idea about my luck; I don't need this."

"Easy, easy. I get it. I'm just saying I'm glad I found you."

"What do you want now?"

"Want? Well, I want to digest this fine meal and hopefully catch me a good night of sleep. You look like you've got some pretty good cover, and I'd appreciate the chance to rest. Nights out there are rough—you never know who might stumble upon you."

Calay's hackles stood up.

"You mean someone like you?"

"Granted you know nothing about me. I'll give you that. But I don't want to hurt you, Calay. I just want to rest. And then I'll be on my way."

"And what do you want in exchange for rest?"

"Good company?" There was that smile again. That teasing in his eyes. *Maybe a bit of hopefulness?* She must have imagined it—she knew nothing about this guy. Or his intentions. She squinted as she peered at him. She directed her attention to the pan while she decided what to do and reached for it. Her arm twanged and a pained moan escaped her lips. She could feel him examining her across the fire. *Damn it.* She wondered if he sizing her up, watching for weaknesses? She couldn't let him near her. For every possible reason It wouldn't just be wrong and unfair to Tess; it would be flat out stupid and dangerous.

Jacob rose and approached Calay, this time without the lure of fresh cooked meat.

"Stop."

He stepped closer.

"Don't come over here."

"Calay, you're in pain."

"What do you care if I'm in pain? I said I'm fine. Stay over there."

"I have experience with this kind of thing. And medical supplies in my bag. I can help you."

"I don't need your help."

"Don't be ridiculous."

"Ridiculous?" The blood in Calay's veins rushed to her head. Her pulse quickened. "You don't know a single thing about me. You've known me for less than an hour! Ridiculous! Fuck you."

He was arrogant for sure, and for all Calay knew, dangerous. He'd already helped himself to her fire. She had no idea what he planned to help himself to next. She'd seen what men do to women in this world, and it wasn't about to happen to her. Between this man and Max, the likelihood of finding two friendlies in one day was just too rare. Too unlikely. Too coincidental. He had to be trouble. She had to take care of this. And she was going to do it or die trying.

He reached for her.

Calay charged.

Striking his stomach with the top of her head, he doubled over on top of her, sending them both tumbling to the ground. The force of their movement sent sparks high into the night air. They landed, hard, the cold dirt doing nothing to comfort their fall. Her fists beat his shoulders. His back. Then one landed square in the jaw. *Yes!* She struggled beneath him to get free and was almost out of his grasp when she felt his strong hands on her legs.

"Oh no you don't!" she countered.

She kicked furiously at his chest, his stomach, anywhere she could connect. She was fast and surprisingly accurate, but he was stronger.

"Stop, Calay." His knees pinned down her arms.

"Get off me!"

"It's useless. Just stop."

Calay fought in the dirt, ash, and grass to get free, but her limbs tired. Her body yearned for rest. Her lungs begged for it. She looked up at him, seething between her teeth. He smirked that non-threatening grin. The amusement migrated to his crystal blue eyes. This close, she could see they had flecks of green in them. He was enjoying this. *What a sicko. And yet...*He hadn't once hit her, punched her, kicked her, or tried to tear off any of her clothing. She allowed herself to catch her breath. She noticed the way his t-shirt pulled across his shoulders. The freckles across his cheekbones. In that moment, she wasn't sure if she was terrified or turned on. Probably a bit of both.

She wanted to trust him. But how?

She thought of the looting in the streets. When everything started, people took what they wanted. They destroyed what they didn't. The riots that occurred all across the country as cities fell and burned. Seattle had been the first, but many others followed. The stories were of assault and murder when resources became scarce, and it had only gotten worse over time. It seemed when the world went to hell in a handbasket, those willing or able to do the most damage flourished, and those who were unwilling fell victim. All that was good about humanity had become an inferno of violence.

Fuck this, I'll be damned if I'm going to burn too.

Calay gathered the strength she had left, bent her leg, and kneed him square in the groin.

Jacob instinctively grabbed himself. Calay scrambled from underneath him. He rolled on the ground, immobilized and without breath. She lunged for the closest weapon she could find—a thick branch sticking halfway out of the now dwindling fire. Calay spun on her heels and clobbered Jacob across the head just as he reached for her. A meteor shower of ash and sparks flew through the night sky.

Jacob was out cold.

CHAPTER SIX

Calay woke with a start.

She didn't mean to fall asleep. She planned to stay awake until Jacob came to, just to make sure he couldn't get loose from the twine she'd used to restrain him.

She rolled over and saw him sitting there, right where she'd left him. Those piercing blue eyes looking directly at her. Fuming.

Rise and shine.

"Are you hurt?" he asked.

"Are you serious?" she spit back.

"Of course, I'm serious."

"You attacked me."

"I attacked you? I tried to help you with your damn arm, and you went crazy." He took a labored breath. "And now you have me strapped to this log like a wild animal."

"As far as I'm concerned, you are a wild animal."

"We're all wild animals," he countered.

"Then it's a good thing I tied you up."

Her arm was crusted with dried blood and her leg hummed with a dull ache. Something had to be done about the pain. *And I'll do it myself thank you very much.* She pushed herself to her feet, wobbling, and snatched his duffle bag.

"You said you had medical supplies. Was that true?" Without waiting for his reply, she opened the zipper and started rifling through the contents, the buckles jingling as the bag shook in her pained grasp.

"Yes, nothing I've said to you has been a lie, Calay."

She pursed her lips together without glancing up and continued to dig. As her fingers scraped the bottom of the bag, she found a variety of medicated ointments and bandages.

Huh, look at that.

He was telling the truth.

"Go ahead, help yourself," he grumbled. She couldn't tell if he was being cheeky or generous. He was in no condition to stop her either way. She didn't answer to him. She didn't answer to anybody.

Calay sat down and nursed her wounds, slathering on more topical cream than necessary. The arm didn't look great. Underneath the dried blood and caked on leaves and dirt, it was red and filled with pus. *That's not good.* The only thing worse than a stranger in her camp would be a stranger in her body—an infection. It didn't take much to take people down now, and proper medical treatment was rare, if not impossible. She again regretted losing her pack. *Suck it up, Buttercup.* She shook off the thought. This time she wouldn't take any chances. Her heartbeat pulsed through her arm. She wrapped a bandage around the wound, securing it with a lengthy strip of medical tape.

"So you weren't lying about the medical supplies. So what? That doesn't mean you were actually planning on using them to help me," she said.

Her gaze met his.

She knew nothing about this man, Jacob, if that was his real name. Except that he knew how to cook rabbit and lost a fight to a girl. A wounded girl, at that. Because he fought…fair. He fought fair, she realized. But now, in this world, fair was a luxury she couldn't afford. She fought dirty.

"Jacob, was it?"

He nodded.

"Why are you here?" she prodded.

"I told you last night."

"Tell me again."

"I was lost. I was looking for…"

"Looking for what?"

"For a chance."

"A chance to do what?"

"To survive," he stressed. His voice was firm. If not a bit abstentious. She couldn't read him. And that was a problem.

"And you just happened upon my camp while I was out. Didn't think maybe it belonged to someone? Or you just didn't care?"

"No. That's not it. I told you last night. It's been days, weeks, even. I'm not sure. You know what it's like on your own out there."

Damn right she did—it was dangerous. Terrifying. Every man for himself. And certainly, every woman. She squared him up.

"I feel like I'm talking in circles right now" he pleaded, "untie me and I'll show you."

"Show me what?"

"I know things."

"Bullshit. What kind of things?"

"You aren't alone in this, Calay."

She stiffened. "Stop saying my name like that."

"Like what?"

"Stop saying it like you know me. You don't know me and this isn't personal."

"You're right, I'm sorry. I don't know you. I…I just want you to know you can trust me. You aren't alone, and we can do this together."

"Do what, exactly?"

He was too risky, in every way. Tess—wherever she was—needed her, and Calay had to get moving again. The birds sang a chorus of agreement. Jacob replied but she didn't hear him. Instead, she shook the tarp off her shelter and dumped the contents of his bag on top. Max investigated the various food items that tumbled out, along with some basic supplies and articles of clothing. She put half the food back in his pack but kept the other half, a rather large hunting knife, and a flashlight for herself. She folded the tarp over the items and using the string from her shelter, fashioned a rudimentary backpack out of the mess.

It would do.

She looked at Jacob.

"I should probably kill you," Calay said, thrusting her hand on her hip.

"I'd prefer if you didn't," he countered, smiling.

"I have no idea what you're capable of."

"We can work together, Calay..." he began.

"Stop!"

She looked at him and straightened her shoulders. She knew her instincts were right—she should kill him where he sat. But she couldn't bring herself to do it. She'd killed plenty of people in the past, because she'd had to. So why was this one so difficult? She always did what she had to do; she survived. *But maybe that was the problem.* Those people didn't deserve to die, but it came down to a 'me' or 'them' situation. Right now, Jacob posed no threat. She couldn't just murder an unarmed man, could she? He didn't even have use of his arms or legs, they were wrapped tightly against the log. The veins in his arms bulged. For a fleeting moment she wondered what they would feel like wrapped around her, that pouty mouth on hers, trailing over her chin and down her neck...

"Stop it," she said again, this time to herself.

She wondered if she should give him another knock on the head? Bury him? Fuck him?

She grabbed a t-shirt out of Jacob's things and walked over to him. He smirked. "You gonna change me?" Calay's breath caught in her throat and she resisted the urge to beg to do just that. Instead, she wrapped it around his face, knotting it in place. She waved in front of it. Held up the knife. He didn't so much as flinch, which meant he couldn't see a thing. *Perfect.* She tossed the rucksack in his lap and started making her way out of camp. She'd made a decision she could live with. She was leaving him behind, trussed up like a Thanksgiving turkey. She didn't kill him, but as she took another step forward, putting more distance between the mysterious man and herself, the thought occurred to her that someone else might if they found him like that. Twigs and leaves crunched under her feet as she walked away from him, toward Tess. Or at least she hoped so.

"Calay! Stop! Calay!" he called from under the t-shirt mask, "I haven't given you any reason to leave me like this!"

"No, you haven't." she called back, "but everyone else has."

※

CALAY AND MAX STOOD AT THE EDGE OF THE BARREN highway.

To the west was the city. It was a dangerous and familiar place. To the east, the unknown, endless trees, and the nightmares that lurked there. Neither option seemed preferable—she didn't want to go to either of those places. She wanted to be in Tess's embrace. Tess wasn't in the city. Not as far as Calay could tell, anyhow. If she was, Calay should have found her by now. She'd interrogated every crack, crevice, and building looking for signs. She'd found nothing but violence and flying spacemen. *Space orbs*. She had to keep moving and cover all ground until she got to where they said they'd meet if they were ever separated. But she didn't know how or when they were separated. She couldn't remember a fucking thing. For all she knew, Tess could be locked in a building, alone and injured, just like she was. Waiting to die. Or live. Or...Calay abandoned the thought. All she knew was that they weren't together and she was going to turn over every single stone to find Tess.

She took a step onto the broken pavement and looked east. Into the wild unknown.

"What do you think?" she asked the dog. Max wagged his tail.

"East it is." She decided.

Her feet—and Max—followed.

They kept to the edge of the highway. Though shielded by trees and hanging moss, the sun still beat down on them. Even their shadows retreated into the cracks of the pavement, melting below the asphalt and looking for a respite from what was promising to be a very hot day. Max nipped and scratched at flies that landed on his fur as they made their way down the highway. Occasionally they'd pass cars, broken and long since abandoned. She checked the backseats and pried open the trunks, searching for water. Food. Anything that might help them. Rarely did she find anything more than a rotting corpse or two inside. Most were so badly decayed she couldn't tell if they'd met their death at the hands of The Others or other people. She didn't look too closely, and frankly, didn't want to. There was the issue of bacteria and infection that could carry to her own injuries, but more than that, the gruesome images buried themselves in your mind and rose each night in your nightmares. She'd seen enough to last a lifetime. Her lifetime. Which, if she didn't find Tess, could be much shorter than she'd originally planned. She wondered if that was such a bad thing now.

She coughed on the dry air and looked down at Max. He was panting heavily. They needed water. Bad.

"Keep moving," she whispered.

And so, they did.

As they made their way through the carnage of abandoned vehicles, Calay felt the weight of the last forty eight hours bear down on her and began to waver. *What have I done?* Physically her body was shutting down, begging to rest and rehydrate. Emotionally she'd already become dust. She began to wonder how she'd ever find Tess; since The Change, they'd never been apart more than a couple days. Now it had been almost a week. Probably more. And that was the part she could remember. What happened before she woke up in that warehouse? Where was Tess then? Where was she now? The sheer distance Calay had to cover to even make it back to their rendezvous point seemed insurmountable.

And then there was the issue of Jacob. She'd just left him. His pleas for mercy creeped through her mind, inching their way ever closer to her sanity. *Did I make the right choice?* He could have been telling the truth about everything. She wondered if she should turn back and hear him out. Give him the chance he'd begged her for. If he could be trusted, his company would be a welcome retreat from her loneliness. Maybe he deserved it, maybe not. But it had already been hours since they'd started walking, and she wasn't sure her and Max would make it back now.

Something resembling a sob escaped her parched lips, but it died as it broached the sweltering heat.

"I'm totally alone," she choked. She was all too aware of her own contributions to that. She had no control over where Tess was or what the aliens had done to them, but she could have stayed with Jacob. Or brought him with her. Or...an urge to cry welled in her throat, but no tears came. Her body couldn't spare them. Instead, she felt the hollow of her chest heave and her vision fade.

Calay leaned against a vehicle, the doors ajar, and the indicator long since run dead.

She began to sink to the hot pavement. If this was the end, this was as good a spot as any. She closed her eyes. The hot air was relentless in its pursuit of her. *Lean into it, just breathe it in.*

A strange hum filled the air.

She stopped mid-crouch, her back warm against the metal of the vehicle. The breath she thought gone from her lungs caught in her throat.

"What the...?"

She listened. It grew louder. And then she saw it.

CHAPTER SEVEN

A CAR WAS DRIVING toward her in the distance.

An actual car. With a functioning engine and headlights and people. Her heart jumped at the thought and then it plummeted. *People.*

Calay considered her options. Many months ago, she would have waved it down and begged for water. But she knew better than that now. That kind of impulsive reaction to live could get you killed. And in her weakened state she'd make an easy target. She knew now survival went beyond basic human needs. But she couldn't deny she was beyond thirsty. She needed water and soon, or she wasn't going to last the day. Which meant she wasn't prepared to make a run for it, either. She knew if she wanted to see tomorrow, she was going to have to be smart. Or at least, smarter.

The car drew nearer, the sound got louder. She scrambled up the embankment, her feet slipping on the loose gravel and dirt. Her fingers grasped at the long strands of grass, pulling herself up the slippery slope. It was only about ten feet to the trees, but it felt like ten miles. The harder she fought the less quickly she moved. She knew the foliage and ferns often made the forest too dense to walk through, but they would make an excellent hiding place. If she could only get there.

Max barked. "Shhhhh..." In the two days she had the dog, she'd quickly grown to love him. But he sure knew the worst times to speak up.

She collapsed behind a fern as the refraction of heat waves cleared and the vehicle approached. A Jeep. Not dissimilar from the one she'd hid under in the alley a couple days ago. She took that as a good omen. It had saved her once, maybe this one would save her again.

It slowed its pace as it converged on the abandoned vehicles in the road, weaving between them. The glare of the sunlight on the cars made it hard to see who was inside or how many.

It rolled to a stop below her, idling. Threat or not, it was there. Between the tumbling vines, she scoured the pavement. Waiting. Deciding. If she didn't get help soon, she wasn't sure how much longer she would be.

A door opened. Then three more. Calay sucked in her breath and crouched lower behind the shrubbery. She pulled Max close.

Three men and one woman stepped out of the vehicle in matching uniforms. Calay wondered if they could be whatever was left of the government. *Maybe some kind of rescue or humanitarian organization.* She let her heart hope, just a fraction. A fracture. A glimmer of possibility there might be something better. She couldn't help herself—it was who she was. She'd always believed the best in people. Despite her many cynical moments, deep down she hoped people were better. That humans were good. It was a shame humanity had proven her wrong so many times. Still, against her better judgement, she yearned for goodness.

"Yeah. Check that group," one of them said as he pointed to a pileup on the side of the road, "might find something in there."

She wasn't sure if it was her desperation or a lack of options, but Calay felt compelled to reveal herself. They could have water. Food. Security. Tess was maybe even somewhere in the safety of their care. She observed them. As they combed the vehicles one by one, they seemed organized and methodic—not irrational and compulsive like other groups she'd come across. Not like Jacob. *Jacob.* She was being unfair. He didn't seem irrational or compulsive either—quite the opposite actually. All he'd done was shown up. His presence scared her and made her realize how much she needed human connection, but he hadn't lashed out at her at all. The relentless ache in her chest reminded her if she'd ever missed Tess, it was now. Between that and the trauma of the last few days, Calay felt unnerved. Risky. Irrational even. She looked at Max, dehydrated, panting, and laying on his side. He wasn't even trying to bark now. Both were breathing heavily. She had no choice.

She stood up.

"Hello!" she called, giving them a friendly wave and a broad toothy smile. She hoped she didn't look as awkward as she felt.

The group trained their guns on her. Big guns. How had she not noticed those before? The severe heat and lack of water must have clouded her judgement. Or her vision. *Now I've gone and done it.* She threw her hands up.

"What the fuck? Get down here!" one of them demanded. It didn't matter which one—they all looked the same to her in their matching uniforms and short hair. With their big guns.

Seriously, what the fuck, indeed?

"I'm very thirsty. I'm not dangerous. I..I don't have a weapon," she stammered, "it's just me and my dog."

"Get the fuck down here now!"

"Can you help me?"

Two of the men brought their gun scopes to their eyes and raised their weapons higher.

"Now!"

Calay considered running back into the forest but she knew she wouldn't get far. She assumed they were well-rested. They looked well-nourished. They had combat boots. They had big fucking guns. She had none of those things.

Oh my God, what have I done?

"Okay I'm coming down. Don't shoot me, please." She made her way out of the forest embankment, her leg cramping as she slid on loose stones.

"Easy! Go slowly!" one of the militias called out.

"Yes, I am. I mean, I'm trying. Don't shoot me. I...I just slipped." Calay shook her head, tried to keep her legs underneath her. This was a mistake. *A big mistake.*

She stood on the road; five long barrels were trained on her head. She could feel them as much as see them. It was like she was a marionette, a string attached to each gun. They could make her dance. They could make her die. They could make her do anything they damn well pleased. *Well, this was a bad decision. Really bad.* She stood there, waiting. For what felt like an eternity.

"Put them down," the man who ordered the car search grunted.

She looked at him, seeing him up close for the first time. He was taller than the rest. Thinner too. She pegged him for a runner in a past life.

"I said put them down soldiers!" he demanded, "Now!"

Soldiers, so they might really be the military. A whisper of hope whistled through her mind. If so, she might just be okay after all. Slowly—reluctantly—the guns slid down the length of her body. Past her chest, her major organs, her kneecaps. But the soldier's cold gazes held strong. Calay knew one quick movement from her and they'd blast so many bullets into her, she'd be more lead than biological tissue.

"I know what it's like out here," she started, conjuring Jacob's voice in her mind as she said it, "I'm lucky I found you."

"Shut the fuck up."

She shut the fuck up.

"You said it's just you and the dog?" The man nodded to Max.

"Yes, just us."

"And you don't have a weapon?"

"No, no weapons."

"That's bullshit," the woman soldier said. The anger in her eyes was unyielding. "Everyone has a weapon."

"Search her" someone commanded. Calay missed who, she was busy gawking at the only other woman on the asphalt. She wanted to reach her somehow, appeal to her better nature. But how?

"I don't have a weapon," Calay explained, "I was run out of my camp by a man. I left everything behind to escape." It wasn't a complete lie. She'd learned that was the thing about sharing disinformation. The closer you skirted the truth, the harder it was to fumble it up.

A stalky man approached Calay. He pulled the makeshift pack off her back shook the whole thing loose. The contents scattered on the ground at their feet. Right there in the center was the hunting knife she'd taken from Jacob.

God damn i--

Calay looked up, eyes wide, her mouth open to explain when the man's fist collided with her mouth. He grabbed her. She felt the weight of his calloused hand wrap around the back of her neck. If he had the inclination, he could snap her spine like a cheap piece of plastic. Max growled, fierce, and leapt for the man's leg but was kicked aside.

"Ouch, please. No!" Calay begged.

"Hang onto that dog," the tall man ordered.

Calay's body slammed into the side of the Jeep, her teeth coming down hard on her lower lip. The scent of metal filled her senses. She wasn't sure if it was the taste of blood or the smell of the hood of the vehicle. Her vision darkened; the bright day faded. The man groped his way over her arms, her back, her ass.

"Okay, Guy..." the taller man said.

The man—Guy—granted himself one more feel of her behind and spun her around. He raised a flashlight in her face and held it there.

"Not bright enough out here for you?" Calay spit. She couldn't help herself.

Guy smacked her across the face with his free hand. "Shut. Up. Or yeah, I'll give you something to make noise about."

Calay's body recoiled with the thought of how he might good on that promise. She looked to the woman standing to her left, pleading with her eyes for help.

The woman walked up to them. She ran her hand down Calay's arm; it was almost tender. And then she twisted it around and bound Calay's wrists together with a zap strap behind her back. Calay blinked in disbelief. The woman stared back. *So much for sisterhood.* But she knew what was between their legs didn't matter for shit. Hadn't for a long time. Maybe not ever. Just because you were a woman, didn't mean you were *for* women. It had always been more about power than it was about people. Or about other women. Before The Change, what you had in your pants meant almost as little as it did now. Unless someone wanted what was between your legs—that was alive and well.

"Why are you doing this?" Calay could feel the tears trying to come again. But she wouldn't give them the satisfaction, and her body wouldn't give her the water. She swallowed hard.

They all looked at Calay. She imagined them sizing up what needed to be done.

Max whined, his head low.

Beside her, one of the men's heads exploded; the spray decorating Guy's face with brain matter. Fragments of skin and drops of blood coated Calay's hair.

Then the tall man; his head popped like a Starburst candy, shooting bone shrapnel all over the woman whose gun had slipped from her hand, her bottom lip shaking.

"What the fuck?" Guy shrieked. His eyes were frantic, scanning the forest edge, the sky. Calay tried to look up as well, but with her neck still firmly lodged between the vehicle's hood and Guy's palm, she couldn't see much. From what she could tell, the sky was empty. There were no pods. No aliens. A person, then. Someone was shooting.

Calay decided to use the distraction to her advantage.

She leaned back and wrangled all her strength to drive the top of her head into Guy's nose. It worked with Jacob, why not now? Guy screamed and as he released her, Calay fell to her knees. Pain shot through her body. *Shake it off.* She looked up and saw the woman who'd bound her wrists was standing there, dumbstruck. Calay pressed herself up from the pavement and kicked the woman in the stomach, forcing her to the ground. Max, now free, snarled and bit hard on the soldier's leg, shaking violently.

Guy's nose was a faucet that refused to turn off. Blood poured over his lips and clung to the front of his button-up uniform shirt. He breathed heavily and grunted with rage. Or fear. Or both. Calay felt his hatred pulsating in the air between them. She crawled backward as he rose, nearly tripping over the woman who was shaking Max loose. Calay looked around. The guns were on the ground, the men who had held them now dead. With her hands tied behind her back they were of little help. She scrambled to stand, took a step back, and then another, putting as much distance between herself and the two remaining soldiers as she could. She didn't dare run. She had no idea where the bullets had come from. Her gaze darted between Guy and the woman, both of them leaning on each other now for support. And then they ran. One moment, they were on the other side of the road and in the next, they disappeared into the forest like two bats out of hell. A trail of blood lingered behind them.

Calay was alone. Or at least, alone with the shooter. Whoever it was. She fell to her knees. Bloody, sweaty, and surrounded by death, she awaited the inevitable. That final pop. A release from the heat and thirst and God-fucking-awfulness of this world. She closed her eyes and sat. For a millennium. Waiting. But the shot didn't come. Max nosed her head, trying to encourage her spirits; they were a pack.

A branch cracked. And then another. *This is the moment. Do or do not.* She looked up, ready to face her would-be killer.

And there he was. *Jacob.* He stepped out of the forest; perched at the very place she'd previously crouched. *That really is a good hiding spot.*

Her mouth became dry, it hung open. She was unable to speak. A million questions whirled in her mind, one lagging as another clamored on top: how had he gotten loose? How had he found her? Did he follow her? Was he going to take revenge on her for leaving him tied up? Was he going to take anything else…? Calay tried to slow her thoughts as fear crept through her veins, one unspeakable horror at a time.

In his hands, Jacob held a very large sniper rifle. His blue eyes were dark and trained on her. And he was descending the embankment, sure footed, toward Calay.

CHAPTER EIGHT

Calay was paralyzed with fear. She trembled as sweat dripped down her neck like a lover's kiss.

Jacob made his way toward her. She noticed his lips pressed together in a thin line. His knuckles whitened as they tightened around the gun. His shadow grew longer on the pavement, a darkness that broadened with each step. The weight of it pressed down upon her, crawled up her body. First, over her toes. Then her thighs. Her shoulders. She shrunk against the pavement as his shadow grew taller, devouring her frame. Finally, he towered before her. And she had nothing left with which to fight.

"I definitely should have killed you," Calay admitted.

Jacob crouched, meeting her gaze. Calay clamped her eyes shut, tears leaked out the side. *This really is it*. There was a loud bang, like the sound of metal crunching metal. And she was suddenly on her feet.

...Wait, what?

She opened her eyes and Jacob's gun was splayed on the hood of the Jeep, his hands around her biceps. He'd lifted her up; the confusion on her face unmistakable. She tilted her head back and peered up at him, furrowing her brow.

Her eyes met his. He stepped closer, trapping her between the Jeep and his body. He leaned in, his hard chest against hers. She caught herself leaning into the connection. It had been too long since she felt the touch of another human. He reached behind her, silent save for the sound of his breath. Her neck tingled, the hairs on the small of her back raised.

Calay wondered what was wrong with her. How could she think about affection with this strange man, when he could quite possibly be there to kill her? *No, not affection—dirty, hot, animalistic sex on the top of this car.* If she was being honest with herself, that was what Calay was thinking about. Tess's face flashed through her mind, and she pushed the thought aside. She would get to Tess as soon as she could. But in the meantime, she had to focus on what was in front of her.

Her hands were free.

Oh…right.

She felt more disappointment than she wanted to admit. She was free, she should feel relieved. Instead, she felt Jacob pull away and couldn't help but feel…unsatisfied. And then the realization hit her like a brick on bone. *I'm free!* She'd already made two stupid decisions that day, she would not make a third because she had an emotional vagina. She had to do something. Now. It was do or die time.

"Just for the record, I wa…" Jacob started.

Calay whipped around and grabbed the gun off the hood of the car. She trained it on Jacob. His face fell as he rolled his eyes, raised his hands, and backed away.

"You've got to be kidding me."

She pivoted and shot both dead men—for good measure, safety, and because it felt damn good. It was something raging in her gut. It had to be done. *Fuck them.* Blood splattered the pavement and Jacob's boots.

"Okay they're dead now," he mocked, but there was that damn smile on his face again. Was he teasing her? She retrained the gun on him.

"How did you find me?"

"I'm glad you're safe," he said, "those people were going to kill you, 'ya know."

"You think I don't know that? You think I'm some dumb chick who can't take care of herself? Look, I was surviving just fine before you showed up."

"I don't think you're dumb at all. Definitely a chick though, but please, correct me if I'm wrong. But not dumb, Calay. Never dumb."

"And then you come into my camp and ask me to trust you? How can I do that? I know nothing about you."

"What do you want to know?" he asked.

"Who the hell are you, for one? And where did you come from? You forced me to leave my own camp. Forced me into this situation. It's your fault. You're dangerous." She shook the gun at him, felt it—and herself—quivering.

His eyes looked concerned. Almost kind.

"What. Do. You. Want?" she pushed.

"I want to help you. And you want to help me."

"What's your angle?" she pressed. *And why do I care?* Here she was again, not shooting him. Max hovered around her legs, eyes trained on Jacob, seemingly ready to pounce should the need arise.

"I don't have an angle, I swear it. I'm just tired of being alone. You know what that feels like."

She knew that feeling all too well and she didn't need him reminding her of it. What she *did* need was to get away from Jacob and find Tess before she did something she'd regret. In more ways than one. She didn't want to kill him. She didn't want to kill anybody. And she certainly didn't want to betray Tess's love. Their commitment to each other. But everything in her body yearned—screamed—to be touched. To run and get the hell out of there. The two urges waged a tug of war inside her. She needed to leave. Now.

"Don't move," Calay said as she began to back away from Jacob, "do not come after me or I will shoot you. Do you understand? If you stand in the way of this vehicle, I will shoot you."

The edges of his mouth teased up.

"And if you smile one more time, I will motherfucking shoot you."

"Well, that'd be a rather severe punishment for saving your life just now, don't you think?" he smiled.

Her knees weakened with lust. She walked forward and shoved the barrel of the gun into his chest harder than she needed to. His face fell, went cold, his body erect. *Erect.* She pushed the image away.

"Got it?" she said between clenched teeth.

Jacob nodded. But barely.

"Say the words, Jacob."

"I got it."

Calay backed away from the body she wanted to lean into so badly. She made her way around the front of the Jeep and maneuvered her way behind the steering wheel.

"Max, come!" The dog jumped into the back and barked.

She looked down to start the engine, wrapped her fingers around the keys still in the ignition, and then she realized the flaw in her well laid plan. It was a manual transmission.

Her stomach dropped.

She couldn't drive the damn thing. Her dad tried to make her learn on the farm over the years, encouraging her to develop that skill. It might just come in handy, he'd say. But she hadn't seen the point. She wasn't interested in farm work so she didn't need to know how to drive the machinery, and any vehicle she'd ever owned was an automatic. She cursed herself for her lack of foresight. *Right, like I could have predicted the end of the world.* She pined for Tess—she'd know how to drive a car like this. Tess was prepared. But then again, if Tess wasn't missing, Calay wouldn't have found herself in this position to begin with.

"God damn it..." she muttered.

Calay tried to turn the key and pump the gas, remembering what little she could of the lessons her dad had given her. The car lurched and sputtered. Then, the engine died. And again. And again. She had to admit, she didn't know what she was doing. The car sat only about three or four inches from where it had been parked. She peered over the dash at Jacob, who hadn't moved, his hands still in the air, watching her embarrass herself. He hadn't shot her. Or attacked her. Or raped her. *Yet.* In fact, he'd actually just saved her life. He was right about that. He also had a considerable amount of food and supplies in his pack before she'd raided it—maybe he had more somewhere. And he'd fed her. The memory of the rabbit, so perfectly cooked, sent a flood of warmth through Calay. There was that, too. So what *did* she know about him? Well, he'd wrangled himself free and followed her—but why? She also couldn't get a straight and clear answer from him on anything, and that was worrying. He was definitely hiding something, but what?

Walking in this blazing heat, she and Max wouldn't make it much further. She knew that and considered their options. She couldn't very well find Tess if she was dead on the side of the road from dehydration. They were also losing daylight, so she needed to move quickly and find some place safe before dark. She surveyed the wreckage of the cars on the highway. So many were littered with bodies. Or what was left of bodies. More like cesspools of disease and infection. It was possible one of the vehicles would start, but highly unlikely. So much time had passed since cars started to break down. Most ran out of gas or the batteries would die. As far as she could see, they were stacked on each other like Legos. It would take ages— and more hands than she had—to move them the wreckage out of the way in the event one of them actually started. She needed a car, and here was one. The only catch was that she'd have to bring Jacob along to get it to move.

She sighed, her fists coming down on the steering wheel. She got out of the vehicle.

"I can't drive a stick shift," she said.

"And you'd like me to...?" He smirked.

"Get in and drive." She raised the gun.

"What makes you think I can?"

That was a legitimate question. *Damn it.* She'd given in to her impulse to ask him for help. Her desperation was betraying her. She was relying on him now. He knew it, and she knew it. She gritted her teeth.

"Well, can you?"

He smiled.

"Can you?" She raised the gun higher and stepped forward.

"Yeah," he acquiesced.

"Then do it."

He nodded. "Now we're gettin' somewhere."

She got in the passenger side door as he slid behind the steering wheel. "If you do anything to me or Max, it'll be the last thing you do. Ever. Understand?"

"Noted," he said, chancing a glance at her out the corner of his eye. This way, with him driving, if he tried anything his life was as much at risk as hers. At least, that's what she told herself. "Ready?"

"Drive." She nodded, her eyes on the road ahead.

And he did. Jacob easily gunned the engine, revved it a couple times, slammed the gear into first, and they were off.

SEVERAL HOURS LATER JACOB SLOWED THE VEHICLE AS THEY approached a gas station, long since abandoned. The sun was almost gone, and it was the first evidence of humanity they'd come across.

"Wait." She hesitated. "Pull off here."

"What is it?" he asked, pulling to the side of the highway. Calay narrowed her eyes as she stared at the building. The sign hung by one chain on its frame, gas hoses were strewn about. It seemed like the perfect place to hole up for the evening. Which, also made it one of the worst. She knew from experience that if she thought a hiding spot looked good, someone else probably did too. The last thing she wanted was another confrontation. She'd been lucky so far; she didn't think she'd make it through another one. Not today.

"We should keep driving. Go, quickly."

"Why?" he asked.

"That's a high-level food zone," she admonished, "we can't stay here."

"A what?"

"A high-level food zone. The Others." Her eyes were growing wide the longer they sat there, darting between Jacob and the building. They were staying too long. They had to go.

Jacob nodded, understanding. They both knew the risk. They also knew there was no gas for the vehicle, and likely very little—if any—food for them. And they knew the sun was about to set and they needed cover.

"Right." Jacob looked at the sun disappearing over the horizon. "But it's going to be dark any minute. We can't risk The Others finding us out here. It looks abandoned. There's probably nothing left in there for them to target us. Let's be careful."

"If there's anyone in there..." Calay started.

"We'll be careful."

She nodded, knowing he was right. They got out of the vehicle and crouched low, watching for signs of life. Of movement. Of anything that might zap them into a glittering cloud of stardust. They stayed this way for a long time, until the first glimmer of stars appeared overhead, and the sky turned dark blue.

"There's nowhere else to go tonight, Calay." Jacob said.

"There's never anywhere else to go," she replied. She felt his gaze on her again. She couldn't tell if he was pitying her or curious. She resisted the urge to ask and ignored him.

The foliage was overgrown and parking lot in disarray, but the structure was small and the windows were mostly intact. They had good line of sight for any uninvited guests, human or otherwise. This would do.

"Alright." She ran a hand over the back of her neck, wiping away the sweat and shadows that had chased her all day. She knew there would be new ones at night. *Rock and roll.* She mustered her courage and pushed her way through the long grass at the forest's edge and across the black pavement.

Inside, Calay found a bag of half-used candles in the back, along with some bottles of whiskey. She brought them out front and arranged the candles as best she could away from the windows. They wanted to see, but not be seen.

Jacob tried the faucet; the water was still running. "Must be a well out back." He called from an open doorway further in the room. She watched him from the corner of her eye as she lit the candles. He was looking for something. He fumbled with some shelving. Banged the cupboard doors. He pulled an empty plastic container from under the till and filled it with water. He placed it gently on the ground near Max, and the dog's tail wagged as he lapped it up.

Huh, didn't expect that.

Exhausted, Calay collapsed onto the floor. Jacob joined her, folding his legs underneath him. Together they sat by the candlelight, passing the whiskey between them, trying to dull the events of the day, and waiting for the eventual moment of sweet escape when sleep would come calling.

"So that was kind of a crazy day," Jacob volunteered.

"You started it by coming into my camp."

"I don't know if that's true, but I agree I didn't give you much of a choice. When it came to how you reacted, I mean. I fucked up. I'll give you that." He looked sideways at her, his eyes catching the light. "I'm sorry I frightened you. I should have introduced myself more carefully. More thoughtfully."

"Yes, you should have." Calay still didn't trust him, but she was beginning to think she could.

"That's on me."

"Yes, it is." She tilted the bottle to her lips, swallowed, and steeled her jaw.

"I get it, okay?" Jacob raised his hands before folding them in his lap. "You were right to react how you did. I was wrong."

Calay handed him the bottle without looking at him and let her shoulders relax. *I'm so tired.* She let her gaze grow soft as she stared into the darkness. A silence fell between them as the candlelight danced along barren shelves and cracked walls. Someone had spray painted the inside black. Shadows scraped along the floor, calling her to sleep. It felt darker than it should have. *Less lonely.*

"I'm sorry I almost shot you," she conceded.

"You didn't almost shoot me."

"Oh, yes, I did. I would have if you tried to come at me." She looked at him, a smirk danced at the corner of his lips. She wanted to mean it. She needed to mean it.

He cleared his throat. "Yeah, I thought you would have."

She knew he was placating her, but she appreciated the gesture. It was a small win, nonetheless. And in a way, a gift.

"So how did you find me anyway?" she nudged.

"Well, after I managed to free myself out of that hogtie you left me in, I figured you'd gone down the highway. The brush was too dense to walk through quickly, and I knew you wanted to get away from me."

"Yet you followed me anyway."

"I meant it when I said I was lucky to run into you." His gaze was inescapable. She fought to still her movements under it but found herself pulled to him. *Sit your ass down.* She pressed her hips harder onto the cement floor and clenched her teeth. He continued., "it's hard out here, alone. I'm wasting away by myself. I can't do it much longer. You seem like you've got your shit together. As much as anyone can now. You're right, I was arrogant coming into your camp like that. But you were wrong to leave. People survive together, and I couldn't just let you walk away when I knew we could be a team."

"A team? You barely know me," she countered.

"Let's just say I have a good feeling about you."

She pursed her lips, narrowed her eyes.

"Anyhow, when I looked down the road, I knew there were only two ways you could have gone—into town, or not into town. Like I said, I know you aren't dumb. The cities are dangerous, there's nothing left in them anyhow. So I figured you went the other way."

"That's not true. I found a stash of medical supplies in a clinic I used to volunteer at."

"Is that so?"

"A whole room full of stuff in perfect condition."

"Did you ever stop to think why those supplies were there?"

"I don't know. Maybe the room was too far inside the building. No one hit it yet."

"Are you sure?"

Calay paused and recalled the scene at the clinic. The vandalism in the foyer. The mess in the hallway. The broken glass throughout. The feeling that someone else was there.

You fool.

As realization creeped across her face, Jacob nodded. How could she have been so naive? She saw what she wanted to see. She'd rationalized her doubts and took what she needed. She'd ignored the risk.

"Someone put the supplies there," she said.

He nodded again.

"But who? Why?"

Hope fluttered again in her chest. *Persistent little fucker.*

"What do you know of it? Was it you? Have you been stalking me?" she demanded.

"I don't know what you're talking about." Jacob eased back on his forearms. "I don't know a lot. Just it seems pretty likely to me that if a place was torn up so bad, it's unlikely a pristine room full of supplies made it through like you've said."

Calay sat there, stunned, shaking her head. Of course. Someone had stocked that room. Someone had been looking out for her. Or at least, looking out for people. Maybe not everyone was as terrible as she'd feared.

"So how long you been on your own?" He changed the subject.

"I'm not on my own," she replied, then reconsidered recent events, "well, I don't know for sure."

He looked at her.

"I have someone I'm with, but she's missing." She took another sip. The whiskey was making her chatty. "I'm looking for her. I think."

"You think?"

"I just don't know where to look."

A gentle breeze wafted through the building's cracked exterior and the windows. After the traumatic events and relentless heat of the day, the cool air felt good. Yet at the mention of Tess, Calay shuddered. *Where is she?*

"I've lost someone too," Jacob volunteered. This had Calay's attention. "Someone I loved very much. I've looked a long time for her. Pretty much everywhere. It's like she never even existed. Just one day she was there, and the next day, poof. Gone."

She still didn't trust Jacob, but something about what he said felt true to Calay. There was a genuine connection between them. Maybe that's why she resisted his presence so hard. He couldn't be trusted, because she couldn't be trusted. His face fell, looking sad at the memory of his loss. Maybe they did have something in common after all.

"You must really care for her."

"More than anything," he admitted.

"You can't ever give up, Jacob. Not ever. She's out there. They're out there!"

"I don't know." His head was low. "It makes it harder; I think. To be alone when you've lost someone. It might be easier to never have had them in the first place."

Calay's insides ached. For him. For herself. For the world. The Change had made them all hard and at the same time, broke their soft hearts every chance it got. She took a deeper swig from the bottle.

"I do know one thing though," he said.

"What's that?" she asked, handing him the bottle.

"Your arm isn't going to heal in a fifth of whiskey. It's bleeding through." Calay looked at her arm. He was right. "Let me help you."

She stiffened at the thought of his hands on her. He pushed himself to stand, inching toward her like he was approaching a wounded dog. Max's head lifted from the pile of old blankets he found in the corner; his eyes wary on the large man approaching his human. Jacob squatted beside Calay. He held out his hands, allowing her to come to him. *He's not wrong.* Would it really be so bad to let someone take care of her for once? Would it be so bad to let him fix her up? She handed him her arm and his smooth fingers lifted the bandage. His hands were strong and warm on her skin.

She stifled a sigh.

"Inflamed and possibly infected," he muttered. She let him rinse away the dirt with tap water. He dried it, careful not to pull on the raw skin. His touch was almost delicate. She watched as he applied some of the ointment from his pack before he redressed the wound. "There. That should do it. At least for tonight."

The feel of his body so close to hers pushed Calay over the edge. Despite herself, she exhaled into his chest. It felt strange. Foreign. Not unwelcome. She wondered if Tess was somewhere safe, with someone safe? Or if she was looking for Calay as desperately as Calay was searching for her? Calay knew she shouldn't be leaning into this man, accepting comfort from his body, if not his help. But there she was, small and lost, and for the first time since she found herself in the warehouse, feeling safe. For a moment—for this moment—she wasn't afraid. So she breathed in the scent of him and closed her eyes.

The whiskey took hold, and Calay fell into a deep sleep.

SHE WOKE AS DAWN BROKE.

I fell asleep. Again. They planned to keep watch in rotation through the night, and he'd let her sleep right through.

"God damn it." She scrambled up. Her arm was noticeably less sore, her leg even better. *Some good rest was all I needed.* But Jacob was kidding himself if he thought she wouldn't hold him to his word. She wasn't sure if she was pissed off or grateful to him. Since he'd shown up, she wasn't sure about a lot of things. She looked around and found the room empty—he wasn't there.

Jacob was gone.

To her surprise, Calay's heart plummeted. She'd been adamant he leave her alone. Then, after one night of conversation, she'd done a complete one-eighty. Tess would shake her for being so frivolous with her emotions. With her safety.

"Stupid." Calay chided herself, knowing better. "Get it together."

The room felt stale in the morning light now that she was alone. Again. She gathered the things she'd collected the night before, palmed a couple candles that still had a bit of wick left, and did one more sweep to make sure she'd grabbed anything of value. She shoved it all in a cloth sack she found in the back and secured a reusable jug of tap water to the straps—she wouldn't make the same mistake twice. Those were errors in judgement she couldn't afford to make. Not since The Change. Not on her own, not without Tess.

The morning sun was already heating the air as she stepped outside and found the Jeep missing.

"Son of a bitch."

She looked out front; she searched behind bushes; she ran around the building. Twice.

"Son of a motherfucking bitch!"

For all his talk of not wanting to be alone, he'd abandoned her without hesitation. Just like her parents. She wondered if he'd just used her to get further. *Maybe closer to his camp?* The thought crossed her mind that perhaps he hadn't been looking for her at all, and his saving her was just a happy accident on his way back to his people. Maybe he'd just stumbled upon them along the highway and used her to gain access to the vehicle. She had taken his gun, after all. She'd thought she was in control the whole time. But he'd used the chance encounter to his advantage. *They could be on their way right now to finish me off.* He was dangerous, and she felt violated and betrayed. She couldn't believe she'd shared such personal details with him the night before. Calay gagged on her own neediness. Her foolishness. Tess would be right to judge her. Last night was a mistake—she shouldn't have let it happen.

"Good riddance," she spit, covering up her pain. She had to move before he came back. Before he brought reinforcements. The thought was alarming. For the third time in twenty-four hours, she pummelled herself. *What have I done?* She knew she had to move now, but which direction? Calay synched the bag higher on her shoulder and she and Max once again tentatively stepped onto the road, prepared to continue on foot. What other choice did she have? She looked left to right, east to west. It was a new day, and she'd be damned if she'd let this traitor change her course. Tess needed her. And she needed Tess. *Onward.*

The bushes beside Calay rustled. So quietly at first, she didn't notice it. Then louder. And then aggressively enough she stumbled back several steps, tripping over her sore leg, and almost landing on her ass. Jacob careened right into her. His blue eyes were wild, almost bulging out of his head. He seemed just as surprised to run into her as she was to run into him.

He licked his full lips like a rabid dog—thirsty and afraid.

"We need to run, and we need to hide. Now."

CHAPTER NINE

Jacob grabbed Calay by her uninjured arm and began pushing her across the road. "Go!"

"What are you talking about?" she demanded. Still stung by his disappearance, she planted her sneakers on the cool morning pavement.

"Calay, come with me." His ordinarily confident eyes were desperate and pleading. He tried to urge her forward, one of his strong hands wrapped around her arm, the other gliding onto her lower back. The weight of his hand on her waist wasn't lost on her. The comforting feeling of the night before rushed through her mind before she pushed it back down. She'd be damned if he was going to tell her what to do, especially after he'd abandoned her overnight.

She didn't budge.

"What's going on?" she pushed.

"I'll tell you later. We have to get out of here."

"Why? What did you do?"

"I didn't do anything. But we have to run. Right now."

"But why?!"

"Fuck!" he shouted.

She recoiled at the violence of his outburst. He let go of her arm, his other hand ran up her back. Tailbone to the top of her spine.

"Calay..." His eyes begged. "Please."

Her resolution wavered. He seemed genuinely concerned. This apprehension—this eruption of emotion—was so unlike what she'd seen of him so far. Something must have spooked him. Something serious. *I can hate him later.*

"Fine."

They took off across the highway and into the trees ahead, Max beside them. Why did it feel like she was always running? Every time she took a breath, she'd choke on the pieces of what was left of her life. What was left of civilization, What was left of her. She just couldn't ever get enough air. There was always something on the periphery. Something bleaker in the shadows. Something just over the horizon that was ominous and dark, pooling around anything she'd built, sucking it down to where she couldn't quite reach it again. Any chance she'd found to relax was quickly smudged out. It wasn't fair. But then again, after The Change, what was?

And so, she ran.

The Bracken ferns and ground cover tugged at their ankles as they pushed deeper into the dense forest. Blackberry bushes snagged at their skin; the remnants of fallen giants blocked their path—spruce, sitka, sequoia. The canopy sprawled above them. One stumbling foot after the other, they plunged deeper into the semi-darkness of the early morning light. Calay could feel her lungs burning for oxygen. She couldn't hear anything but the roar of her own breath. Chancing a glance over her shoulder, she couldn't see anything either.

Her ankle caught on a root, and she fell face down in a pile of moss. It tasted like mushrooms. She spit out the mouthful that forced its way between her teeth. Her leg ached. Jacob stopped, picked her up before her mind had the chance to calibrate that she'd even fell, and they were off again.

"Jacob, stop. I think we're okay." Her body screamed to rest.

He wasn't slowing down, and he didn't answer her. He just kept going. It felt like they were running forever—forever into a dark hole of never-ending pain and subterfuge. This was her life now. Running. It was relentless and unceasing. Between gasping breaths, she wondered if this struggle was any life at all.

They came upon a small clearing in the trees. A rolling waterfall pooled before them. The sunlight just starting to poke through the trees. It was so tranquil. So serene. So ineffable. He pushed her toward the large outcrop of rocks at the base of the falls.

"Behind there. Go."

He waited for her to slip behind one of the taller rocks, the updraft from the falling water danced in her hair. Then, he pressed himself between them after her.

Aside from the gentle rush of the water, it was absolute silence.

Be silent, be still.

"What's going on, Jacob?"

"Shhhh…"

They waited. Her anxiety turned to exasperation. Once again, he wasn't telling her anything. All her questions were just bumping up against evasion or non-answers. For all she knew, nothing was chasing them. Nothing was coming for them. And suddenly she found herself alone in the woods with a man who was for all intents and purposes, a stranger. A stranger who had abandoned her only moments earlier. Pressed between his large, hard body and a bunch of cold rocks, she had nowhere to go. Calay wondered if she'd just made the impulsive decision that would be her last.

"This is ridiculous." she fumed, pulling Max by the collar. "I'm going. You can't make me st…" He put his finger to her lips and held it there. She fought the urge to both pull away and put it in her mouth. How she could feel so angry and so turned on at the same time, she didn't know.

He shook his head and mouthed the word, "no." She watched his eyes leave hers and linger where his finger still lay, heavy on her lips.

They waited.

And then she heard it. The hum. The whir. The throaty mechanical sound. Calay's stomach dropped. *The Others.*

She peeked around Jacob's shoulder as the shadows of two pods gathered just beyond the falls. Her breath caught in her throat. She'd never seen more than one at a time. She didn't even know if they traveled in packs, had always thought of them more as lone gunmen. Did they communicate? *Of course, they did you idiot. But how?* She couldn't help but shake the feeling they were talking about her and Jacob right now.

Was this it?

Still heaving and out of breath, they slid deeper against the rocks, tucking their bodies closer together behind the waterfall. Sharp edges of granite cut at their sides but still, they pressed further inside the swell. Calay's foot slipped on the wet ground. Jacob caught her. Held strong. The cold dampness of the wall behind seeped through her shirt. His hard, masculine body warm on her front. Her skin tingled with goose pimples. With lust.

The noises got louder as the machines approached the falls. Beyond the water she could see the refractory shadows of the blue lights, searching.

"Can they see us in here?" she whispered; her voice barely audible against the backdrop of the plunging water.

He looked at her, his lips pressed together, and shook his head, but he didn't look convinced. In fact, he looked uncomfortable. Almost like he was in pain. It occurred to her that his being so close to her might not actually be something he wanted at all. She thought back to the distance he'd maintained from her at camp. The space he'd given her at the gas station. The way he wasn't there when she woke up. And now, their bodies damp and warm and packed together, he looked like he wanted to escape from *her* more than he wanted to get away from the aliens.

She'd manufactured the whole desire thing. *Like it was even an option.* Calay felt silly.

Silly for wondering what it would feel like to be underneath this waterfall in more regular circumstances—where maybe they'd make love, and silly for thinking he'd be interested her. He didn't want her. That much was evident. She was so confused. In that moment, she didn't know if she was scared for her life or excited by the possibility of passion and connection. She felt guilt for Tess and lust, in spite of herself. She didn't know if she felt safe or unsafe. She didn't know if he was a bad boy or a good guy. She didn't know where Tess was or if she was alright. She didn't know if they were going to make it out from behind these rocks alive to even find her. She just didn't know.

She released a breath and tried not to cry against the heartbeat she felt in his chest.

"I think they've left," he muttered into her hair. Jacob peered down at her, but she couldn't read his expression. He looked uneasy and she caught herself wishing there was something more to his expression. The ache of being truly alone rose in her throat. She swallowed it.

"We have to go," she said, "I have to go."

Calay's eyes darted to the ground as she slipped around him and out from behind the falls. Carefully, silently, they made their way back the way they came to the highway. They could still hear the whirring in the distance. It seemed to be getting quieter. No flashing lights. No rumbling. No bodies pressed tightly against each other. They were in the clear.

"What do you think?" he asked her.

She cleared her throat and directed her gaze down the highway.

"The road is more direct. But the forest provides cover."

They stood where the grass met the pavement.

"If you want to find Tess, maybe we should take the Jeep. It's faster."

"Do you see the Jeep, Jacob?" Calay condescended, still feeling wounded. "The Jeep is gone. I don't know where. It doesn't make any sense. None of this makes any sense. I think I'm going to stick to the trees. It'll take longer, but it gives me a better chance of getting to her. I hope."

Damn the aliens. Damn them and everything they'd taken from her. From the planet. From this moment. When her parents kicked her out, she'd thought that was the end of the world. She'd felt lost and trapped at the same time, unable to tear herself away from her family and yet, forced to. Because of their judgement. Their ignorance. Their inability to love her because of who she was. It wasn't the end though; it was the beginning. She'd built a new life with Tess, and they were happy and good. Until The Change.

She didn't deserve this. None of them did. It was true that the human race could be truly awful to each other. To their planet. But they didn't deserve to be wiped out, their cities burned, their entire civilization extinguished.

The Others had no right coming here and doing this to them.

They had no right to do it to her.

"Fuck this." Calay resolved.

"I'm sorry?"

"This. Fuck this. They can't keep doing this to us."

"What do you mean?"

"I'm going to follow them. I'm going to stop them."

"Uh, what?"

"This is our planet. Our home." She fumed. "I'm tired of running, Jacob. This planet is ours and I'll be damned if I'm going to let them…"

"Let them what? I get how you're feeling, but have you gone mad? We just spent the last hour running from them. Calay, they can wipe you off the face of the Earth with a single swipe of blue light. There's nothing we can do to them before they do us in."

"Of course there is, there has to be. There must be! You've heard the rumors. There are ways to take them down. If others have done it, we can too."

"Yeah, crazy girl, but they're just rumors. Nothing's been proven."

"So let's prove it."

"No, Calay. I'm sorry, but no. It's too dangerous. Let's just keep moving."

"Oh, I'm going to keep moving, but I'm going that way." She pointed in the direction the fading sounds were coming from.

Jacob blinked at her, ran a hand over his forehead. She knew he wanted to change her mind, but didn't know how. *That's because I'm doing this, and he knows it.*

"Maybe I can figure out how to stop their pods. Maybe I'll follow them and find out something important. Or maybe I'll figure out how to put my life back together so I don't have to run anymore. I'm tired of running. I don't know how to stop them, but I won't know unless I try. There's a chance we can actually live again, Jacob. Like, really live."

"Or maybe you die trying."

"Or maybe I die trying," she conceded.

Calay stood straighter, pressed her lips together, and set off. She was determined to do something other than run and cry and wish for a better life. *This—whatever this was—wasn't a life.* Not one she wanted. *Not like this.* She thought of Tess and the home that had crumbled that first day. The horrors she'd lived since then. The pain of never feeling safe. If humans could just come together, they could take their planet back. Take back what had been stolen from them. But make it better. *This is our chance for absolution.* She was sure of it. It had to be. What else was there?

Calay pressed on, toward the unknown, Jacob trailing reluctantly behind her.

CHAPTER TEN

The distant sound of alien pods was terrifying and constant. The instinctual need to flee teased at the edge of her mind, but Calay's feet drove her forward as she stole through the forest after them. She placed one foot in front of the other, mindful that one wrong step could send her face first back onto the forest floor. Or worse. Slippery roots and sharp rocks punctuated her way, and it would only take one slip to land on one of them and shatter a bone or cut deep into human flesh. And then where would she be? The idea of losing the pods—of losing her chance to get some semblance of a normal life back—frightened her more than the threat of what they could do to her. At not quite a run, she moved forward through the dense forest because this was what she was prepared to do. And she'd do it, with or without Jacob's help. Without anyone's help.

Despite herself and the risk beckoning her deeper through the overgrown greenery, Calay couldn't help but think about her family and the home they built for her. The home she was forced to leave. She'd loved her family more than anything. When she was young her father tucked her into bed every night, smelling of clean laundry that just that afternoon had dried on the line in the sun. At her incessant pleading, he'd tell her stories of brave foxes who went on grand adventures. They climbed the highest trees and burrowed the deepest tunnels. They explored deep caves and ran free under the stars. These stories enthralled Calay and nurtured dreams that she, too, would one day be like the fox—clever, daring, not afraid of anything. Her mother would stand in the doorway smiling, a silhouette against the gentle light creeping in from the hallway. She'd watch the two of them do their nightly dance—her husband telling and retelling fairy-tales about woodland creatures, her daughter fighting the weight of her eyelids so she could embark on just one more adventure as he told it.

Calay's mother had always been warm, but distant. Loving, but slightly out of reach. Calay didn't understand why or what had made her mother that way. And she didn't mind for the most part. She enjoyed the freedom their relationship offered her. The space to explore and become the woman she was growing into. As she got older, the nightly ritual of bedtime stories became less frequent. Though she found new ways to find closeness with her dad. Sometimes she'd help him with tasks that needed doing around the house or the barn. And there were the camping trips she'd enjoyed so much. But most days, they'd sit together, delaying the inevitable start to the day, and drink too much coffee at the kitchen table. All three of them. A family.

For all intents and purposes, Calay's childhood was a good life. A safe life. A happy one. But it wasn't her life; it wasn't her; it just didn't fit. She tried for a long time to breathe in their way of living. To toe the line, as it were. Work on the farm. Go to church. Meet a nice boy, get married, have three kids. The Walt Disney happily ever after. For someone who dreamed that dream, it would have been paradise. For Calay, as she got older and found herself resisting these things more and more, it was a prison sentence. She'd never married, though she had come close, once. All the while, feeling like something wasn't quite right. Nights had passed—months—where she could hardly breathe. The air was ripe with ill-suited responsibilities and obligations. It took her a while to figure out what she needed, and once she did, there was no denying who she was. These were things her parents didn't approve of. People. Experiences. Women. As she grew into herself it was no secret Calay took a liking to beautiful men. It turned out she had a penchant for beautiful women too.

And one woman in particular—Tess—was the most beautiful woman she'd ever seen.

For the first time in her life Calay felt heard. Happy. And exposed. In the best ways possible. She'd tried to come out to her parents. And then she'd tried to convince them to accept her. To love her. As she was. But try as she might, she'd become an outsider in a home that she was once *so* inside, she thought it a part of her. Like an arm. Or a leg. Or a heart.

As she navigated building something she could call a life of her own, she was bombarded with reminders about what she'd lost. Whispers chased her as she walked the aisles of the grocery store hand in hand with Tess. Stares from the other young women who only a short year ago were attending high school together, their bellies plump with children, followed her when they went out for dinner or to the movie theater. Her father's truck passed down Main Street, and he pretended not to see her. Her hometown was an archive of rejection. Of judgement. Of loss. It was then that she knew she had to leave. It was a self-banishment, of sorts. To build a real home she could call her own. To find her own kind. Then, like now, as she pushed deeper into the forest, she'd worried she'd be alone forever.

But then, there was Tess. And Tess changed everything. On their first date they'd stayed up until dawn, talking, laughing, and fucking. It was that rare kind of night that happened when you were both totally in the moment, not worrying about the future or what might happen—it just didn't matter. The only thing that mattered was that they had found each other. They were just fully and completely together. She could still remember the fruity smell of Tess's hair and the sweet taste of her mouth as Tess kissed her for the first time. And for the first time in her life, Calay felt like she'd found herself. That in this woman—in Tess—she'd found her purpose. Her love.

As the days turned into weeks, they moved quickly, falling in love and falling into each other. They ran from that small town and into the city together, where they remained. Until The Change. They'd clung to each other like life-rafts, and as The Others exterminated entire cities, they'd supported each other. Through the loss of friends. Through the loss of strangers. Through the loss of humanity. They'd stuck through it even while everything around them collapsed into ash. Into fear. Into regret.

Into nothingness.

Calay regretted a lot of things in her life, but she never regretted loving Tess. Not once. And now, it had been too long since something felt comfortable in her life. Too long since she'd held Tess in her arms. And if chasing down these aliens and figuring out a way to take them down was her path back to her, she was going to do it.

She was going to fix this.

Somehow.

"Calay...stop."

She chanced a glance back at Jacob, panting and thighs burning.

"Do you hear anything?"

She listened, stopped, waited.

It was silent. Dead air. The whirring was gone.

"Where did they go?" she asked.

"I heard them a second ago." Jacob shrugged, straining to listen beside Calay.

She surveyed the darkness ahead, the trees so thick they blocked most of the sunlight. They were deep in the forest, deeper than she'd gone since The Change started. She forgot how quiet it was. And how isolated. Moss billowed out of fallen tree trunks, large mushrooms cascaded along the forest floor. The wind rustled the leaves in the canopy. But that's where the airflow stopped. Dense ferns and vines scaled toward the treetops, blocking it from reaching them. The air smelled clean and fresh with an underlying hint of dirt and decay, untouched by humans for who knew how long. She used to love that. Tess and Calay would find a reprieve in the woods. It was a place of comfort and peace.

Now, it was a dangerous place, full of threats. A place of shadows that harbored the pregnant risk of losing oneself. As she peered around, Calay realized they were in fact, lost. And the pods seemed to be gone.

Her head swiveled in the opposite direction, venturing a glance back the way they came. She squinted, but any evidence of their trail had already been erased by the thick underbrush. Just as the aliens wanted it.

"Where are we?"

Jacob looked around, shook his head. "Your guess is as good as mine."

To the left, Calay spied a trickle of light through the endless columns of trees. She pushed forward, ignoring the scraping pull of ferns and thickets on her legs and arms. They came to an opening where the sun made its way to the mossy woodland floor. Jacob pulled up alongside her. Her breath caught in her throat.

A heaping graveyard of human history unfolded before them. Piles were stacked twenty feet high with old furniture, burned out cars, and mangled slabs of wood and concrete. Old photographs, binders with what looked like hand-written notes of some kind, and stamped envelopes littered the ground. Then, bodies. Oh, the bodies. Reeking of death. Ephemera and proof of a species that had once existed, but now struggled to remain. On the edge of extinction. Among the wreckage Calay counted several fried alien pods. Discarded like toys. It was a surreal scene—the familiar and the foreign. The then and now. The nostalgia and desolation of their world. All of it, destroyed and lost to...what? Was history still history when there was no one left to record it? No one to notice. Or to care. Calay thought about the dinosaurs and prehistoric man. How humans recorded their existence long after they were gone. *Would another era do the same for us?* She wondered if they found the televisions, cell phones, and computers, would they document and preserve these things? Would this history become their history?

...Or is this all that ever was? All that ever would be?

"I had a necklace..." she choked out, but stopped. Jacob's piercing blue eyes rested on her, the pain in her face reflected in his.

She thought about that memento. About the Jeep. About Tess. About her family, her home, herself. Her desire—her need—to trust the man standing in front of her. It was all so broken. In that moment Calay hated The Others more than she ever had. She swallowed a sob and stood, tiny and fragile in the mountains of broken stuff. Tears silently streamed down her face. She swiped furiously at them.

"Hey, hey..." Jacob pulled her into his strong arms, his muscular shoulders enveloping hers, shielding her from the scene. "We'll get through this." For a moment, she allowed herself to hear his words. To smell the fabric of his t-shirt. To feel the comfort of his embrace.

"I've got you," he told her, "you need to--"

Calay stiffened. "I need to what?" she spoke into his chest, her tone hardening, "I told you before, you don't get to tell me what I need."

Just like that, Calay's walls were back up. Her defenses armed.

Jacob released her and let his arms fall to his sides, seeming to acknowledge the moment had passed. She pulled away from him and focused her attention back on the wreckage.

"Do you think this was a battle of some kind?"

"I don't know," he admitted as he gazed around, his jaw tight.

"There's so much of it. Maybe someone dumped it all here?"

"I don't know." There was no impatience to his voice, just despair.

"We don't have time for this. We have to keep moving," she said, shaking off the weight on her shoulders, "Max! Max, come!"

They waited.

The dog didn't come.

"Max!" they both called.

"Where is he?"

"I don't know," Jacob repeated for the third time.

"Oh no. Oh no no no no no..." Calay searched the area, winding through the piles of garbage.

"MAX!"

"Shh, Calay," Jacob urged her, "keep your voice down. We don't know who else is out here."

She stopped. Blinked at Jacob. Her mouth fell open and then closed again. She wrapped her arms around herself. In an instant, she knew he was right. The onset of vertigo tilted her vision. For a few excruciating moments the forest spun on its axis. If the dog was anywhere close, he'd have come when she'd called. *We are a pack.* She'd told herself that how many times? *A pack sticks together.* Her eyes glazed over as she waded through the mounds of debris and the thick feeling she might faint.

Max, it seemed, was nowhere to be found.

She blinked away a new set of tears.

"We have to find shelter." She pointed to the fading light above them.

"Are you okay? We'll find him. Tomor…"

"Let's go."

※

SEVERAL HUNDRED FEET IN THE OTHER DIRECTION, JACOB and Calay came across a cabin. The windows were dusty but intact, firewood stacked under the sweeping veranda. They tucked behind the trunk of a giant Sequoia, watched, and saw no movement from within.

"This will do." She nodded.

They closed the door and secured it with a chair bolted under the handle. She pulled on the knob. The door wasn't opening.

"It won't stop someone who wants to come in, but it might deter someone who isn't sure," she said.

"It's a good idea." Jacob nodded. "The best we've got."

Calay walked past him, not giving herself permission to accept the compliment. She surveyed the room. Old sheets draped the furniture and the floors creaked, but it was a comfortable enough place to spend the night. A safe enough place. *Whatever that means anymore.* She made her way to the bathroom and shut the door.

The lights were out. *No surprise.* She turned the taps on the sink, no water, either. *Of course.* Most of the grids went out in the first month of the attack. Systems failed when there was no one alive to run them. She braced herself on the sink, felt the welling deep within her chest, the pain pulling her into an abyss of darkness. Loneliness. Fear. And she released the tears she'd been holding back, allowing them to ping on the dry porcelain.

She cried for all that was lost in The Change. All that she'd lost that first day. And all that she'd lose tomorrow. She wasn't sure what else there was to lose but somehow there always seemed to be something else that could be taken from her.

And so, she cried.

***

When she came out of the bathroom, Jacob was leaning against the refrigerator with the half-empty bottle of whiskey in his hand.

"Are you okay?" he asked.

She stood taller and rubbed her eyes.

"I could hear you in there," he explained, his eyes half shut, turned down toward the floor.

"I'm fine."

"You're strong, Calay," he said, sincerity dripping from his tongue. He lifted his gaze to meet hers. "Stronger than you think. Whatever you need, I want to give you. I want to help."

She sized him up as he took a gulp from the bottle. She felt vulnerable and naked as he peered at her. Empty. And he had something that would fill her up. She tugged on the hem of the t-shirt that was a little too tight across her chest, and smoothed her long dark hair, conscious what she must look like to him. *A mess.* Even though she loved Tess, the world had collapsed around them, and she didn't know what to do next, she still wanted to feel pretty. To feel like a woman. To feel wanted. *Old habits die hard.*

"I don't know if I am," she admitted, "it's all gone, Jacob. The entire fucking world. I don't know what I was thinking going after the aliens like that."

He stepped closer.

"You were right," he told her, "we can do this. It's dangerous as hell, but it's possible."

"If it isn't…"

"It is," he reassured her.

"It has to be." She nodded.

Calay examined him, watched his movements in the stale light that filtered in through the dusty curtains. He took another step toward her and passed her the whiskey. Her eyes traced the scars on his knuckles, the veins in his forearm. The fleshy bulge of his bicep. She knew what she was thinking was wrong. That she'd be betraying Tess. And in that same moment she also knew she needed some kind of solace. Some comfort. Something. She just wanted to feel connected. Even if it was just for a short while. Tess wasn't there; Calay didn't know where she was. But Jacob was right in front of her. She knocked back a swig of booze, and a big inhale of his body. He smelled like pine, sweat, and man. He was within arm's reach.

Her eyes trailed up and met his. He held them. Maybe Jacob did want her after all.

She released a breath and stepped forward, and before she could say 'kiss me,' his mouth was on hers. Hot, wet, and tasting faintly of bourbon, his tongue ravenously passed her lips. It was a hungry kiss, their hands weaving around each other's bodies as if they could somehow save each other if they just hung on tight enough.

Jacob's hands cupped her ass, grazing the inseam of her jeans, and he lifted her onto the counter behind them. She readily opened her legs and pulled him to her, needing to remove as much space between their bodies as possible. She could feel him hard against his zipper; she could feel him hard against her. She pulled him closer still.

His fingers wrapped around her hair and he closed his fist tight. Pulling her head back, her throat exposed, his teeth grazed her collarbone before closing over the vein in her neck. She released a low moan. She needed more.

Their clothes were off in seconds, their naked bodies melting together. His hard stomach sweaty and pressed against the soft curvature of her belly. She pushed herself off the counter and into his arms. They sank to the kitchen floor, there was no time to make it to the bedroom. The need to have him inside her, to feel something other than despair or hopelessness or loss, washed over her like a tsunami.

He placed his hand beneath her head as his body rose above hers, their eyes trained on each other, their mouths thirsty for more. Skin to skin and heart to heart, he kissed her passionately as he slid deep inside her. Her hips rotated to meet his and everything else fell away; there was no space for anything but them, together. He pounded her, the scruff of his chin on her neck, her nipples. Gently biting and then sucking, hard. Her lips found the round of his shoulders, her fingers tightly wrapped around his arms, her legs around his waist. They clung to each other, unable to stop themselves. Not wanting to stop themselves.

He breathed sweet nothings into her ear. She moaned in reply.

She had no more words. No more thoughts. She was fucking for all she had lost. She was fighting for her life. And she was living for this moment. For this.

It was all she had.

They made love until they both collapsed into a pile of sweat and ecstasy there on the kitchen floor. Calay looked up and noticed the roof was peeling and stained. It was oddly comforting—proof that human lives had once called this place home. They peeled themselves off each other and off the floor. She reached for the bottle of whiskey and took another sip. It tasted like Jacob.

He picked up her t-shirt, folded it, and handed it to her. "I'll take first watch."

"Are you sure? I can do that. You didn't get much rest last time."

"I got it," he said and pushed himself up off the floor.

※

IN THE MORNING CALAY BLINKED HER EYES OPEN TO FIND Jacob next to her on top of the blankets. At some point during the night, he must have collapsed beside her. She peeked at him through the curtain of her eye lashes and felt something in her chest give way. He looked peaceful now. Not so pained. She allowed herself to hope for something more for herself. For them. For their species. She wondered about the possibility of salvation in this world. A little normalcy. Humanity had proven itself to be fundamentally awful, but was it not also human to hope for goodness, too?

Goodness. *Tess.* A river of guilt ran through Calay. *Tess would be heartbroken over what I've done.* It was them against the world and Calay had jeopardized that in a moment of passion. She looked at Jacob again, sleeping peacefully beside her. *No, not passion. Not at all.* It was a basic human need to feel connected. To feel safe. To not be alone when loneliness was threatening to drown her. *It was human.* Calay didn't feel good about her decision to use Jacob this way, but she felt better thinking he had used her too.

She pulled herself up off the mattress and stole one more glance at him and smiled. Today, she'd watch the sun rise. Her bare feet padded across the wooden floor, to the front of the cabin. She pulled the chair out from the doorknob—still firm where they'd lodged it—and opened the door wide. She breathed in the fresh morning breeze. It had always been her favorite time of day. Fresh dew. Cool air.

A new start.

She stepped out onto the porch. She felt something beneath her feet. Calay looked down.

"Oh my God!" Her stomach retched.

She was standing in a chaotic pile of fur and dismembered animal parts.

And it looked an awful lot like Max.

CHAPTER ELEVEN

The sound that escaped Calay's mouth was not human.

She sunk down to her knees as Jacob bounded toward her.

"Calay!"

"Holy fuck." His eyes scanned the carnage.

Calay sat in a thick pool of dark blood on the porch, her hands fumbling with the pieces of Max like she was trying to put him back together again.

Humpty Dumpty sat on a wall...the rhyme played over and over in her head.

"Calay, get up," he told her.

She didn't get up.

Humpty Dumpty had a great fall...

"Calay," he said more firmly, glancing around the property, "get. Up."

All the King's horses and all the King's men...

"Calay!"

Couldn't put Humpty together again.

Calay became vaguely aware of Jacob's face appearing before hers as he crouched down. *Humpty Dumpty sat on a wall*...It began again. Jacob was saying something but she couldn't hear him. She felt his hand rough on her chin as he forced her gaze to meet his. His other on the side of her face. And then, he was there.

"Who could have done this?" she whispered through tears, "Max."

"Calay, I need you to come inside. Now."

"This is my fault. I did this. I shouldn't have brought him out here."

"It's not your fault."

"And you, you should have been watching!" she accused.

"I...I didn't..." he stammered.

"You said that you'd watch! Why didn't you watch?" Her tears gave way to hysteria. "We didn't look hard enough, Jacob. We gave up too easily. This is our fault. We abandoned him. We abandoned Max!"

"Calay! Whoever did this is probably still here. Still watching. We don't even know if it is Max."

"How can you say that? Of course it's Max!"

"Calay, you need to get up." He reached for her, pulling the pieces of dog carcass out of her hands. He lifted her to her feet. "Come inside." He led her into the cabin and shut the door. Blood and tufts of hair coated Calay's clothes.

She paused, looked up at him. Her hands coated in red. She folded her palms together, staring. *It's red. So red.* Her eyes grew wide.

"Jacob," she started, "it's still warm. It's still fucking warm."

She gaped at him, tears pouring out of her eyes.

"Do you know what this means?"

"I know." He pulled back the curtains, surveying the perimeter. Whoever it was could be outside, waiting for them.

Calay ran to the other side of the room and did the same.

"He hasn't been dead long. They must have done it right here. Right now."

Jacob only looked at her from across the small room, any trace of that slick smile smeared clean off his face. His thick lips pressed together into a thin line. He looked angry as hell.

"We're not alone." She concluded.

The creeping feeling of isolation that had haunted her the last several weeks washed away. Before The Change, loneliness was something she avoided. Most people did. Entire industries were built on the very essence of not being alone: online dating, sex work, the wedding industry, pop music. Now, she realized, solitude was a measure of safety. Instead of feeling comforted by the company of others, she felt dread. She had to get away. From whoever did this to Max and from Jacob. People just weren't safe, and Tess needed her more than ever. Or rather, the realization dawned on her, she needed Tess.

"I was a fool," she told him, "for thinking people could be better."

He looked at her, empathy clouded his eyes. *His judgement. And mine.*

"I have to go," she announced.

"You can't be serious."

"I can't be here," she snapped, "I have to get back to the road and find Tess. Now."

"You can't go now, Calay. We don't know who's done this. Stay here. At least until we figure some of this shit out."

"I have to go, Jacob. Last night was special, but it's too dangerous. I can't be here."

"Calay...Stay. Stay with me." The pleading in his voice was almost unbearable. And unexpected.

She turned her body and full attention to look at him. His beautiful blue eyes were tinged with hurt and confusion. He genuinely wanted her to stay with him. She realized his protests weren't really about the dog, they were about her. Last night hadn't been a temporary reprieve for Jacob like it was for her. It had meant something more. Her heart ached for him and for the mistake she'd made. He seemed to actually care for her, but her goals were never his. He wanted to be with her, and she wanted to be with Tess. He'd only slowed her down.

"You need me," he said.

"I don't know what I was thinking." She grabbed her things and headed for the door, both wanting to hug him and run from him. "I'm so sorry."

As she reached for the knob, his hand thrust hard against the frame. It was a violent move, but when she brought her gaze to his, she saw a wave of sadness wash over his face.

"Please..." he begged.

"Don't follow me." She pulled on the door; his arm resisted.

"Don't." She steeled her jaw, forced herself to maintain eye contact.

His lips parted, but he said nothing, and then his hand fell away from the wood.

"I told you, whatever you want, it's yours Calay."

"Why, Jacob? Why is it mine? Why do you care?"

Jacob simply blinked at her in response, unable to speak. Or unwilling to. His eyes said it all.

Calay's shoulders deflated. She couldn't stay. Not with him. Not after all she'd seen. Not when Tess could be somewhere close. She opened the door and took off down the steps, without looking back. As she trudged through the long grass toward the forest, she acknowledged she did care for Jacob. More than she wanted to. It had only been a few days, but it had been enough. She was only starting to trust him, but she saw the possibility of something growing there. *Another time. Another life. Another world.* She'd fractured Tess's trust by being with him, by being selfish and impulsive. But she'd be damned if she'd miss her chance to repair what she'd broken. She needed to get to Tess more than ever and that drove her forward into the trees.

She didn't have to look behind her to know Jacob was standing in the door. Alone, brooding, and watching her back as she walked away from the house. Away from him.

✳

CALAY HAD NO IDEA WHERE SHE WAS GOING. ONCE THE cabin was out of sight—or rather, once Jacob was out of sight—she stopped to get her bearings. Fighting back tears, she looked around. Every direction was a crapshoot. It was all just endless forest. Bark, leaves, and dirt. She decided to go back to the ephemeral graveyard—the last landmark she could identify. The only direction she knew to walk. It wasn't far and she was pretty sure she could find it again. *Hell, given the size of it, it'd be hard to miss.*

And she was right.

It took over an hour to get there, but she was back. The heap of rubble rose in the forest as she made her way closer. The legacy of humanity, broken. It was all just made up. Everything. And so easily destroyed. Until there was nothing left. But there was something ahead. Calay approached the clearing. There was movement amongst the wreckage.

People.

She crouched behind a patch of ferns and tucked herself against the trunk of a nearby tree, praying to a God she no longer believed in, that they hadn't seen her. Yesterday she and Jacob had walked the better part of a whole day and not come across one single person; the likelihood these were the people responsible for Max's death was high. Max...she pushed the grief and fear down. *Now is not the time.* She stretched her neck around the tree and braved a glance.

It was a man and a woman. They were talking.

"...bodies on the road," one of them said.

They were dressed in the same kind of clothes as the soldiers she'd run into the day before. The soldiers she and Jacob killed. This was not good. She considered running back to the cabin to warn him. She may not have been able to stay with him, but she didn't want harm to come to him. The thought occurred to her there may be more of them in the area. She couldn't risk getting caught on the way there. Besides, she'd seen him in action; he could take care of himself. *Just like I need to now.* She contemplated announcing herself, but that hadn't gone so well last time. And if these were the people that had killed Max, it was certain they'd kill her too. She knew she couldn't hide there forever, that left running as her only option. But run to where?

It didn't matter. *Anywhere but here.*

She risked one more glance forward. Their attention was focused on sorting through a pile of garbage on the far side of the clearing. She backed away, stepping cautiously over the twigs and leaves so as to not cause a sound. One step. Two. Another. *Just keep moving, almost there.*

A hand clamped over her mouth and another around her waist from behind.

Fuck.

She struggled against the attacker and they fell backwards, the foliage enveloping and closing around them. He pulled her tight against him. She could barely move. She tried to bite at the hand, to wiggle free. Her legs flailed and fought as she tried in vain to connect with whoever was holding her.

Oh no!

"Shhhh..." he whispered in her ear. The scent of him became familiar, and she felt her body lean into his. It was Jacob. *I just can't shake this guy.* Relief poured through her. Then, resentment.

"Come with me, quietly," he instructed, "and stay low."

Calay—though rightfully pissed—nodded in agreement. Right now, the bigger threat was the strangers only a few meters away. She could discuss the finer points of stalking with Jacob later. And she would. They rolled over, crouched in the underbrush and looked back. The group hadn't noticed them. *Good.* They were still lasered in on whatever they were digging through.

"Let's go," Jacob urged. They turned to crawl forward, then, stopped short. Poised in front of them were a pair of black military boots. That, and a sub-machine gun pointed inches from Jacob's nose.

"Well, look what we have here boys."

"You..." Jacob sneered, his mouth curling into a snarl.

Guy, the man who'd fled when Jacob started shooting up the highway, was standing in front of them with two gaunt men. Calay gasped, remembering his thick face and the way he'd cupped her ass when he patted her down. He seemed bigger—broader—beside the other two, his body blocking her entire line of sight. He ignored Jacob and peered at Calay. "Did you like the present I left you this morning, little lady?"

It had been him, Calay realized. Her heart ached; her stomach turned. "You're a monster." Calay spat.

"Oh, honey. Oh, baby. Yeah. You assholes killed three of my guys, so I killed one of yours. That still leaves two more to make up for." He smiled. He had a slimy, lopsided, toothy mouth. She shivered despite the rising morning heat.

"I'm going to kill you," she promised.

"Yeah no. Unlikely sugar," he said. "You didn't stand a chance before and you don't stand one now. Your dick friend here isn't so tough without a big gun in his hand, is he?" Guy wound up and cuffed Jacob in the chin with his boot. Spit flew from Jacob's mouth as Guy's foot connected.

"Fuck you!" She lunged, reaching for Jacob. Guy stepped forward, placing a heavy boot between them.

"No darling, Fuck. You." His eyes trailed along her body, his pointy tongue darting in and out of his mouth like a lizard's. "I bet you like it on your knees, huh?"

Calay shrunk further back into the brush. She saw Jacob's body tighten; his eyes burn with rage.

"Yeah. You're both coming with me."

CHAPTER TWELVE

Night fell. They walked for hours. Over an ink-black horizon, the compound rose from the asphalt in a wave of brick, the buildings low and sprawling. Chain-link fences ran the perimeter, lined with barbed-wire and sharp razor. Florescent lights and small CCTV cameras scoured the corners. Even from a distance Calay could make out rows of metal grates on the ground, thick bars with foot-wide gaps, perfect for…what? Disposing of what was left over? What remained? The thought turned her stomach. It was the kind of place nightmares were made of. Or rather, made nightmares come true. Calay shuddered and wrapped her arms around herself. The place looked like a death camp.

"Yeah, keep moving." Guy nuzzled the cold barrel of the gun into the back of Calay's neck. She fought the urge to run. To spin around, take it from him, and blow his ugly face off. *Would I be fast enough? Probably not.* If she wasn't, she'd never make it to Tess. She'd never make it anywhere but probably through the slats of those grates. *Escape—revenge—would have to wait.* The risk was just too high.

A wide moat ran the perimeter of the compound. It looked cold, dark, and foreboding. They crossed the bridge, flood lights casting strange shadows and illuminating guard towers Calay hadn't noticed on their approach. Were there more soldiers in those towers? Were they being watched? The questions overflowed in her mind, swirling like the water below their steps.

"How do they have electricity?" she whispered to Jacob.

"Maybe they power it with the water," he said, as he looked around and shivered.

"I don't think it'd be powerful enough."

"Then they must have a generator."

"Or several."

"Do you think it's to keep people out?"

"Or keep them in."

"Shut up or I'll shut your mouths for you, yeah?" Guy spat.

As they made their way through the gate, Calay noticed a camouflaged network of tarps and foliage concealing the stars above. *They're practically invisible under all this netting.*

The good news was they were seemingly successful in hiding from the aliens. The bad news—they were human.

Guy punched a code into a flat access panel in the side of one of the buildings. The door slid open.

"You're going to be processed," he told them.

"What does that mean?" Calay asked.

Guy grinned that reptilian smile in reply.

"What does that mean?" she pressed. Two other men in uniforms took her by the arms. "Stop! What does 'processed' mean? Where are we? What are you doing? Get off of me!"

Guy stood to the side. The doorway Calay was being dragged through was a gaping bright hole about to swallow her. The hair rose on her arms, a spark of panic flashed down her spine. She looked at Jacob, restrained and deathly still. He was unable to move with multiple guns trained on him. He was powerless to stop what was happening. And Calay knew it.

"Jacob!"

He nodded, silently reassuring her. She struggled against the men. It was futile.

Guy looked from Jacob to Calay and back to Jacob. He blew them both a kiss and stalked off as Calay was dragged inside the brightly lit corridor, away from the cool night air. Away from Jacob.

She found herself sitting alone in a small room. It was padded and sterile. A small round table was at the center. Sprinkler heads garnished the roof every few inches. She wondered what the room used to be. Before. Maybe it had been an office. A hospital. A school. Now it was something else. Whatever it was, she hoped it wouldn't be the last place she ever set foot in. It had been hours since she'd seen or heard anyone. *It must be soundproof.* She considered why they'd need soundproofing in the first place and glanced at the sprinklers again. *Maybe this is where I'm going to die.* She pushed the thought away.

Instead, she distracted herself. She'd sat in rooms similar to this after she'd crashed her car and was mandated by the court to attend therapy. The police report stated alcohol was a contributing factor. And they were right. In the end, the court dropped the charges—there'd been no injury but that to her pride. That, and her Volvo. Still, she was required to see a shrink to learn proper drinking and driving behavior. That was, don't do it. She'd already known that. What she didn't know was how to deal with the judgement and persecution from her family because she'd fallen in love with someone who happened to have the same genitals as her. So she self-medicated, sometimes to excess. *Who didn't?* And that night she impulsively made one of the biggest mistakes of her life.

Impulse control, who needs it? Jacob's face flashed through her mind.

A man in a lab coat opened the door.

Calay straightened and watched him enter. In his hands he held a flashlight not unlike the one Guy shone in her face back on the highway when they first met, what looked like a taser, a notebook, and a glass of water. *No gun.*

"Drink."

Calay blinked at the technician.

"You've been sitting here a long time. You must be thirsty."

He stretched his arm holding the glass of water to Calay. She peered over the edge, sniffed it.

"Look, we have you. You're here. You aren't going anywhere."

She brought her gaze to meet his, leaning over the table, her hands tucked in her lap.

"There's no need to drug you. It's just water."

Calay considered what he said. He was right. If they wanted to kill her, they didn't need to do it with poison—they had more than enough guns. She was parched. She released the grip in her lap and grabbed the glass from him. Calay drank. Her throat opened to the cool liquid and relaxed. While tension nestled in her shoulders, the heat in her throat dissipated. She'd needed that, but she wasn't about to thank him.

"Better?"

She nodded, cautious. She set the glass on the table in front of her. He placed the other items next to it and lined them up in perfect symmetry.

"Good." The man sat across from her. "Now, tell me who you are."

She sat, silent. Still. Just as Jacob had done outside.

"Where did you come from?"

She gave him nothing.

His brow furrowed. "Did you kill our men on the road?" he pushed, "do you know who did?"

Calay shifted, uncomfortable with the barrage of questions but relieved he hadn't used the taser on her. Yet.

"How have you survived? Who is the man you're with? How do you know him?"

The questions seemed to never end, but the man never repeated himself either. The lab coat looked at his watch and sighed. He shook his head.

"This isn't going to stop you know. If you don't talk..."

"You'll what?" It was the first thing Calay had said since he'd come in. And it was the only thing she was giving him.

"Well, let's just say this will go better for you if you cooperate."

Calay sealed her lips and turned up her chin. Between the law proceedings and social justice activism for the women's health clinic, she was no stranger to political standoffs. So she sat there. And would continue to do so. *For as long as it bloody well takes.*

Calay was escorted out of the room by another man in a uniform. As they made their way down the halls, she surveyed the surroundings, trying to memorize the landscape of the building. Through a far window, she caught a glimpse of the sun rising. It was morning. They'd made it through the night; or at least *she* had. She didn't know where Jacob was or what they'd done to him, but she'd made it. One day at a time.

"This is yours." The man gruffly shoved her inside a barred cell. The space was not unkind. Inside she found food—toast and eggs. *Actual eggs!* More water. *Thank Christ.* And neatly folded linens on top of a cot. It wasn't exactly the Four Seasons, but it was infinitely better than laying on the hard ground under a tarp. *It's almost hospitable.*

The door closed with a loud clang and the man locked it from the outside.

"Wait," she pleaded, rushing to grip the bars, "where's my friend?"

The man narrowed his eyes, scrutinizing her question. In reply, he tapped her knuckles with his baton and walked away.

Calay rubbed her hands together and glanced around the cell. The confinement felt defeating. She was caged like an animal and there was nothing she could do about it. At least, not yet. She picked up the plate and inhaled her breakfast before making the bed. She laid down. The last real bed she'd been in was with Jacob. In the cabin. And before that? Blank space filled her mind. She had no idea.

Jacob. Where was he?

Despite her current predicament, she couldn't help but worry about him. She knew the fondness she felt for him could never last—how could it possibly? He wanted her, and she needed Tess. But for the moment—in this moment—she wanted to be with him. If for no other reason than she was lonely, and he was there. Strong. Safe. Sure. There was a solace in his company. Something oddly familiar. He was a respite from this hell. The way his body curled around hers was a cessation from pain. It was true—the moments with him were tenuous and she still wasn't ready to trust him completely. But she thought that she might, if given the right circumstances and amount of time. She wondered if she'd ever see him again. If she'd ever feel him again. With her. On her. In her.

Oh stop.

She stood. Paced. Dozed in and out of consciousness. Hours passed. Her exhaustion and anxiety fought a war for her mental capacities. One that neither side would win.

The telling *click* of the cell unlocking cajoled her attention. A tall man entered. He had a stronger presence than the others. Bolder. Blonde with dark eyes and a strong jaw, he was downright handsome. In that classic Hollywood kind of way. Except there was no Hollywood anymore. No movies. No love stories. No heroes.

"Hello Calay."

"How do you know my name?"

"I am Smith." Smith pulled a small padded chair from the corner of the room and perched on it. His perfectly manicured hand gestured to the cot. Calay followed it and sat.

"How was your breakfast? Are you well rested?"

"Where's my friend? Why are you holding us? Why won't anyone tell me what's going on?"

"I understand." He smiled, though the shine didn't quite reach his brown eyes. "This has all been very confusing and unfortunate. I am sorry for the rough treatment my officer gave you earlier. Guy—he is a bit like a wild dog, that one. I shall deal with him once you and I have a little chat."

This man—Smith—was put together. He had great teeth. He was well spoken. She wondered if he'd worked in politics or some kind of government before all this went down. And what his role was here.

"Let us go."

Smith looked at Calay. Cool and calculating. That was how she'd describe him.

"We are The Resistance."

She looked back at him, blinking. Her mind raced through the possible answers of what The Resistance could be and came up with only more questions.

"What the fuck does that mean?"

"I understand," he repeated. He leaned forward, rested his elbows on his knees. "You have not heard. Sometimes stories about our conquests make it beyond our gates, sometimes they die on the field." He nodded like he'd just made some kind of joke.

"Those guys on the road. The ones that died..." Calay began.

"The ones you murdered."

Her breath caught in her throat. "Uh, yes. No. I mean...they were going to kill me."

"I apologize for the inconvenience they caused you. They did not know who you were or if you were a threat to them. They behaved... inappropriately. Like I said, Guy and his pack of animals will be dealt with."

"Inconvenience? Is that what you call assaulting and killing other people? A fucking inconvenience?"

"You are not dead. You are here. You are fine." Smith nudged the empty breakfast tray as proof. "We want you to join our cause, Calay. The Resistance."

'Fine' is up for debate. She wondered if these people could really be the good guys. As good as they came, anyhow. No one was clean in this mess. Not anymore. How many times had she herself pulled a gun on someone or taken what she'd needed, leaving others wanting? It was the way of the world. The way of humanity. And if these were the good guys, what did that make her? The villain? The lines of good and evil were marred by the need to survive and she wasn't sure on which side of the wall she fell.

Where any of them fell.

"Where's Jacob?"

Smith rose. "He is still being questioned."

"When can I see him?"

"You will both be moved to a more appropriate space when they are finished."

"When will they be finished?"

Smith stepped out of the cell.

"Smith, when will they be finished?" she pressed. Calay was desperate for answers. She needed something—anything—to give her some kind of semblance about what was happening. This man Smith was smart, she could tell. Arrogant too. He evaded her questions without trip. And now he was evading her. They could do anything they wanted to her. To Jacob. And she was powerless to stop it. *How will I ever get to Tess now?* A chasm of loneliness opened in Calay's heart. In her mind. In this fortress of strange men. And now she was locked up like a common criminal. Like a dog. *Max*. The memory of him spurred her forward. She had to get answers.

"When will they be finished? Please!" she begged, lurching toward the door that was now swinging shut. Her opportunity to learn more was closing swiftly. She didn't know when she'd have the chance again. "Where am I? What is this place?"

Smith locked the heavy barred door. It grated against the concrete floor before it shut with a final clang. He looked calm. Poised, even. He smiled, his teeth straight, gleaming white and strong. His lips curled into dimples at the corners.

"We are fighting the aliens, Calay. And we are winning."

CHAPTER THIRTEEN

The motion of sheets scrubbing against the washboard cleaned away the dirt under her nails, but not her fear. Water, a bit of soap, sunshine. Flashes from her childhood flickered through Calay's mind. They were the makings of a clean, simple life but not a useful one. Not for what she needed. Not now.

She braved a glance up when she dared. When the voices of men quieted and the shadows grew smaller, when she thought they might not be paying her attention. Or at least less attention. The courtyard was bathed in sunlight. If it weren't for the forced confinement and lack of answers, it would feel like a peaceful, safe place. A possible sanctuary. A place to call home.

Men were raking leaves, harvesting lettuce, and moving supplies from one shed to another. Men went about their tasks, heads down, except to nod at one another when they passed. Men. It was all men. *Where were the women?* Surely, there had to be more than just her. And if not, what happened to them? Calay thought back to the woman on the road. She had existed among them. *A lone siren? A wolf? A prisoner?* It had only been days since then but it felt like a lifetime ago. No one nodded at her. It was quiet here. Shadows haunted her thoughts, though those on the compound grounds were chased away by flood lamps at all hours of the day. The perimeter of the compound was lined with razor sharp wire, cameras and tasers dotted the barbed fencing, and high-level bunkers shrouded in mesh and branches housed dark clothed men with guns. The moat—dark, thick, ominous. And then there was the general population. *The men. Dangerous.* All of these things were reminders this place wasn't quite what it seemed.

She could feel their eyes on her. All the time.

But they weren't the only ones watching. Calay took solace in that. She heard whispers among them. They called this place The Society. And as Smith mentioned, they referred to themselves as The Resistance. For the past three days, she'd been paying attention, leaning on her ears and eyes to guide her movements. She'd surveyed the buildings and courtyard. Memorized layouts and routines. It was like clockwork. The same people came and went from the smattering of buildings on the property. Meals were served on a strict schedule. Lockdown of the grounds was firmly at dusk; everyone retreated to their dens. All voices spoke in hushed tones.

The smell of distrust—fear—in the air was thick.

She yearned for the comfort of Jacob. The trust issue was still a question, and she didn't know much about him, but the warm feel of his body against hers and the safety he'd proven thus far was a respite from this fresh hell. Whatever this was. She couldn't say what this group's intentions were. No one had touched her or threatened her. No one would even make eye contact with her. Ever. And Jacob was still missing with no word given on when they'd be reunited. She wasn't even sure if he was still alive. When she asked, they brushed off her questions with gruff replies. Grunts, really. She was starting to feel as if she were a ghost.

Calay looked up from her chores to see Guy coming straight for her, his eyes transfixed on hers. Unblinking. His mouth pressed into a thin line of rage.

Damn it.

His stride didn't slow as he reached Calay. Instead, he thrust her backwards against the chain-link fence, knocking the wash basin over and spilling water all over the pavement. He bullied his broad torso against her, his legs on either side of hers. He jabbed his knee into her thigh and held her there.

Calay's pulse quickened, her fear rose. She hadn't seen him in three days and she would have liked to keep it that way. Surely, he wouldn't do anything here—in the open and in front of everyone; she was safe. And yet, the toxic cocktail of anger she drank from his eyes told her otherwise.

"Feeling cozy, yeah?" he sneered.

She held her chin up and met his gaze, but her eyes betrayed her bravado. She looked at him, stone cold and silent as death. She hoped she wasn't about to meet hers. Her strength quivered with her breath, but she wouldn't let on how scared she was. How furious. And how badly she wanted to run from him straight into Jacob's arms. Who, she didn't need reminding, was nowhere to be found.

He smirked, buried his nose in her neck, and inhaled. "Yeah, I can smell it on you." He started, "you should be scared. I'm going to do to you what I did to your little dog."

Calay forced down the urge to vomit.

"What's your problem?" She. Would. Not. Break.

"You're my problem, bitch. You killed my men. I'm not ab…"

"Your men?" Calay say her chance. "You're right! I did kill your men. What about the woman you were with? Where's she?"

Guy's eyes grew dark and he smiled. His teeth were yellow and stained by years of tobacco use and beer. He leaned in and sighed. His breath was heavy and stale against her skin as he released a breathy moan. Calay's stomach dropped out from under her at the realization that he'd done something to the woman. Calay didn't care about her in particular, but the fact that Guy was capable of what he promised sent a shiver of terror through her body.

"You killed her."

"Not before she and I had a little fun first, yeah. If you get what I'm saying. The same kind of fun I intend to have with you."

His hand traced her thigh. Calay swallowed hard and resisted the urge to push him away. She would not yield to his threats. Wouldn't give him the satisfaction.

"So you have a problem with women, huh? You have to force yourself on them? What's wrong Guy? They don't want you? Or maybe your mother hated you. No, she abused you. She made you her little bitch!"

"Shut up." His voice like gravel in her ears.

"Or maybe she didn't love you at all. She hated you. You disappointed her and she lef..."

Calay felt the sting of Guy's palm across her face more than she saw it. *Bingo, that's the string.* A trickle of blood crawled out the side of her lip as she drew back her shoulders.

"That's it isn't it?" she said, gaining steam. She ignored the burning sensation radiating through her cheek. "You have mommy issues."

"You cunt," Guy sneered, "The Leader won't be hearing about you. Or your friend. Yeah, I'm going to slice you both up real nice and feed you to these sheep for supper."

"The Leader already knows," she spit back. He raised his eyebrows. She had no idea if The Leader knew or not. Until now, she didn't even know there was a Leader. Could Smith have been the one she needed all this time? The key to all of this? To getting answers? This was the first piece of potentially useful information she'd heard since she arrived here. If she could push Guy, maybe he'd give up more.

"Dog shit. You think I don't know who you are? I'm going to pull every single last whisper from your mouth before I turn your bitch parts into..."

"Step away from her, Guy."

Calay and Guy tore their gaze from each other to see a tall dark-haired man approaching them.

"Walk away Adam," Guy replied, his eyes trained on Calay, "or yeah, I'll..."

"You'll what? Don't think so, buddy. Come on, you know the rules. Step. Away."

This Adam person seemed nice enough, wanting to protect her. But like she'd told Jacob, she didn't need anyone. Calay looked at Adam from the corner of her eye. Smiled big for the camera. And raised her knee to meet Guy directly—and firmly—in the balls. Her fingers dug into his scalp and wrapped around his greasy blond locks as he doubled over.

Out of the corner of her eye Calay saw Adam blanch.

She leaned into Guy's ear. "Get the fuck off me. And stay the fuck off me. Or I'll turn *your* bitch parts into dinner. Got it?" She pushed him away from her and he rolled on the ground, writhing in agony. She raised her boot and connected with his ribs. He coughed. Calay stepped over Guy as he groaned in pain.

"For good measure." She shrugged and walked off, leaving Adam standing with his mouth agape.

As she walked away, she appreciated the sentiment of Adam's offer. He meant well. But when push came to shove, she could take care of herself. She learned early on if you get the chance to take the shot, dirty or otherwise, you damn well better take it. It was how she and Tess had survived. In this new world, people didn't play fair. Men didn't play fair. In many instances, a woman's body became just another battle ground. Something to conquer and control. Something to plant their flag in. Something to own. So when the need to fight presented itself, she wouldn't deny her instincts. Her intuition. Her ability or skills. Hell, she'd made it this far on her own, she wasn't about to go down without a fight. *Not here. Not now.*

She was just getting started.

*

POTATOES. GRUEL, REALLY. WARM LETTUCE. A SIDE OF GREEN beans. That was what served as dinner in the cafeteria.

Always with the green beans. "Ugh." She pushed them around her plate, lamenting their existence and at the same time, finding comfort that they persisted. *Resilient little fuckers.* A bit of home in an otherwise foreign place.

"Hey."

Calay looked up from her supper to find Adam holding his dinner tray close to his chest at the end of her table. Where she sat, alone. She was beginning to like it that way.

"That was quite the display out there," he said.

She looked him up and down. His frame was delicate but strong. Like a cyclist. His dark hair flopped clumsily around his face. He looked hopeful. Awkward. Kind.

"Sorry if I..." He didn't finish the sentence.

"Sorry if you what?" she pushed.

"I, uhm..."

She let him hang there. Dangling without a net. Unsure of what to say or how to approach her. It was a game she used to play with men she dated, in another life, after she'd had too many drinks. To get the upper hand and feel like she'd had some control. When in reality, most days she felt like she was in a perpetual downward spiral. When she'd still been trying to fit into the mold her parents made for her.

His eyes darkened and his body shifted, looking hurt and confused. She could tell he didn't want to walk away. He also wasn't a threat. A pang of remorse jolted through Calay for being so curt. So unfair. He had tried to help her, after all.

"Do you want to sit down?" she offered.

"Yes." He stood straighter, his smile widened, shining and his eyes bright. "I'm Adam."

He slid onto the bench across from her.

"Calay."

"Are you okay, Calay?" he asked, avoiding eye contact as he dug into his dinner.

"I'm fine." She refused to let her vulnerability show. Then, thought different. Her stubbornness the past few days had yielded few results. Maybe it was time to try something else. To open up. At least, a little.

"No, I'm not okay," she started, willing her voice to sound more sad than angry, "I'm being kept here against my will. My friend has been missing for three days. And no one will talk to me. I don't even know where I am."

"You're here now. You're safe."

"The incident in the courtyard today would prove otherwise." Calay paused for dramatic effect, pushed the food around on her plate. *If he wants someone to save, I'll give him someone to save.* She batted her eyelashes, took a breath. "Why did you help me?"

"You looked like you needed it. Clearly, I was wrong." He completed the sentence this time. "Sorry if I assumed otherwise. I just...what some of these guys are like. It's not okay."

"Like Guy."

"Like Guy."

"He's an asshole."

"He's definitely that. But you should know it has nothing to do with you being a woman. He's a bully. He's like that with everyone. I don't know if this new world made him this way—broken, or if he's always been like that. I haven't had too many deep conversations with him, 'ya know? But you showed him, that's for sure. He'll know better than to mess with you again."

She didn't know how to explain what it was like being a woman. Before The Change, or after. He didn't understand the kind of risks men posed to them. What kind of damage that kind of violence leaves in its wake. Or how women spent a good portion of their waking lives avoiding situations or places they were afraid to occupy. Policing what they wore. Policing what other women wore. It was a perpetual wheel of fear and yet, despite how strategic— how futile—their avoidance was, the issue was never really about what women did or did not do. It was always about men. Adam had no idea what she had to live with. It was sweet he thought Guy's actions weren't about her being a woman, and in a way he was right. But he was missing the bigger issue. She wondered what his story was and how someone so naive could make it so far in this world. One word came to mind: privilege. She yearned to pass through the world as easily. Then, and now.

Calay reached out and touched Adam's hand. She let it linger. He stopped eating, his spoon halfway out of his mouth, and looked at her.

"Thank you for helping me." Though she was playing the part to get more information out of Adam, she half-way meant it.

He smiled from ear to ear. "You're welcome."

He was cute when he smiled.

Around them, people were finishing their meals. She glanced at the clock. *I'll have to cut to the chase.* She didn't have much time.

"Where is my friend? The one I arrived here with."

"I think he's being held for questioning."

"Where?"

"I'm not sure. One of the other buildings, probably," he said between bites, "what about you though? Where did you come from?"

Calay recounted finding herself in the warehouse, the terror she'd felt when she ran into the alien ship outside the clinic, and how she'd come to know Jacob. Adam listened, asking gentle questions about how she survived along the way, and how she felt about this event or that. He seemed genuinely interested in her journey. Like maybe he was tired of being lonely too. It was nice to talk to someone.

"What's your story?" she asked.

"Kind of similar, actually. I lost the group I was with when The Others shot up our cottage. We'd found an old summer camp. You know, the kind you used to go to over the summer? When you were young?"

Calay stared at him. *Yes, yes, get on with it already.* She nodded and forced a tight smile, hoping the gentle encouragement would seem authentic.

"Yeah well, I survived with one other person, but she was injured in the fight and..." He paused, the spoon in his hand shook. His eyes lined with tears and he looked down at his now almost empty plate. Calay heard many stories like his. She didn't know what happened, but she knew where he was going before he said it.

"I'm sorry."

"She died from an infection."

"I'm really sorry, Adam."

"Me too."

He took his last bite of food and set the spoon down.

"I was alone for a long time when these guys found me. Hungry and exhausted. Finding good water was starting to be a problem. I was tired of running from The Others. This place is well hidden. It felt safe. They had everything I needed. So I stayed."

"And now you're here."

"And now I'm here." He brightened. "So are you, Calay. It's a good place to be. To stay—it's a good thing to do."

"A man named Smith came to me last night. He said this place is called The Resistance. What does that mean?"

"What do you think it means?"

"He said you're fighting the aliens. Is that true?"

"Yeah, it's true!" he said. The clang of his spoon on the tray sounded louder in the now almost empty cafeteria. It would be lights out soon.

"How?"

"The guys that go out, they have this test. To find them."

"Wait. What do you mean to find them?"

"They're learning more about them. What their weaknesses are. How they function."

"But how do they know? What's the test?"

"I guess it's more like an experiment. I don't really know the details."

"How do they find them? I've never seen one. Only the pods. Are there actually aliens piloting them? What do they look like?"

"I don't know. I've never seen one either. Never stuck around to find out." He grinned like he said something funny. "I just know we're winning."

Calay considered this. That's what Smith had said last night—that they were winning. Now, Adam too. *What does that mean?*

"We've even captured one." Adam said, as if in response to Calay's thoughts.

"What? Wait."

"We're holding it here."

"We...They have an alien. Where?"

"I don't know. There's a place."

His lack of knowledge was infuriating. She wanted to press harder but didn't want to alienate him. Her mind shifted to Jacob and the way he often left her with more questions than answers. She shook it off. This man in front of her—Adam—was the closest thing to a friend she had in this place. The closest thing to a reputable source of information. She had to be gentle.

The cafeteria lights flashed then dimmed. It was the signal that it was time to go back to their rooms. Her cell. No sirens, no announcements. Everything was kept as quiet as possible as to not alert The Others to their whereabouts.

"Guess it's bedtime." Adam stood. "It was really nice talking with you Calay. I hope you'll stay."

"Do I have a choice?"

He smiled again and walked out the door, dropping his tray in a bin as he left.

Calay sensed she wasn't quite out of the woods yet. There were too many unanswered questions. Too much secrecy. Too many men. She pawed her fork and knife and some of the sugar packets on the table into her pocket. She wasn't sure what good they would do her, but one thing she'd learned in this new world was to take what you could get. You never knew when you'd need it.

And hell be damned, she was going to take it all.

※

CALAY PADDED HER WAY BACK TO HER CELL. THE HALLWAYS were quiet now, everyone having retreated to their rooms. Her conversation with Adam ran hamster wheels through her mind. It was the most information she'd gotten in days. She wondered about the alien they had stashed away somewhere and hoped it wasn't Jacob. But how could it be? Hadn't he run with her from them? Wasn't he trying to avoid them as much as she was? Besides, he was human. But then again, where was he? Why hadn't they released him into the general population as they had her? And if it turned out he was a threat, what had they decided about her? She raised her fists to her eyes and she rubbed. She was starting to feel like she could maybe figure this place out. Yet even as she uncovered more details, she was left with only more questions.

A hand reached out from the shadows and grabbed Calay by the throat.

Another, closed and hard, punched her square in the cheek. Calay saw sparks, and the hallway closed in around her as her mouth filled with blood. Pain coursed through her face and down the side of her jaw. It seemed the ground was rushing up to meet her, not the other way around. The supplies she confiscated from the kitchen decorated the concrete.

Guy stepped forward and heaved her up off the ground.

"Thief!" he accused, his face in hers, spit flying out of his mouth, "you greedy, lying, alien-fucking, traitor."

She felt his hand on her belt buckle. *No. No no no no no. Not like this. Not here.* She coughed, swiped at him. But his hand around her throat kept her at a distance. "Are you an alien too, you bitch? Do you have an alien cunt? Yeah, let's have a look."

Calay's pants were ripped down around her knees. Guy spun her around, exposed. She clenched her eyes shut against the pressure of his hands on her skin, prying, pinching.

"No, you look human from the outside..."

Calay's tears poured down her cheeks. She tried to cover herself, but he held her hands back, pulling her against his grotesque body. The feel of his uniform was rough against her skin. She choked back a yelp.

He reached for the knife on the floor, pressed it against her abdomen. She braced herself against the jagged sting as the metal dipped into her skin. "Yeah, maybe I need to pry you open and examine you from the inside myself?"

A guttural sob erupted from somewhere deep inside her, spit and blood dripped out the corner of her mouth. *This was it. This was how it was going to end.* She had to do something. Anything. "They'll catch you; you know!" she begged. She had no idea if that was true, but she'd seen enough men coming and going, she knew they wouldn't be alone for long. "They patrol down here."

"You think I don't know that, you dumb bitch?"

He leaned closer. He pressed his mouth next to hers.

She whimpered under the strain of his control.

"Soon," Guy promised. He cackled too loudly in her ear and released her.

Calay fell into a heap on the ground. The concrete was cold and hard, her tears pooled beneath her. She covered her face with her hands as she heard the knife drop beside her head.

"Castrated bitch."

Guy's footsteps led away down the hall. He chuckled to himself until he was out of earshot.

Calay was alone.

So alone.

She brought the tips of her fingers to where the knife had been pressed against her stomach. It was rubbed raw but there was no blood. Just the scrapes remained, evidence of his violation. Of this life. Slowly, she gathered her pants around her waist and collected the items she'd taken from the cafeteria.

Her shoulders shook with humiliation. With terror. And with grief.

She closed the cell door. The reverberation of the reassuring click vibrated up her arm as it shut behind her. She dragged her body onto the bed, and she cried herself to sleep.

In the morning, she was undecided if the nighttime terrors were worse than the daytime ones. Her cheeks were tearstained and bruised. Adam, while well meaning, was wrong. *He was so wrong.* This place wasn't safe. Not for her. And she knew there was more happening than what appeared on the surface. There always was. You just had to dig a little deeper.

She would have to dig a little deeper.

She had to. For herself. For Tess. For the life she intended to return to. It was tough— running from the aliens and constantly hiding from people—but anything was better than this place. As long as the two of them were together.

Calay resolved she wouldn't be made to feel the way Guy made her feel, ever again.

He will not break me.

She resolved to find out where Jacob was. *Then, we have to get the fuck out of here.* She couldn't leave him behind. Not in this place. She couldn't leave him to suffer the consequences of her escape. Whatever they would be. She cared for him but couldn't stay with him. Once they were free, they'd go their separate ways. He could do whatever he wanted at that point, and she'd find Tess.

Once and for all.

CHAPTER FOURTEEN

Calay was bruised, broken, and generally pissed off the next morning.

She eyeballed the damage in the bathroom mirror. If it weren't for the irrefutable swelling that marked her face, she'd have thought it was all just a bad dream. But her tear-stained face and swollen jaw were evidence of the previous evening's encounter. *Attack.*

It's not real, she'd told herself when she'd rolled off the cot and padded her way to the small, stained mirror that hung above the sink in her cell. *It's not real. It's not real. It's not real.*

But it was. She could lie to herself all she wanted, but the truth was marred on her face. And she couldn't deny that.

This is as real as it can fucking get.

She splashed cold water across her cheeks, rinsing away the salt and dried blood at the corner of her mouth. Today was the day. She had to press on. The cuts and scrapes would fade, but she refused to let her resolve do the same. Guy could break her body all he wanted, but she wasn't about to let that coward weasel break her spirit. She meant it when she decided to get Jacob and then get the hell out of there. Regardless of whether The Resistance was winning against the aliens or not, they could do whatever they were doing, without her. Calay knew she'd never make it within these walls. Among these men. And even if she managed to survive here, she'd never again be reunited with Tess. And that was all that mattered. She had to find a way out. She needed to talk to Adam.

The sun glistened above the military-camouflaged canopy, creating checkered shaped shadows across the compound. It seemed colder today, harsher. Even in the warm sunlight. Something changed last night for Calay. Whether it was inside of her or outside here, it was irrelevant. Now more than ever, she needed to keep her wits about her and figure out an escape plan.

Adam was gathering wood at the far side of the pavement, loading armfuls into a wooden cart. She ignored the whispers and stares and made a line straight for him.

"Adam!"

"Oh, hey Cala..." He stopped short when he saw her face: a contortion of pissed-off and bruises. His face went pale with worry. "Oh man. What happened to you?"

"Guy jumped me last night."

"Are you serious?"

"He popped out of the shadows like the boogieman." She flung her hair back over her shoulders, shaking off the mental image of last night. "But that's not why I want to talk to you."

"He's not going to get away with this, Calay. I'm going to take care of it. Right now." Adam started to stalk away; his usual lightness gone. Calay grabbed the log he was holding and clenched his wrist.

"No. Don't. I'm fine," she stressed, lightening her grip on Adam's wrist, "I need to know more about this place."

"You most certainly are not fine! Look at your face, Calay. He beat you!"

"I know what he did, Adam. Believe me."

"Then you know I can't let it go. What kind of coward creeps up on a woman and attacks her? No. This goes against the rules..." He began to pull away from her grasp. She couldn't let him walk away. Not now.

"Wait," she said, pulling him closer to her. She lowered her voice, "that's what I want to talk to you about Adam. The rules."

He looked at her, his eyes brimming with anxiety. "I'm not sure what I can tell you, Calay. I don't know much more than what I've already said."

"That's bullshit Adam and we both know it. You've been here for how long now? I know asking this of you is a risk. For both of us. But I need your help."

"I haven't been here that long. I know it's safe. That's what I know. And I'm not about to upset my stay here—or yours—by putting my nose where it doesn't belong. You'd do right to do the same."

"Adam, please. How will I ever get out of here and find Tess or Jacob, if you don't help me? I'm begging you."

"I know as much as you do, I swear. I wanna help you Calay, but I've told you everything I know. Is staying here so bad? Once things settle down and we sort Guy out, you'll see. It's a really good place to be." Adam pulled his wrist from her hand and distracted himself, bending over to gather more logs, gently tossing them into the cart.

"Adam…"

"Calay, please don't ask me to do this. To jeopardize my place here. I'm sorry for your face and what Guy did to you. I really am. I'd kill him myself if I could. If you ask me, this place would be better without him. But we have rules we all have to abide by. There's a process."

"See? Right there! I don't even know the fucking rules! What process?"

He stood up and looked her square in the face.

"In good time," Adam levelled, "Smith will relay them to you. But that's not my place. I can make sure Guy gets what's coming to him. There's protocol. That's how I can help you."

"But that's not the help I need. I thought I could trust you!"

"Of course, you can trust me. Because I follow the rules, like you should. If you follow the rules, it works. It all works."

Calay stared at him, both their eyes wide and agitated. Then, disappointment flooded Calay. It was futile. "Nothing works." She shoved a log at Adam's chest and defeated, started making her way back across the yard. She heard him call to her, but she kept walking. He didn't chase her down. He wasn't a man of action, she concluded, he was too scared to make a real move. To give her the help she needed. But scared of what? *He has to know more than he's letting on.* Something was going on here and she was going to get to the bottom of it. And if he wasn't going to tell her, she'd find out herself.

She'd made it before on her own, she could damn well do it again.

She just had to pick her moment.

※

THE LIGHTS DIMMED THAT NIGHT AT THE USUAL TIME, AND the residents of The Resistance retreated to their rooms. Or in Calay's case, her cage. The door clanged shut as the guard secured the lock and walked away, barely giving her a cursory glance goodnight. The echo of his boots faded down the hall.

She waited until she was sure she was alone.

Then, from behind the mirror, she retrieved the things she'd taken from the cafeteria the night before.

The lock wasn't particularly sophisticated—a classic spring style. Early after The Change, she'd learned how to jimmy locks just like this. It proved useful when searching homes and buildings for supplies or food. This one was a bit more complicated than she was used to, but not too dissimilar. She could work with it.

Calay bent the prongs of the fork down except one and began clipping the latch. It was stiff. The fork slipped several times, puncturing and scraping her knuckles in the process.

"Come on…"

She tried again, carefully sliding the prong between the spring and the wall.

It clicked and popped open.

Just like that.

It took Calay a few moments to realize she'd done it. Like, actually done it. In disbelief, she gasped. *No way.* She set the fork down and took hold of the bars. Slowly, she slid the door open a few inches. *Yes way! So much for gated security.* She was free.

The sound of heavy footsteps approaching from down the hallway put a pin in her great escape. Her breath caught in her throat and a trickle of sweat dripped down her back.

"Shit," she whispered.

Calay placed a sugar packet between the spring and the locking mechanism to keep the door from re-latching, and slid the door shut. She tucked the fork into the waistband of her pants. And then sat on the bed and waited.

A guard came into view.

She crossed her fingers he wouldn't check the bars. The door would come right open, the sugar packet would land on the concrete floor. It would be clear evidence of what she'd done. She had no idea what they would do to her then. She just needed a little luck. A little saving grace. She needed him to walk on by.

He paused just long enough for his eyes to linger on every place she wished she'd hid under the covers. Guy may have been the only one to touch her, but she felt all their eyes on her, all the time.

Then, he was gone. The sound of his boots echoed as he retreated further away, each step a reminder that this was her chance. Her moment.

It's time. Now or never. Do or do not. Do or die.

She got up, rushed the door, and slid it open. She didn't want to alert anyone that she was on the move so, she left her boots tucked behind the bed before springing barefoot into the hallway. Learning from her captors, Calay was as quiet as a gun silencer. Her feet bare against the concrete, she made her way down the corridors, up the stairs, and right out the door.

In the cool air of night, the yard was dark and open. Almost peaceful.

She looked up and thought she could see stars. She thought back to hot summer nights with Tess. After late dinners, they'd walk down dirt country roads serenaded by a chorus of frogs. The sky glittered with silver and gold—stars and fireflies, dancing around them. They talked about everything; they talked about nothing. It was just them and the infinite universe, ripe with possibilities. With their future. On those nights, they'd felt destiny brought them together; they were meant for each other. Like two stars themselves, part of a constellation the universe had designed just for them. For all eternity.

Now? Now, Calay felt more like dust in a sea of ash. *The Big Bang wasn't the beginning of the universe, it was the end of the world.* Her heart ached at the memory. *This isn't helping.* She focused her gaze forward, urging her body to move. *I can't stand here all night.*

She pitched from building to building, dodging flood lights and curling through shadows. Door after door, locked. Unsure of where she was going or what secrets each building contained, she tried her dumb luck, hoping something would give.

And then voices. Male voices. They were getting louder. Calay made herself as small as she could and pulled herself into the corner of the nearest building, just as two men in dark blue lab coats walked past. They were close enough she could see the creases in their leather boots and their breath in the night air.

They entered through a door she hadn't noticed before, hidden and tucked back almost as tightly as she was. Afraid she'd miss her only chance to get inside, she lunged forward and grabbed the handle right before it latched shut.

She swallowed. Took a breath. Hoped the men weren't standing on the other side. And let herself in.

The space was surgical. White with bright lights—sterile. And the two men who'd just entered before her were nowhere in sight. *Thank God!* Aside from the horrible metal whirring noises and screams coming from some distant room in the building, it seemed deserted. But those sounds were all she needed to keep moving. The last thing she wanted was to be at the business end of whatever machine that was.

Calay started making her way through the building. She wasn't sure where she was going, all she knew was she had to take control of her fate. It's what Tess would have done. She was sure of that. *Tess. Jacob. Tess. Jacob.* Their names tumbled in her mind as she padded along corridor after corridor, making her way deeper into the building. She wondered if she was running a fool's errand, trying to rescue him. He could be dead for all she knew. Not only that, but it was delaying her mission to find Tess. To escape. And yet, she couldn't leave him behind. She felt a softness toward Jacob. He'd treated her kindly and she cared for him, despite herself. There was an undeniable connection between them and a certain level of safety. Of comfort. And wasn't that the thing about being human? People wanted to feel connected. They needed it. She needed it. Humanity may have turned on each other, but she'd be damned if she let The Others—human or alien—take away whatever goodness was left in her. If Jacob was alive, she couldn't let him rot in a cell. She owed him this. Owed it to her species. To herself.

At the end of a long hallway, Calay reached a textured glass door with a big red sign. A strange glow emanated from beyond. The sign read Restricted Access. *Bingo.* She gently pulled the door open and peeked through the crack. No one was there. But if it was restricted, some*thing* definitely was. Maybe that something was Jacob.

You aren't going to find out just standing here.

She slipped through and found herself in an identical looking long white hallway, but with a single door at the end. The linoleum cold on her feet, Calay made her way to the door. The metallic sounds she'd heard when she'd arrived were inaudible now. It was just her, the stark white lights, and whatever was behind that door.

She reached for the handle. *Locked.*

Her hand fumbled with the waistband of her pants. It was still there. The fork.

The lock gave way almost as easily as her cell had. A sliver of light crawled across the carpet as she slipped through. Inside, Calay found a mass of equipment. Screens. Refrigeration modules. More of those weird taser looking things. Vials of liquid. A desk piled high with papers and boxes. And several filing cabinets.

She approached one and opened a drawer. Inside she found folders labeled with various codes and symbols, none of it making any sense to her. The urge to get out of there and find Jacob pulsed through every cell in her body. She knew she should get all of this over and done with. But at the same time, whatever was in this room at the back of the building, behind a Restricted Access door, stored away behind lock and key, could be her only chance to get some answers about this place. To find out the truth. *Just a few minutes.* The reward was worth the risk.

"Might as well start somewhere" she exhaled.

Calay reached in, pulled out a few folders, sat down, and began reading by the moonlight of the monitors.

CHAPTER FIFTEEN

The reward was most certainly not worth the risk.

"Oh my God..."

Calay's body was shaking. Her hands fumbled to turn the pages. She wished she had never opened the damn cabinet. The symbols on the folders may have not made sense but the information in them was clear as crystal; it was horrifying. She'd wanted information, and she'd sure as hell gotten it. *Careful what you wish for.*

She found the rules Adam talked about. Instructions on how they tested for aliens. Details on how they recruited new members. And the scariest things she'd ever read: a Crimes Against Humanity manifesto. There were memos from The Leader promoting Us vs. Them propaganda, valuing duty, purity, and blood. Letters espousing the mission—and death in the name of it—to be the ultimate loyalty. That any order should be followed without hesitation, regardless how old—or young—the victim was. They were to cause chaos to bring order. Pamphlets encouraged total war and insisted on an eradication of anyone not fit for the master race, including what they called 'hygienic methods' to dispose of the inferior and pseudo-scientific plans to build a pure, more moral society.

It was like someone collected the worst parts of every genocide in human history. And then created a map to implement it.

It had been minutes—or hours?—since she'd started digging through the files. It was all a blur of horror and death, and foolishly, she'd lost track of time. They'd notice her absence soon if they hadn't already. Calay didn't know how she fit into their plans or why they were holding her, but if history did in fact repeat itself, she wanted no part of it. She understood the role of women in rebuilding a society. And she wasn't about to become a human incubator for the rest of her child-bearing years. She had to keep moving. She had to get to Jacob. She had to escape.

She tossed the papers aside and peeled herself up off the floor. Her body moved slowly. Heavily. As if she were moving through mud. As she fought against her instinct to burn the place to the ground, she noticed one cabinet she hadn't before. Smaller and almost hidden behind the others. The label on the front was displayed in small black type. It read 'Intake.'

Unable to stop herself, she pulled open the drawer and found dozens of files. Hundreds, perhaps. Organized alphabetically. This made a lot more sense than the other cabinets. How much time did she have? *None.* She glanced toward the door. Her fingers tightened around the drawer. She swallowed. *I have to know.* She began leafing through. It didn't take long to find what she was looking for. She pulled it out.

She had Jacob's intake folder in her hands.

Calay flipped open the cover. She sank down to the floor like lead as she read page after page. Overcome with emotion, the papers slipped from Calay's fingers and tears streamed down her bruised face. She couldn't believe it. Yet here was the undeniable truth, in all its horrific, gory detail. How could this have happened to her? To him? To them? She tried to stand up and instead, doubled over. She lost everything in her stomach.

"What are you doing in here?" a voice from behind her commanded.

Calay, hands and knees on the floor, turned to find Adam standing square in the center of the doorway, a pistol at his hip.

He definitely knew more than he'd let on. Or he wouldn't be here.

The room spun.

"Calay. I asked what you're doing in here?"

"Adam."

"How did you get in here?"

"Do you know what they're doing?" She pushed herself to stand and shook a fistful of papers at him. "Do you know what they plan to do?"

He frowned at her, sadness washing the surprise from his eyes. His body shifted and stood stronger. Taller. The realization hit Calay. He didn't have to say it. And now, he couldn't just let her go. She knew too much.

"You knew."

"I'm so sorry," he said, pained. His hand moved to the gun and rested on it.

"So am I, Adam." Her head hung like a yo-yo at the end of its leash. She wiped vomit off her chin. Her hair dangled across her face.

"I told you to leave it alone," he said.

She solemnly nodded.

As Adam's fingers wrapped around the butt of the gun, Calay charged. Knocked off balance, he fell backward onto the desk. She rushed past him, making a break for the door. He lunged forward and grabbed her hair. The room turned upside down as he flung her into the open cabinet. Her head collided with the drawer, lolled side to side. How many concussions could one person sustain in a twenty-four hour period, she wondered?

"You knew," she repeated, mumbling more to herself than him.

"I'm sorry Calay. You made me do this." His slim physique seemed much bigger as he walked toward her, several zap straps in one hand, the gun in the other. Calay realized she needed to get her shit together or she was about to die.

Adam reached for one of her arms. She wound back with the other and clocked him hard in the jaw. The force was enough to catch him off guard. Calay grabbed the back of his head and slammed it into one of the blue monitors, smashing the glass in the process. His body dangled from it as blue light sparked around his dark hair. The gun dangled from his fingers.

She wasted no time. She grabbed the weapon and sprung for the door. Frantic, she burst into the long, narrow, and very brightly lit hallway.

One foot in front of the other. Adam would be close behind. *Keep moving. Just keep moving.*

Don't panic.

White wall after white wall, bright light after bright light. It all looked the same, and yet it all looked so different. Had she been here before? Was she running in circles? Calay found herself deep within the building, with no sign of a way out. In her fervor, she'd taken a wrong turn and ended up somewhere new, where the whirring, clunking, and screaming noises were louder. Much louder.

It seemed, in fact, they were coming from the other side of the steel door straight ahead of her.

She planted her feet on the cold linoleum floor. She didn't want to go near those sounds, but what other choice did she have? She hadn't found a way out and going back the way she came was impossible. *If* she could even trace her steps. Besides, if Adam wasn't coming for her yet, someone else definitely was. It had been too long since she'd escaped her cell. Somebody was sure to have noticed her absence by now. If they figured out where she was, she was in real trouble. If she was being honest with herself, even if they hadn't figured out where she was and just searched the buildings, they'd find her in due time. She now knew how they worked. Systematically. Methodically. Forcefully. And they'd come straight for her.

Calay looked down at the gun in her hand. She stepped forward. Grabbed the door handle. Took a deep breath. And walked through.

She found herself in a small empty room, with another door a few feet in front of her. Smaller than the other, made out of heavy plastic and barred by vinyl. It reminded her of the plastic curtain in the warehouse, and the pain and panic she'd felt as she fled then. A vision flashed through her mind. The taste of sawdust appeared in the back of her throat. The never-ending staircase. The blinding sunshine. And the long fall off the end of the short rooftop. That door led to freedom, maybe this one would too.

She moved forward on the balls of her feet. She leaned into the plastic. She peeked through.

The room was large, empty, and for the most part unused. But in the far corner, she spied a gurney. A tray with what looked like various medical instruments. A heart monitor beeped. Beckoning her forward. And a large figure strapped to a vertical table. Her blood rushed to her ears and her vision blurred, threatening darkness.

Jacob.

Calay pushed through the plastic to find his blue eyes already trained on her.

Seeing him clearly before her, her legs began to shake. After what she'd discovered, all she wanted to do was fight him. Or run from him. Or save him. Jesus, she'd never been so unsure about anything in her entire life. The metal instruments gleamed beside him. His lips tight, his body entirely naked.

"Jacob," she whispered across the room.

"Calay...you're here," he said, "you can't be here." His words slurred. He was out of it, but lucid. *What had they given him?*

Calay moved as close to him as she dared. Her body vibrated as she fought the conflicting urges to both hold him and punch him.

"Who are you, Jacob?"

"It...it doesn't matter. You have to go—now! Run! I can hear them; they're coming!"

"Who's coming?"

Jacob tried to talk, but only a wheezing sound escaped his mouth.

"Is it Adam?"

He shook his head.

She remembered the manifesto.

"Is it The Leader?" She paused. "Do you know what they're trying to do here? Do you know about the tests?"

"Run."

"What about you?"

"Go five miles, north northwest. You'll come to a road," Jacob continued. He struggled for breath; his chest heaved with the effort. "He will be back soon. I can hear him. You have to go now."

"Who will be back? Why are they holding you?"

"You'll find the Jeep. Drive as far away as you can, Calay."

"The Jeep?"

"Please Calay. Do. As. I. Say. Go."

"Yeah, no. I vote the bitch stays," Guy announced as he marched through the plastic door. He looked vindictive. Psychopathic. Predatory.

"You," Calay spat.

"I see you've been a busy girl," he started, a long nail flicking something from his teeth. He stretched his arms above his head as he made his way across the expansive room. "Messing up my records archive. You gave Adam quite the head wound, too. He's going to take weeks to heal. He may never be the same. But let's be honest yeah, that guy could use a bit of a personality adjustment anyhow."

Guy selected a long instrument off the table and approached Jacob. The muscles in Jacob's chest tensed. Guy raised the shiny object to his skin and took a deliberate swipe. Blood slowly trickled down Jacob's pec and over his hard nipple.

"Fuck you!" Jacob hissed.

Guy took a second swipe on the other side.

"Stop it!" Calay begged, backing away from them both. "He's not one of them! Do your test!"

"Ah, yeah. I guess you read some of those files, didn't you?"

"Is it true? If the test is true, just test him. You'll see. He's not an alien."

"Oh, we did test him. Just like we tested you. You passed; I might add." Guy wiped the blood off the blade with a white cloth. The blood—Jacob's blood —was glaringly red. "That doesn't mean I'm not going to split you in half after I finish with him. Yeah, and test a few other things. For fun."

Calay's body stiffened, paralyzed by the thought of Guy's slimy body anywhere near hers.

"And because you're a fucking traitor. We've been ordered to dispatch anyone who allies themselves with the inferior races. It's immoral."

"He's human you idiot!"

"Oh, yeah no, that's where you're wrong honey. The Resistance, we value loyalty."

"I read his file…"

"Oh, I know. Did you read yours?"

"It wasn't there," Calay admitted.

"And do you know why?"

She shook her head. Guy transfixed his gaze on her and stepped forward.

"Because I removed it. I can't have a record of you existing here. Not with what I'm going to do to you."

"Please, stop." She felt the tears welling up behind her eyes.

Another step.

"Whore."

And then another. She could smell his sweat. It was tart and rancid.

"Yeah, why don't you just put down that gun and we'll get started?"

The gun. Calay had forgotten she was holding Adam's gun. *Use the damn gun woman!* She lifted the revolver and aimed at Guy's chest.

He stopped walking. His jaw clamped shut, fists balled at his sides. Through clenched teeth he said, "don't go getting any smart ideas now. It's really not your style. Put it down, Calay."

She had no intention of putting the gun down. She knew if she killed him, she and Jacob could escape. They could get out of there, as she'd hoped, and then she could get back to finding Tess. But what if Guy was telling the truth and Jacob really was an alien? What would that mean? The Others had eradicated the human race, leaving the rest to struggle and brutalize each other. If Guy was right, maybe the work they were doing here was good and just. Maybe she'd misunderstood everything. Then again, if she just turned the gun on herself, then this bloody fucked up mess would be over, once and for all. The options spun like a cyclone through her mind.

She had to choose.

Now.

She heard herself pull the trigger more than felt it.

The smell of gun powder was thick in the air, and the recoil only a memory in her bruised muscles. As she stood there, numb and in disbelief, the scene unfolded before her.

Jacob stood strapped to the board, bleeding out of two holes straight down the center of his chest.

The grape Jell-O that was Guy's head exploded in a spray of purple and red, and what remained of his body slumped in a heaping mess on the floor. Warm blood pooled, creeping along the cold tile floor toward her toes.

Calay dropped the gun, turned, and ran.

CHAPTER SIXTEEN

Calay burst through the panelled exterior door and the cool night air grasped her lungs.

Somehow, she'd made it outside. All she could think was she needed to keep moving until she found a way out. Or until she was dead. Or both.

"Oh God," she gasped, choking back sobs, "what have I done?"

She peered through the netting and mesh designed to conceal the compound and squinted up at the stars. Was Jacob among them now? Particles of organic matter, a universe of dust. Was Guy? *Fuck him. Fuck them both.* They were exactly where they belonged, and it wasn't up on high. At least, she didn't think so. Already, she was beginning to waver. Before The Change, she used to wonder where the universe led. What kind of adventures were to be had in the galaxy? What mysteries were hidden there? Now she wished she didn't know anything about it. All she wanted was to have her life back. She sealed her pain and focused on what she needed to do next.

Waves of nausea flowed through her. Flashes of pink, red, and brain matter clouded her vision. The sound of blood rushing through her ears was louder than the becalmed night. The perfect stillness of the stars. The raging of her heart. As she stood there, looking up at the twinkling sky above her, she realized the night *wasn't* calm. The stars were moving. En masse.

"What...?"

Round beams of light danced across the dark, landing on her, one by one. Fear gripped her body as she realized they weren't stars at all. They were lights of some kind. She pushed herself further into the recesses of the shadows. They'd found her. She'd fought like hell to get out of that building and she wasn't about to be taken down now. She was so close to escaping. So close to freedom. She could taste it. She had to move.

Calay forced her legs forward, away from the relative safety of the building, and like always, she ran.

Daring a glance back, she couldn't tell if the beams were the search lights or if the compound had been discovered by The Others. The question of human or alien rounded her mind, but she pushed it back. It didn't matter. Either way, if she didn't get out of there now, she was a dead woman. *One foot in front of the other, as fast as you can.*

She ran faster than she ever had before. Faster than when she'd escaped the two men in the warehouse. Faster than when she and Jacob escaped the pods. Faster than she'd run into Tess's arms before The Change. Her body screamed to stop; her legs begged to give in, to let whoever was pursing her take her and have it all be over.

Ahead, the chain-link razor-lined fence beckoned. If she could get herself up and over without splitting open every vein in her body, she might have a chance. Or if she couldn't, at least she'd go out by her own hand. Her own way. She could die on her terms.

She heard men's voices barking orders, their boots slamming into the asphalt behind her. What choice did she have?

"Fuck it."

Calay gathered every ounce of energy she had left and leapt for the fence.

She barely felt her leg scream in pain as she leveraged herself to the top. She didn't notice the wire dig into her arms and rib cage. But she sure as hell felt the icy water wrap around every inch of her body as she plummeted into the dark moat below.

The fresh night air she'd so greedily inhaled was seized from her lungs. Pins and needles penetrated every cut and scrape on her skin. Darkness was on her heels and all around her. She began to lose consciousness, drifting deeper into black water. She felt the Earth reclaiming her and calling her home. It was peaceful, really. Away from the beams of light, the whirring of pods, and the pain of being alone and unable to trust anyone. It was still, here in the darkness, where she would sleep. A long sleep. Forever. Tess would have to go on without her; Tess was tough, she'd make it.

But the thought of Tess stirred something in Calay. Against her will, her arms and legs began pulling her up toward the surface of the water. *No.* It seemed she couldn't even trust herself. Because her body, as usual, was stronger willed than she'd ever been. Sex. Alcohol. Survival. Through it all, her body seemed to get exactly what it wanted. She on the other hand...

Calay broke through the surface. Her fingers clawed at the grass on the far side of the moat. Her body was heavy in the water, her lungs grasped for air. She hauled one numb leg onto the embankment and then the other. She was on flat ground, for what it was worth.

"God damn it." She coughed. She knew blaming her body was a false idol. She'd made every choice to survive. To drink. To fuck. To fight. To live. She wasn't separate from those choices—she was one and the same. Her faults were what made her who she was. They also made her human. But at what cost?

Through the haze, Calay noticed dark figures approaching. She tried to pull herself up. If the water wouldn't take her, her legs must. She couldn't go back there. To that compound. To the men. Where Jacob was strapped to a table with holes in his chest. Where she was completely and utterly alone. There was nothing but pain there. She had to get away. But a strong hand was on the back of her neck, hauling her up and across the damp ground. Dirt and rocks grated her skin. Then, she was standing, her legs limp with water and exhaustion. The building looming ahead. Bright white lights invaded the night sky.

"No..." she begged of her captors, "no, please."

"Calay." Smith was standing in front of her, poised as ever. "You knew how this was going to end."

"No. I can't go back. Let me go! Please!"

"Oh, Calay..." His soft hand wrapped around her chin. He roughly brought her face to his. He narrowed his eyes at her, evaluating. Calculating. "You did this. I told you I was sorry for the inappropriate treatment you received when you arrived. But now you have given us no choice. You've given *me* no choice, Calay."

"There's always a choice!" she said, "we always have a choice. I'm nothing. You can let me go. What would it cost you? Show your troops how it can be done! Lead them th..."

"This is how it must be done, Calay. Do you not see? Letting you go could cost me everything. I told you we are winning, and I intend to keep it that way. With you on our side, or with you in the ground. We have rules for a reason. And you broke one of them. Several of them, actually."

He dropped her face and turned, leading the way for her retrieval. "Bring her," he commanded. One of the unidentified, uniformed soldiers aimed his rifle at her back harder than he needed to and pushed her forward.

Calay heard the growl before she saw him.

"What the hell is that?" the soldier asked, his voice evaporating into the night. The men stopped and listened. It came again, deep, low, rumbling.

"Everybody shut up and listen," Smith said.

Then, a mass of dark fur lunged for the man leading Calay. His gun flew in one direction and him another, deep into the wet grass. His throat let out a guttural scream as a beast laid into the man's thigh, shaking its head back and forth, ripping tendon from ligament and bone.

"Max!" Calay shouted with surprise. She didn't know how it was possible, but there he was. Very much in one piece. Whole. Alive. Jacob had been right! Whatever was left for them on the front porch of the cabin wasn't Max after all. The dog's head perked up at the sound of his name, his haunches bristled, teeth bared and red. He began to growl again, blood and drool dripping from his incisors. She never thought she'd be so relieved—or lucky—to see those golden eyes.

Smith and the other men stared in shock at the carnage, unsure what to do next.

Calay knew this was her last chance. She bolted.

"Stop her!" Smith yelled.

Max lunged for one man, then another, before catching up with Calay. Her legs carried her to the edge of the forest where tree trunks and ferns concealed their path. She didn't dare look back. The sound of panicked shouting and gunfire was at her heels. As she ran, Max close beside her, she allowed herself to think about nothing but what Jacob had said—the Jeep. Judging by the position of the moon and stars, she figured she was running in the right direction. His instructions were embedded in her mind. Five miles, north northwest. But the forest was dense, and it was difficult to be certain.

Then, she was at the road.

The moonlight was blue and bright above the canopy of green and black. Straight ahead, the Jeep was right where Jacob said it would be, tucked against a rock behind several branches. She'd made it. Calay had to stumble through sharp blackberry thickets on the side of the road to reach it, but it was there.

He'd told the truth.

She opened the door to find a couple pairs of clothes and sneakers stacked on the driver's seat. That, and her backpack on the passenger side. The one she'd lost in the city days before.

"What is going on?" She reached for her bag. Checked the contents. Everything was as she'd lost it. Safe and sound. She clutched it to her chest, breathed in its worn leather scent. It occurred to Calay Jacob had hidden the jeep—with her backpack—all along. But how? Did he know Max was still alive too? Why would he have hidden all this from her? Didn't he trust her? If she was being honest with herself, she hadn't trusted hum. So why would she have assumed...? Like usual, whenever Jacob was involved, the questions circled around her head like a typhoon, but there wasn't time for answers right now.

It was time to go.

Calay strapped the sneakers to her feet and fired up the engine. She struggled with the shifter. She remembered this was why she'd brought

Jacob along in the first place. *Fucking stick shifts.* The vehicle lurched forward. Stalled. She restarted and repeated the process several times before she got it moving. Inching painstakingly forward, she heard the shouts of men.

Many men.

"Oh no..."

In the dark down the road, she saw movement. The silhouettes of dogs, soldiers, and guns. The very identifiable shape of Smith charging the pack. Leading them straight to her.

She leaned on the gas and stalled.

Again.

She glanced at Max, who licked his jowls and whined before longingly looking at the vehicle's console. There wasn't time for this. They'd be on her any minute. And she knew her luck wasn't going to get better from here. In fact, she was pretty sure her luck had all but run out. She'd already defied the odds more than once. Vehicle be damned, if she was going to get out of there and find Tess, she had to play the hand she was dealt.

Calay grabbed her bag, opened the door, and ditched the Jeep.

She ran for what felt like forever. Her feet hit the pavement with such force it sent shudders up her spine and into her still concussed head. She paused but a moment to catch her breath. As she fought for air, the thought crossed her mind that if she could move quickly down the road, so could her pursuers. *Let's make this a little harder for them, yes?* She dove into the forest, braving branches and roots. She kept going well into the night.

Until she couldn't go any longer.

Her body was exhausted. Her brain, fried. She saw herself collapse in the middle of a wooded area, deep in the forest, surround by brush. Pulling her legs into her chest, she curled up the way she used to under the tarp she called home for so long. Max tucked himself into a ball in the arch of her lower back.

And they slept.

✳

It was still dark. She didn't know if she'd slept for five minutes or five hours, but her body ached with stiffness. Max was pulled in tight against her stomach, his warmth gentle against her belly.

She listened.

"I think we lost 'em," she whispered. Her hand caressed the dog's head. He leaned into her touch—a welcome and needed comfort for both of them.

Her arms stretched out and she shimmied from under the brush. The thought of running from the alien pod in the city only days earlier, flashed through her mind. This wasn't so unlike when she had to pull herself from under the vehicle. Only now, it was a thicket of ferns and thorns. The ground scraped against her already raw skin. She'd lost her bag in her panic that day and yet, here it was beside her now. How? It felt like every day since The Change started was Groundhog Day. *Wake. Run. Sleep. Repeat.* Over and over again. The rawness of everything that happened between then and this moment barraged her senses. She began to cry.

Her sobs started deep inside her and shook her whole body. She released a wail that was more animal than human. She knew she should be quiet. That she might alert someone to their presence at any moment, but she couldn't stop. The pain was too much. She was no closer to finding Tess. All she wanted in the world was the love of her life back and right now that woman felt like a cruel, distant memory. She had just killed two people. One of whom was her comfort. Her lover. If she was being honest with herself, her friend.

An alien?

She didn't know what he was, and now she never would. Because she'd shot him. Murdered him in cold blood. *Can I live with that? Do I even want to?* She was lost, alone in the forest. A metaphor for her life. And the stark reality of it too.

Max sat up, sniffing her tear-stained cheeks and laid his head in her lap. If nothing else, she still had the damn dog. The loyal, scrappy, beautiful dog. "What happened to you?" She leaned down and nuzzled his face. "Where did you come from?" But it didn't matter. All that mattered was they were together again. Calay reached for her bag and pulled out the necklace. She didn't know if she could live with the knowledge that she'd killed someone who quite possibly didn't deserve it, but she did know she didn't want to live without Tess. Not in this world. Not since the aliens arrived. Not anymore.

The hair raised on Calay's arms. Every stitch of skin lifted with it. She swallowed hard. Everything she'd read about The Resistance's experiments to test the aliens—to find out if someone was human or inhuman, circled her mind. *Self or Other.* She released a loose breath and reached deep into her backpack. She pulled out a flashlight and mirror. Seemingly innocent items, but useful tools when traversing the cities. How many times did she used both these things to see around blind corners or signal Tess?

She held the flashlight up to her face, forcing her eyelids open against the brightness. She placed the mirror below them to bounce the light back.

Her eyes ran cold with tears at what she saw.

A voice from behind—"I was going to tell you everything..."

CHAPTER SEVENTEEN

Against her better judgement, Calay dropped the mirror and flashlight she was holding and turned to face him.

Jacob stood nearby, one foot in front of the other on the uneven, mossy ground. His blue eyes almost glowed in the moonlight. He ran a hand through his dark hair, sweeping it up and out of his eyes. His chest heaved with each breath. He should be dead. But here he was. He'd somehow found her again.

Calay reeled. In every possible way.

"I shot you."

"Yes, you did."

"Twice."

"I'm aware." He grinned, but his eyes grew darker.

"Then why aren't you fucking dead? How are you even here?"

"That's the thing about us. We regenerate."

Calay's vision swam, she stumbled back, increasing the distance between herself and Jacob. She blinked, refocused her eyes. She couldn't believe this.

"Regenerate? What are you talking about? I watched you die."

"Well, I did sort of die." Jacob smiled, his blue eyes shining through the hood of his eyelashes.

Then, it dawned on her. The way he suddenly appeared at her camp. How he found her on the road with Smith's men. When he appeared out of the bushes that morning at the gas station. That time he tracked her down in the forest after she'd left the cabin. And just now...

"You've been following me." Her hands travelled up to her very dry mouth. She gasped, desperate for words. The truth was in front of her this whole time. She just had to open her eyes. "You've been stalking me."

"I wouldn't call it stalking, exactly. More like strategically locating your person."

"Wha...Why?!" she wailed, "why me? Of all people, why are you following me?"

He smiled again. *Damn that smile.* It was an infuriating, beautiful, ear to ear smile. She wanted to melt into it. Into him. But she couldn't. Not now. He took a step toward her.

Calay grasped for the gun, desperate to maintain the distance between them. She scoured the thick mossy ground. She groaned, remembering she'd dropped it after shooting him at the compound. There she went again, giving into impulse instead of thinking things through. *God damn it; God fucking damn it.* She loathed her carelessness and promised herself she wouldn't make that mistake again.

Jacob waited, looking at her. She at him. She snatched her bag and fumbled for her Swiss army knife.

"Stay away from me." she said, a tremor in her voice. She unfolded it, one tiny utility at a time. She thrust her arm forward, waving it toward him.

He sighed.

"Cut me."

"Don't think I won't, Jacob!" Her voice was shaky but resolved.

"I have no doubt, you shot me earlier. Why not stab me too? Do it. I'll prove it to you. We heal faster than they do."

"Stop saying 'we!'" she yelled back, though his words—the truth of them—stung deeper than she let on.

He waited.

Calay lunged for his gut but ended up in a backward embrace, the arch of her back to his stomach. He was quicker than her. Stronger too. His thick arms restrained her tight against him. Any weakness he showed back in the compound was gone. He was, for all intents and purposes, fit.

"Let me go!" She thrashed against him, her arms waving wildly.

Jacob plucked the knife from hand. Calay scowled as he gently ushered her away from him.

"I can show you, Calay. I can make it real."

Jacob brought the knife to his arm, his veins pulsing and masculine. Pushing the tip firmly into his skin, he traced the curvature of his forearm. Blood trickled in a thick stream onto the grass below.

"Oh my God! Jacob. Stop." Calay rushed forward, despite herself, grabbing the wound to stop the bleeding. "You'll need stitches!"

She wrapped her hands around his arm, but taking care to not hurt her, he pried them away.

"Give it five minutes." He nodded.

Calay searched his face, her mouth agape, as the blood slowed to a trickle, and then the skin began to close itself up. His blood still dripped from her hands, but no longer his arm.

"But...how?" She swallowed, realizing Guy was right. "You're one of them."

He nodded, his full lips pressed into a thin line, eyes trained on hers. She needed to hear it, but she was afraid. Afraid she might flee like a wild animal when all she wanted to do in that moment was stay.

"An Other."

"Mm-hmm."

"An alien."

"Yes," his voice croaked.

The ground spin beneath Calay. Or maybe it was her head spiralling off her body. *If this is true...*She shuddered at what she'd just seen in the mirror...she could see the words forming on his lips.

"Don't say it."

"Calay." He started, reaching his open hands to her. As if he could lesson the blow. As if he could make it alright. He couldn't. He never could. Nothing would ever be okay again.

"Don't you fucking say it!" Her shoulders shook with emotion. She gripped the edge of her shirt, twisted it in her fists. Tears steamed down her cheeks.

"And so are you."

"Fuck you I am!"

"Want me to cut you so I can show you how fast you heal?" he asked in a sardonic yet pitiful tone.

"Stay away from me. I won't let you hurt me."

"I would never hurt you. In the short time I've known you Calay, you've suffered some pretty serious injuries, yet you've been able to keep going. You've sustained multiple physical attacks and managed to pick yourself back up without missing a beat. You've run marathons around city blocks on a leg that should be in a sling. You've been sliced open and caught on wire fences. Saved yourself from drowning. Got yourself here. Do you really think you could have done all those things if you weren't one of us?"

"My body has never recovered like that." She pointed, nodded toward his arm. "You're insane."

"You're right. You wouldn't heal like I do. You are part human, after all."

"Part human? What the fuck does that mean? Part human! I'm human. That's it. I've always been...strong. It's who I am."

"No. It's what you are, Calay."

"I don't believe you. I'm not one of Them. I grew up here. I have parents. A normal life!"

"You just did the test yourself. What did you see?"

"I saw..." Her voice started to give way to the truth she knew, deep within her soul. Her body. That wasn't human. Not entirely. "I don't know what I saw."

"Calay, when you shone the light into your eyes in the mirror's reflection, what did you see?"

"No!"

"Calay."

"It can't be true. I passed the other tests! I passed them! It was a trick of the light."

"What did you see?"

Calay's entire body was shaking violently. Her breath shallow in her throat, her voice disbelieving, yet the reality was undeniable. She knew it to be true.

"I saw stars."

"Yes, you saw stars."

Calay felt the Earth give beneath her feet. She was falling to the ground. To some unknown universe. Into Jacob's arms. He caught her and gently placed her on the forest floor. Then, there was darkness.

When she came to, her head was in his lap and his hands in her hair.

"What happened?" She blinked.

"You passed out. Understandable, given the circumstances." Any of the irony or sarcasm she usually heard in his voice was gone. He was all kindness and empathy. "I won't let you fall, Calay. I won't drop you. Ever."

Calay sat up, woozy but alert. She'd never been more awake in her life.

"Tell me everything you know."

"Well, that would take several human lifetimes." His smile crept in the corners of his mouth.

Calay went white.

"Too soon?" He laughed. "Okay, let's start from the beginning."

"No, start from today. From the stars."

Jacob nodded, and began: "the stars you saw behind your eyes are the constellation where you're from. A road map to find your way home. We all have them."

"But why do I have them? How did I...why can't I remember coming here?" As they came out of her mouth, the words sounded foreign and somehow, incomprehensibly right.

"Several dozen Earth years ago, there was an enormous electromagnetic storm in our home galaxy. A galaxy called 3C303." Jacob explained. His voice was steady. Calm. He knew this story well. "Its strength was almost inconceivable by human standards. 1,000,000,000,000,000,000 amps, I believe, is the unit humans use to measure it."

Calay blinked at him. Granted, math had never been her strong suit but she couldn't even picture that number in her head.

"Or the equivalent to eight trillion bolts of lightning you'd find here on Earth. When the energy charge exploded, there was a sudden change in the alignment of space waves."

"Space waves," she echoed.

"Yes, basically, electromagnetic waves. This change generated a super massive black hole. Most galaxies have one of these at their center—including Earth's. But this was bigger. Much bigger. It makes the one in this galaxy look like a marble.

"Inside this black hole, at its core, is a highly magnetic field. Your mother–Elora–happened to be returning from a mission not unlike the one I'm on right now. She was in the field of activity when the storm occurred. Inescapably, she was sucked into the colossal black hole event horizon. It would have been impossible for her to avoid it—the jet itself extended out some 150,000 light-years. That's longer than the diameter of the entire Milky Way, Calay.

"The radiated electromagnetic power shot through her ship and atomized her particles, tunnelling them to another galaxy, where they were reassembled. That galaxy is this one. Normally it would have taken 30,000 times the amount of time the universe has been in existence to get from where she was to Earth. Impossible. Even for us. But she made it here in a matter of days.

"You still with me?"

Calay nodded, her lips pressed together so hard her jaw hurt, her knuckles balled up so tight they turned white.

"Galaxy 3C303 is a very small community. If we were animals on this planet, we'd be considered endangered. So you must understand we can't afford to lose anyone. It's my task to find, track, and bring home those who get lost. In your mother's case, teleported to other regions of space. Or in your case, Calay, born on another planet."

"Wait, you're here for me?"

"I wasn't originally. It started out as a mission to find your mother. Instead, I found you."

"You found me."

"Yes, I found you. You don't remember how you got here because you've always been here. So I watched you."

"You watched me? Do you have any idea how creepy that is? What an invasion of privacy?"

"Please, Calay. I had to be sure you were who I thought you were. *What* I thought you were. I tried to make contact a few times. I'm the one who's been leaving medical supplies in the clinic. Occasionally, when it was safe, I left bags of food in alleys I knew you frequented. I was hoping to introduce myself to you on one of your trips into the city, but then *they* found you too. That's why the pod chased after you a few days ago. In the alley. I knew I was out of time. I had to do something."

"So you came into my camp," she concluded.

"Yes."

Calay blinked, trying to make sense of the information Jacob was giving her.

"You saw the pod come after me...why didn't you stop it? Why didn't you stop them?"

"When the war started...it changed everything, Calay. We were never meant to travel so far. And when we did, we came into an ecosystem—this ecosystem—completely unprepared for the environment we found. The life within it. The hostility."

"The hostility? You blew up my apartment building and eradicated my entire fucking neighborhood! Did children—did any of us—do anything to deserve what you did to us? You exterminated people, one by fucking one!"

"Only when we had to. When I signalled to 3C303 that I'd located our kind on Earth, others joined me. It became a rescue mission. And a dangerous one. For us. Not just because of humans. But unlike most life as you know it, we can't be touched by water. It's poison to us —like acid."

"But water is one of the building blocks of life. You can't have life without water."

"You can't have life without water as *you* know it, Calay."

Calay let the gravity of his words set in. The reality of how infantile their knowledge of the universe really was. Not only was there life in other galaxies, far beyond anything they'd ever be able to reach, but they existed without water. *Water, of all things!* As if reading her thoughts, Jacob continued.

"Water doesn't exist in our galaxy. It's believed water was part of our ecosystem at one point. A long time ago. But it hasn't been now for millions of years. Yet somehow, life found a way. We've evolved to exist without it. Over time we've actually developed something of a reaction to it."

"What kind of reaction?"

"The best way to describe it would be we suffer an allergy. Or maybe more like a burn. If you touch a hot surface your skin reacts, right? The skin breaks, you get blisters, it's all very painful. Water does more or less the same thing to us."

"You get burned by water?"

"All our kind do, Calay. A substance forms under the skin, like a chemical interaction. Now, if it's processed enough, we can withstand some contact with minimal side effects. Like with alcohol, for example."

"The whiskey we shared at the gas station," Calay said, putting two and two together.

"I drank from the bottle, but it wasn't something I'd call pleasant. I needed you to trust me. And it felt like an opportune moment to build some rapport."

Calay's eyelashes flutter. She rubbed the tears—the water—from her eyes. She stared down at her hands. *Water.* She wiped them on her pants. "The moat around the compound."

"Water in its pure form is the most damaging. It will kill us on contact."

"And our planet..." she started, realizing the magnitude of his revelation.

"Is over 70% water, Calay."

A wave of emotion rolled through Calay's body. She started to assemble the pieces. The cup of water she'd been forced to drink after The Resistance captured her. How uncomfortable Jacob had been when their bodies were pressed together behind the waterfall. She'd read about the test in the records room, but hearing Jacob explain it out loud was like hearing it for the first time.

It was all so real now.

"We came in peace. We just wanted to take you home. And others like you. But humans..." Jacob shook his head, wrung his hands. "When they discovered what we were, they became afraid. They attacked our ships, started taking us to facilities. Experimented on us. Tortured and dismembered us. It was a fluke that they figured out they could identify us by the stars in our eyes. Just needed a bit of illumination and something to reflect it back.

"The flashlights and mirrors," she said.

"Exactly. They could see them in our eyes, just as you saw them in yours. Then they used water to mutilate us. Every time a new ship dared to make the journey through the black hole, it was immediately seized and destroyed. So we sent more ships. Bigger ships. Like the one that, regrettably, took down your apartment building. We began to defend ourselves."

"This can't be right. No one has ever seen an actual alien," Calay protested.

"They have. And your people in charge did a pretty good job of hiding it. They kept it from their citizens. Acts of war are always covered up by governments—they don't want the truth getting out."

"What truth?"

"That they're the monsters."

Calay didn't know if she should laugh or cry. *Can this really all be true?* Were humans responsible for their own demise? They'd been doing it to themselves for decades, her included. Look at the human race: substance abuse, global pollution, political and social corruption, genocide, flagrant disregard for their own planet. Hell, look what the every day Joe did to their neighbor when it all went to shit. She'd experienced it firsthand. Was it really that much of a stretch to think they wouldn't do the same to a species that was unfamiliar? That was foreign? That was so...Other?

"When they came to retrieve me, I hadn't yet made contact with you. The pods, as you call them, that have been chasing us for the last few days are looking for us. They're here to retrieve both of us. To take us home, Calay. I wanted to tell you the truth, but I couldn't. Not yet. If I'd said 'hey, I'm an alien and so are you, and humans are the ones attacking us and I'm going to beam you to another galaxy now,' you never would have believed me. All that time and energy and life lost on Earth—it couldn't be for nothing. I had to get you to trust me before I told you everything. I didn't want to—I couldn't—leave without you, Calay."

"I knew our time was up. I had to make my move. So that day, I showed up at your camp. And since then, we've been running. Hiding. Doing what we've needed to do to survive until I could convince you to come back with me. To come home."

Calay sat on the cold ground. She began to absorb the information Jacob was feeding her. She looked up at him, searching his face for a fragment of evidence that would betray what he was telling her. She desperately needed to refuse what he was saying. To refuse him. But she felt the truth of it in her core. It all made an eerie kind of sense. Somehow.

All the news reports claimed they were attacked by The Others. But why would they say any different? Whether the media was privy to the other side of the story or not, history had shown time and again that The Other—those who were different from us—were to be feared. *When people are scared, they do some pretty fucked up shit.* She recounted her encounters with the pods. The ships, as he called them. Not once had one actually attacked her. Ever.

"But I passed the water test."

"Because you're half human, Calay."

She let that sink in. Half human. *That makes me half something else too.* Half alien. Half Other.

"So The Others. They know who...what...I am?"

"Of course, they do. We know our own kind. We protect them. It's a core tenet of our society—to our own selves be true. The whole is greater than the sum of its parts. We are all one. Whatever way you want to phrase it, we take care of each other. So yes, they know."

"And all the times they've chased me..."

"They were trying to do the same thing as me, albeit with a heavier hand. Subtlety is not usually our strong suit."

"You'd think for such an advanced alien race you'd have better communication. Have you ever thought about loudspeakers? PR releases? Telecommunication with your own kind?"

Jacob smiled. His gaze was tender. "You know as well as I do messages are often lost in translation. Especially during a crisis. It's no different across galaxies. Besides, would you—would humans—have listened?"

So he was trying to save her. He hadn't tried to kill her; he had successfully protected her. Several times. And now he was offering to take her away from all this.

All this.

"It's everything, Jacob. Everything I've ever known to be real. It's all been a lie. "

"It wasn't a lie Calay. It was just half of the truth." His eyes glistened; his jaw strong.

"Half of the truth. So you're saying I'm part human. My dad...?"

"Your father is from this planet. He's human."

"So my mother. She's...alien? Does my dad know? Did my mother tell him? Why didn't they say anything to me?"

"I don't have those answers."

"Did you bring my mother back with you?"

"I never found her."

"What? Why not?"

"I don't know. But I did find you. And I have to protect you."

Calay exhaled, stood, and steeled herself for what she was about to admit.

"Just so we're clear, what you're saying is I'm an alien-human hybrid. Is that what you're telling me?"

"That is true." Jacob steadied his feet and prepared himself for another physical attack. Instead, Calay stood straighter and looked him square in the eye.

"We have to go home."

"I think that's best and I'm glad to hear you say it, Calay. We can contact The Others." He moved forward and took her hands.

"No," she interrupted, allowing his palms to rest against hers, "we have to go to my home. To the farm. I have to talk to my parents."

"I don't think there's time for that. We're already pressing into dangerous territory evading our collection. And we know what Smith or The Resistance will do to us if they catch us. I can regenerate from death, but you can't. Not fast enough, anyhow. If they kill you, you will most certainly die. We have to go."

"Go if you have to." She drew back her shoulders. "But this is something I need to do. My whole life was just ripped apart at the seams from every possible angle, Jacob! If you want to go back to Them, that's your choice. But if you really want Us to survive together, if we really are all one, then you can come with me. Either way, I'm not going anywhere until I talk to my parents."

Jacob nodded, solemnly.

Rays of sun were starting to peek through the canopy of the lush forest. Small bugs danced in sunbeams; long shadows were chased away in the light of a new day. The fear from the night before was beginning to dissipate with the cheerful sound of bird song.

Calay had no idea what lay ahead of her, but she knew one thing for sure. She refused to go backward. She wouldn't make the same careless mistakes she'd made before. The more information she had, the better she could navigate her choices. And now that she knew what she knew about herself —that she was one of Them—she had to move forward. Into doubt. Fear. Hope. Not having a place to belong. These were things she'd grown accustomed to living with since The Change. Since The Others showed up. Only they weren't The Others, anymore.

They were Us.

CHAPTER EIGHTEEN

"Well, the Jeep's gone," Calay announced. She stomped her foot on the pavement where the vehicle had been. "Again."

"Not a surprise, I suppose. There's no way they would have left it for us," Jacob said, placing a hand on Calay's shoulder. She let it linger. Max whimpered. Calay's heart warmed as she watched Jacob's other hand scratch the dog behind its ears.

"Probably for the best. Makes too much damn noise anyway." Calay reached down, patted Max on the head, and started walking North down the road—the opposite direction of the compound. She wasn't sure she was heading in the right direction to get to her folk's place, but she sure as hell wasn't going back so The Resistance could make good on their promises.

"How did you find me, Jacob? I mean, I know you were looking for my mother. But how did you connect the fact that I was her daughter? I haven't spoken with her in...years." Calay's heart ached with the thought. She yearned to get back to the farm as soon as possible. Despite the pain they caused her, she never stopped loving her parents. Needing them, even.

Their footsteps padded lightly on the pavement, the trot of Max at their heels a reassuring sound that they were on the move. On their way to getting more answers. She was sure of it.

"Just like the cosmic map behind your eyes, we all have signature heat signals. We can track those indefinitely. If you're alive, we can find you. I found your mother's and began following it, making my way toward her. I got to the farm where she lived, but then it disappeared. I never saw her."

"The farm where I grew up! I can't believe you've been there. You know where I grew up." Calay laughed and ran a hand over her face, the idea seemed absurd. It was too normal. Too ordinary. Too not of this world.

"I did. It's nice." Jacob's face brightened as he watched the amusement play over Calay's.

"Wait. What do you mean my mother's heat signature disappeared? Where did it go?"

"I lost it before I could make contact," Jacob admitted, his gaze fell to the road.

"What does that mean?"

"I don't know."

"Does that mean she's dead?"

"I don't know, Calay. A lot has happened since we came to this planet. A lot we can't explain yet. It could be she's been here long enough the signature faded. Or maybe she was discovered, and they extracted it from her. Or maybe she somehow turned it off."

"Turned it off? Can you, uhm, we, do that?"

"I wish I had more answers for you."

They kept walking. Calay contemplated Jacob's words, rolling them over in her mind.

"But if she was injured," she continued, "if they removed it, or she was killed, you said we regenerate. If we can heal ourselves, how do we die?"

"The same way humans die," Jacob replied, scanning the forest for signs of danger, "but the trauma has to be pretty extensive."

"More extensive than being shot twice in the chest?"

"Much more."

"Oh..."

"We're not that different from humans. We bleed. We feel joy. We fuck." He paused at that. A fire ran through Calay, a brief distraction her from the emotional turmoil of the last few days. Jacob cleared his throat. Evidently the words had an affect on him too. She wondered what it would be like to kiss his throat. Here. Now. In the open. He continued speaking, pulling her out of her fantasy. "We're sentient beings. Just like you."

"Do...do they, do we, look like humans in the other galaxy?"

"Galaxy 3C303."

"Right."

"Yes. Or at least, we would to you. But we're brighter."

"Brighter?"

"Yeah, like we shine. It's like our connectedness to each other, our inner kindness—our inner beauty—emanates through our skin. It also increases our pleasure."

There was that flame again, flickering deep inside her. Yearning to get out.

"Pleasure?"

He nodded.

"You mean, sex is better...?"

"Much better."

"Better than when we were together in the cabin?" Her breath caught in her throat.

"Calay." Jacob grinned at her with a side glance, his full lips curling toward his ear. "We're just getting started."

They stopped walking and faced each other. The heat between them rose from the asphalt and whirled between their bodies. Their breath shallowed. Calay felt herself being pulled to Jacob, wanting him, needing him. His hand grazed the side of her body, running up the length of it. His fingers danced on her neck, caressing the bruises.

"I want to kiss them better," he whispered, leaning in closer.

"So do it." Her voice was hoarse with wanting.

Max barked, jolting them both back to the task at hand. To the present.

They looked up. Ahead, several abandoned cars littered the road. Along the side, a big green sign. Calay's heart nearly jumped into her throat. *A highway exit sign!* Now they'd know where they were and where they were going. As long as no one got in their way.

"Do you think anyone's there?" Calay asked, striding forward.

"Only one way to find out." Jacob resolved. His mouth turned upward, a glimmer of a smile. He reached to squeeze her hand. His fingers grazed hers, but she was already on the move.

Half the vehicle doors were open, spewing clothing, empty beer cans, and old photos on the ground. In one, they found what appeared to be a family of four, shot point blank. Their dried blood smeared on the dash and windows. Calay gagged at the stench and gently closed the doors, as if that were enough to lay them to rest. Burials were reserved for a different time. A time before The Change. Now, they simply left the past where it belonged. Behind them. They continued scanning the cars for signs of life. There were none.

There was no evidence Smith or any of his men had been through there. Or anyone else for that matter. They were alone.

"Think we can take one of these?" Calay asked.

"Do you think it's a good idea?"

"I think it's a better idea than trying to walk the next hundred miles."

"How do you know it's a hundred miles?"

Calay grinned, pointed at the big green side on the side of the road. It was clear as day. Her hometown, Forks Washington, was only ninety-eight miles from where they stood.

"It'll take days to get there at this rate, Jacob. We can save time. And the less time we spend out here, the better."

He nodded.

"Pick a car, any car..." Jacob joked, but the brevity in his voice was gone. Calay had explained what she needed to do. And she'd meant it when she said he could come or stay. Though she'd be lying if she didn't hope he'd make the journey with her.

They started searching the vehicles for one that would start. Luckily for them, the third try was a rusty old pickup truck. The engine revved on the third try.

"Got one!" Calay called, sticking her head out the busted window, "now how do we get it out of here?"

Jacob and Max joined her, assessing the mass of vehicles.

"We can push the others out of the way. Clear a path. It shouldn't take long."

"Right. Let's do it," Calay agreed.

They shifted the remaining cars into neutral and pushed them into the ditch.

"Your chariot awaits," Jacob offered, winking as he opened the passenger side door of the truck.

She was grateful for his lightheartedness, but reluctant, too. Nothing seemed right anymore, but that didn't mean she couldn't try to enjoy the moment while they had it. *Go with it. Soon this will be over, and you'll both be moving on. Enjoy his company.* Calay laughed, curtsied, and hopped into the truck, the slightest flutter of delight in her chest.

Jacob drove fast. Faster than she would have. But then again, he was used to flying spaceships. *Wild.* In only three hours, they sped by the crumbling blue and green 'Welcome!' sign and then, bypassing the town, turned down the dirt road that led to the home where Calay grew up. Surrounded by apple orchards and corn fields, it almost felt surreal. Peaceful. Like The Change had never happened. Tractors scattered across the countryside, birds perched on the extended arms of scarecrows.

She thought about the news reports, before the media went dark. When the war erupted, rural areas saw far less devastation than the cities. She figured that was because there were less people. They didn't need to destroy entire communities. Fewer places to hide made it easier for The Others to pick them off later. Now that she knew the truth—assuming it was the truth—Calay knew it was because the countryside didn't pose a threat to The Others. To her kind. There was no armed guard out here. No military. It was humans fighting them in coordinated attacks that posed a risk for the aliens, not some small farmer in the middle of nowhere who just wanted to tend to their families and their cows.

Small town values. They were traumatic for her—for someone who dared to question the status quo as she had, but not to an alien invasion.

A tiny girl, with a big mind, it seemed, was much scarier to this small community.

She sighed.

She was happy on the farm as a child. Hauling bales of hay, helping her mother bake fresh bread, and feeding the baby cows out of giant milk bottles. It was a simple life. A good one. And then Tess changed everything. In the best possible way.

The day she met Tess was the best day of her life. The day she brought Tess home to meet her family, the worst. 'That kind of thing' wasn't right where she was from; 'those kinds of people' weren't normal. She vowed her love for Tess. They vowed she had no place in their house. Calay thought it ironic she was judged and rejected so harshly for being different, yet her mother was in fact, far more different than she could have ever been.

So she'd packed her bag and left. It was the most painful thing she had ever gone through, but she and Tess were meant for each other. And even if they didn't have a place to go home to, they could be each other's refuge—each other's homes.

She hadn't spoken with her family since that day. Not because she didn't want to, but because they just didn't speak. Calay carried that damage and rejection with her over the years. As she looked out the window, she realized they didn't escape unscathed from The Change after all. A scorched barn on one side of the road, and what looked like a makeshift graveyard on the other. Pasture fences were snapped into stunted pegs, and fields normally brimming with goats and horses were empty. In the distance a dark pile of something smoldered. Her stomach churned at the possibilities. She hoped it wasn't human.

It wasn't quite the picture-perfect agrarian utopia she remembered from her childhood. But it never was a safe space for her, as it turned out. After the told them she was gay. She began to wonder what she was thinking coming back here. To this place. To them.

"This is it." Calay pointed.

"Welcome home." Jacob was already turning the truck into the long driveway.

"Oh, right." The realization Jacob already knew where he was going because he'd been there before, for her mother, was a strange feeling. She felt like she was constantly playing catch up with Jacob. Like he was always two steps ahead of her and she couldn't quite get her footing. Even in her own world. *Well, that's going to change now. That's why we're here.* The large three-story house rose before them. He turned off the engine and waited.

Moments later, a dishevelled older man walked onto the porch. He scratched his head, ruffling his short dark hair as he peered out the porch screen door. His clothes were wrinkled and a little too loose. He wasn't quite how she remembered.

Calay stared at him through the windshield, gathering the courage to exit the vehicle. It was seconds, but the moment seemed to last an eternity.

Calay braced herself, reached for the handle, and stepped out of the truck. The jumbled knot of butterflies buzzed in her stomach. The door slammed harder than she meant.

"Hi Dad."

"Ca-Cal-C," the man stuttered, and cleared his throat, "Calay. What are you doin' here?"

"We need to talk."

"It…been years," he said. His hands hung heavy at his sides. His face drooped, but his eyes seemed to light up as Calay took a few steps closer.

"Five, actually." Calay fought to keep the sadness and disappointment out of her voice. She failed. Her eyelids grazed her pupils. Breathing was hard. Everything was hard. *You can do this. You have to. For Tess.*

Jacob stood with Max kept their distance next to the truck.

"Dad, this is Jacob. Jacob, this is my father, Peter."

"Honor, sir." Jacob nodded. His voice was cautious, Calay noticed. Guarded, even.

Peter looked from Calay to Jacob, Jacob to Calay. He choked back a cough and tried to stand straighter. He smoothed his button-up plaid shirt and tucked his hands into the pockets of his cardigan.

"Well, come on in then. I'll make tea."

"No, Dad," Calay said.

Peter shrunk before them. Calay's heart ached for him. For herself. For their family.

"We're going to need something stronger," she explained, daring to take another step forward. She couldn't go anywhere now.

Peter nodded. He waved them forward as he went back inside the house.

They followed him through the swinging porch door. The familiar smell of wood polish and burning logs a comfort Calay long ached to experience again. She'd lost count of the mornings she indulged in a book in the family room as a child while her mother cleaned the house and her dad worked at his desk, paying bills or planning crops. The fire was warm and the furniture soft. It had been her favorite spot in the house, until it had all been taken away from her. Because she'd loved someone they didn't approve of. It wasn't fair. Resentment rose in Calay's throat. She caught herself and swallowed it. *Now is not the time.* She had a bigger purpose here.

"Whiskey?" Peter asked, entering the expansive kitchen.

"Lots of it." Calay slid into her old seat at the kitchen table. It was easy, being back. Almost too easy. It was also hard as hell.

"Seems like some thin's don' change..." Peter countered, his drawl lagging more than usual.

"You're not a saint yourself, Dad," she spit back.

Peter set three rocks glasses on the kitchen table and poured a generous amount of whiskey into each one. Peter took his usual seat at the head of the table. Calay nodded to Jacob to sit. Calay was unsure where to begin. She looked around and noticed most of the windows boarded up and reinforced with metal bars. She wondered who it was they were trying to keep out—the aliens or looters? Probably both. She wouldn't ask. She didn't need to. She knew it didn't matter who was coming for you now, just so long as you got them first. She took a swig from her glass. The familiar burn down the back of her throat was almost better than the childhood memories. Drinking was a habit that helped numb the pain of her family rejecting her. While it could be harsh, too, it was consistent. In a world of inconsistencies, that comfort remained.

"Where's Mom?"

Peter looked at Calay, pain raw in his eyes. He opened his mouth, but only a gentle groan escaped. He looked down at his drink, swirled it.

"I'm sorry I don' have any ice. Tryin' to conserve energy. The freezer is better used for meat, and the solar panels and generator only create so much power." His eyes shifted around the room clearly looking to focus on something—anything—other than his daughter.

"Dad. Where's Mom? I'd like her here for this too."

Jacob shifted in his seat, waiting for Peter to confirm what he already believed to be true.

Peter's eyes transfixed on the table between them.

"Dad…"

"Your mother is dead."

Calay went cold. She stifled a sob. Tried to breathe. Loss flooded her limbs. "How?"

Her father's hands began to tremble. He downed his drink. Jacob slid Peter his, and Peter drank that too. *The apple doesn't fall far from the tree.* Calay didn't have time for this, she needed answers. If The Others lacked subtlety, maybe she should too, considering she was one of them.

"I know, Dad."

Peter looked at her, his eyes wide with surprise.

"I know what I am. And I know what she was too. Do you know what I'm talking about?"

He swallowed.

"Do you?" Calay pressed, leaning across the table.

He nodded, knowingly.

"We didn' want ya to know." A tear ran down his face. "We didn' want ya to struggle. We…oh God Calay, we only wanted to protect you. And then you were gone."

Calay sat upright, careful with her tone. "Are you saying I'm one of them?"

"I am, my daughter."

"Say the words, Dad."

"You're alien 'an human, Calay."

"Us and Other. Neither and Or," she confirmed.

Peter again, nodded.

"Yeah, somehow you exist. As both."

The impact of that truth was like a punch in the guts. She'd evaded it when she held that mirror up to her eyes. She'd felt it when Jacob told her. But now there was no denying it. This was her proof. It was who she was. It was what she was. And she was more confused than ever. She only had one other question for Peter and she was determined to get the answer. She steadied herself on what felt like an unsteady raft in a stormy ocean, thrashing her world into jagged rocks, smashing it into splinters, and leaving her with the carnage of shattered truths.

"Dad...how? How did Mom die?"

Peter sighed and reached for the bottle.

"When they come for her, she was already gone. At first, she tried to get people in the area to 'ccept them. To understand they weren' dangerous. That they would never hurt people. She printed pamphlets, organized meetings, hosted rallies. She was doin' good work. She was organizing somethin'—puttin' together a movement. I thin' she was tryin' to make a bridge between our two kinds.

"But then the news reports started comin' out. That folks were bein' killed. That the aliens were huntin' us down. It didn't take long for everyone to think she gone crazy. And then, to think she gone crazy dangerous."

Calay knew where this was going before he got there. *Humans proving our inhumanity. Again.*

Jacob sat still as a board in the chair across the table.

"They started callin' her a traitor. A witch. A collaborator with the aliens. They chanted 'Elora the destroyer', like she was personally responsible for the deaths of other people. They wouldn' listen to her, so she decided to show 'em. Show 'em how peaceful they really were. That they could live in harmony, despite their differences. Or maybe because of them. So one night, she organized a big meetin' in the center of town.

She asked me to perform the test. In public. I told her I couldn' do that. I couldn' risk losin' her. She insisted this would be what changed their minds. That we could coexist. That all this senseless death didn' have to continue. She convinced herself it was gonna work."

"And you did it." Calay couldn't hide the shock in her voice. The outrage. Her fingers wrapped around the glass in her hand. It took everything in her not to smash it within her fist.

"She convinced me." Peter's voice shook with regret. "One night, in front of a crowd in the center of town, we did it. And then she proved it further by cuttin' herself in front o' everyone. Of course, she healed right away. They were on her in moments, Calay. I fought 'em off as hard as I could, but it was a mob. A frenzy. An entire county of people who wanted to tear her limb from limb.

"And they did," Calay finished.

Peter's face was soaked with tears. He nodded.

"She couldn' heal herself. She couldn' come back. There was nothing to come back from. As it happened, didn' take long for 'em to come after me. I had to hide. To board up. Eventually they took their anger elsewhere. To the aliens. I didn' ever get to bury her properly, Calay. When I got back there, she was gone. I been alone here ever since."

Peter poured himself a third drink, took a mouthful, and dropped the glass back on the table. Jacob reached over to keep it from tumbling to the floor.

Calay understood her father's pain. Intimately. But she resisted consoling him. Or to wilt before him. Her father. The man who was supposed to protect her from the evils of the world, the bad men, and the things that go bump in the night. Instead, he turned her out into that world and it did nothing but abuse her. *I didn't need him then, and I don't need him now. He can wallow in the shadow of a monster he made.* She refused to show him mercy.

And yet, her heart was breaking for him. *God damn it.* Even after all he had done, he was still her father. The man she'd called Daddy. The man who'd told her bedtime stories, taken her on camping trips, and drank coffee with, at this very table. He was, in his own broken way, a version of home. Home. It was all she ever wanted.

"Will you stay the night?" Peter asked, interrupting her train of thought. His hands were folded on the kitchen table. His eyes trained on Calay's. He ignored the tears that clung to his chin.

"Of course not." Calay put the glass she was holding back on the table. She pushed it away.

"Calay, it' late. It' dark. There's nowhere else you'll be able to go tonight. Please, stay."

"I'm sure we'll figure something out." Calay stood, ready to break for the door. Jacob reached over and touched her hand.

"I think we should spend the night," he said.

"What?"

"You aren't the only one who lost someone," Jacob's voice cracked. He looked between father and daughter, around the room. Calay realized he meant her mother. Jacob was feeling the absence of one of his own. His eyes met Calay's, and she understood. How could she say no to him? To this?

"Fine," Calay relented, her shoulders slumping with exhaustion, "it's safe here. Whatever that means. But in the morning, we go."

Both men acquiesced.

※

THE SMELL OF FRESH BREWED COFFEE AND SUNSHINE wafted into her old room. She'd initially refused to sleep in her bedroom, opting to take the couch. There were too many memories among her stuffed animals and bookshelves. But Jacob wouldn't take the bed and it was ridiculous to let it go to waste. So when she reluctantly went upstairs, she discovered her parents had left her room exactly as it was. Posters from teen magazines and photos of friends she was sure were now long dead, lined the walls. Half-burned candles and fake flowers decorated the desk. When she pulled back the yellow comforter, her sheets still smelled of the laundry detergent her mother used. Only mustier. And so, she crawled under the covers, reliving memory after childhood memory. And she slept better than she had in as long as she could remember.

God that coffee smells good.

She made her way downstairs and into the kitchen. Jacob and Peter were cooking breakfast together, making casual conversation and laughing at what seemed like nonsense. Max was close at their feet, begging for what turned out to be a third piece of bacon. Her dad tossed it to him and the dog greedily scarfed it up. He waited impatiently for another.

Despite her mood and the revelations of the last two days, Calay was surprised to find herself smiling. Her father looked more like the man she remembered. Sometime overnight he had shaven. His eyes were clearer and the patches of fly-aways on the top of his head were combed. Jacob looked more like the kind of man her parents hoped she'd bring home than she ever thought he could look like. It was a happy scene. The events from the last week felt like a lifetime away. For a moment, Calay wondered if it was all really going to be okay. If there was a salvation here.

As they sat down to eat, Peter offered a proposal.

"Maybe you kids can unpack? Stay a bit longer. Maybe for good."

Calay glanced at her father and then at Jacob, evaluating how to respond. It all felt so wonderful this morning, she didn't want to spoil it. Even if it was just a fantasy.

"No pressure of course." He scooped a ladle of scrambled eggs onto his plate, topped them with ketchup. "I just...it' good to have you back, Calay. I'm sorry for...what happened. I can' change it. I need you to know I do love ya. We missed you over the years. Your mother and I, we realized our mistake. But we didn' know how to take it back. It seemed fruitless. And once everything started happenin', we thought you were dead. Honestly, I didn' do so well after I lost your mother. I'm still not doing well. I know now, Calay, I need you in my life. My daughter. And it took you comin' back into it to make me realize I never want to lose you again."

"I'll think about it." Calay directed her gaze outside as she sipped her coffee.

After breakfast, Peter went to do chores. "Never ends 'round here, end of the world or not." He joked as he walked out the door, Max close on his heels.

Calay watched them cross the yard. Jacob cleared the dishes from the table.

"Why don't you go outside?" He suggested, taking a plate out of her hands. "Relax for a bit. I've got this."

She looked at him and chanced her second smile of the morning. The sun lit up the entire yard, mist hung in the air. It felt clean. New. *It feels like a fucking fairy tale.* How long had she wanted to allow herself to believe in those again? The past four years had been hell. They weren't what she wanted, but maybe they were what she needed. Maybe it all led back here. To a place where she could make a life. And feel safe. A place she could belong.

She hoped against hope, against all that remained good and pure and beautiful in the world, that was true.

CHAPTER NINETEEN

"I'M A FUCKING ALIEN."

She couldn't stop saying it out loud. It seemed too crazy to be true. And the fact she had gotten all of it so completely wrong made it utterly devastating. How did she miss so much? About her family. Her relationship with Jacob…herself? The paint peeled on the edges of the chair and dug into her bare thighs, but it was nothing compared to the pain of what she'd come to know in the past seventy-two hours. Because people feared what they didn't understand, she'd lost her mother. The world lost billions. And as a species they'd lost their humanity. Whatever that meant. Humans did horrible things to each other for centuries—probably since the dawn of time. It wasn't shocking it amplified as their very existence was being snuffed out. Over time, they'd got it all so confused and fucked it up.

They were their own undoing. She was her own.

Who would save us now? Who will save me?

Calay sipped her coffee, the questions churned in her head.

Given their peaceful nature, she wondered if The Others—if she could she even call them Others now—would extend an olive branch. Maybe she could somehow bridge the gap, like her mother had tried to do. And failed. Calay's eyes teared up at the thought of never seeing her again. Never hearing her voice. Or seeing her silhouette in the hallway. She wrapped her hands around the cup and pulled the coffee close to her chest, letting the warmth melt the icy edge of loss in her heart. Maybe the human race had already blown their last chance. Maybe they got exactly what they deserved. Maybe she did too.

"How's your coffee?" Jacob padded up behind her on the deck, a smile hanging on his words. She turned. It was strange seeing him in socks, his hair clean and his face so at ease. It was nice.

"Glorious." She beamed back at him, raising the mug. "Want some?"

"Water," he said, winking.

"Oh, right. Water." Calay's face fell. "What do you think that meant for my mother?"

He eased himself down into the chair beside her, squeezing her shoulder with a familiarity she didn't want to turn away from.

"I imagine she took some pretty careful steps to avoid it."

"What about rain though? Are you telling me she never got caught in the rain? We're in the Pacific Northwest. Or what used to be called the Pacific Northwest. We basically live in a rain forest."

"I mean, we can handle a little bit of moisture. We've spent millions of years traveling the universe. There's water in space. And we've developed some pretty advanced training and tools to detect help detect the presence of H_2O. And avoid it. It's necessary for our survival."

"What kind of tools?"

"Well, our ships for one," he started, peering at the puffy clouds in the sky. Calay followed his gaze, imagining the pods as she'd known them. It was hard to believe the machines that destroyed everything she'd ever known, were also acutely responsible for maintaining life. Like everything she'd learned in the last day, this was just another truth she'd have to get used to. "They're completely sealed from the inside. Nothing can get in. Ever. They keep us contained and safe, no matter the environment."

"But you said humans were capturing you. Torturing you."

"Yes."

"Well, how? If they're so self-contained?"

"Well, we aren't perfect. Sometimes ships break down. Something goes catastrophically wrong and we need to exit them to fix the problem. Sometimes we need to make contact. Like when I needed to introduce myself to you. There are a million reasons our technology is flawed. It doesn't help, that humans are flawed too. Many civilizations aren't hostile, you know. Many are peaceful by nature and decree so there's no threat to our kind when they have to leave the ship. Flaws compounded. Earth is a very dangerous place for us to be."

"It's a dangerous place for anyone to be."

"You're not wrong."

"My mother wasn't in a ship to protect her though. She raised me. Bathed me. Cooked for our family. Gardened. All of that involves water."

"We have other methods to stay safe. To protect us from your atmosphere. From the elements of Earth."

"What methods? What other technologies do you have?"

A grin spread across Jacob's lips and his eyes lit up as he peered at her.

"It'll make much more sense in person. I'll show you when we go back."

Go back. She couldn't go back. She had to get back to Tess. Maybe repair the relationship with Peter. Figure out how to rebuild their lives. The mug trembled in her hand. "I'm scared, Jacob," Calay confessed.

"Of what?" He kicked his heels up onto the table and looked out onto the farm in the morning light.

"I feel almost happy."

"That doesn't sound 'scared' to me."

"What if it's all a mirage? Another lie? We're fooling ourselves into thinking this could work, but what if my father will always be my father? He threw me out of the house because I fell in love with someone who he didn't approve of. Because I was different from him. From others in our community. That's only gotten more complicated since we came here. What makes us think he's changed at all?"

It was the most honest she'd been with Jacob—and herself—in a long time. She almost couldn't believe the words made it past her lips. A wave of nausea rose in her throat. Panic tried to follow in its wake. She resisted. *No, this is the right thing to do. I have to tell him.* She had to tell the truth. Otherwise, she'd never become the woman she wanted to be. A woman who knew who—and what—she was. He looked at her, his blue eyes soft and dark.

"It's been two days Calay. I think he's genuine. He means it when he says he wants you here. The question is, do you want to stay in this place? Or do you want to come home, with me?"

She shook her head, pulled her gaze to her lap. The coffee steam caressed her face. She closed her eyes. Sighed.

"Who's to say they won't come for you—for us—any day? Do we even have a choice?" she asked.

"We'll figure that out," he reassured her, nodding.

"I can't stop thinking about your mission. Theirs. That they're supposed to bring us back to 3C303."

"The planet is called Téras."

"We have a planet?"

"Of course we have a planet. What do you think we live on? A shooting star?"

"Huh…" Calay frowned, her brows knit together. "I guess I hadn't thought that far yet."

"And you don't have to. It will all be a surprise for you!"

"But Jacob, I can't be the only hybrid. I'm willing to bet I'm not the first. Nor am I the last."

"A race of mixed alien-human babies? Sounds like fun to me." He smirked and reached for her free hand and squeezed. "Or rather, making them sounds like fun." He leaned forward and raised his eyebrows in her direction. She grinned despite herself and pushed him back, a wave of coffee spilled out of her cup and onto the deck. She swiped at it with her sock.

"I'm serious, Jacob. Look what happened to my mother. Do you have any idea what people would do to me if they knew what I was? To my father? If more hybrids like me exist, the chaos we've seen so far will look like an intergalactic toddler spat. People react badly to different. They react even worse when they feel tricked or betrayed. Especially by their own kind. This could be really, really, bad."

"Hey." His strong hand rested on her shoulder, his face turned serious, all joviality smeared clean out of his eyes. "We're safe here. Safe now. That's what matters."

Calay wrinkled her nose and sighed. She wasn't sure if he didn't get it or didn't want to get it. He'd seen firsthand what people were capable of. Their violence had managed to single-handedly bring an entire army of aliens across multiple galaxies and start a war of the worlds. *Jesus Christ, humans are a violent species. But maybe he's right.* Whether it was the calm before the storm or the eye of the hurricane, maybe feeling happy, even for just a few minutes, couldn't hurt.

"You wanna see the farm?" she asked, setting her cup down on the table in front of her. Calay slipped on her old sneakers. The ones that still lived in the closet by the front door.

"An opportunity to explore the place that made you into the force you are today?" He smiled, already rising to his feet. "Let me get my boots."

They meandered across the yard, mooing at cows, climbing on tractors she used to ride when she was a little girl, kissing in the gazebo where she and Tess first kissed. Calay couldn't help herself. And she didn't want to. She knew she was betraying Tess by being with Jacob, but this was different. He was her own kind. Alien. Other. And whatever it was that was growing between them, she decided, was temporary. The love Tess and she shared was forever. And when they reunited, she'd make sure they were never separated again.

"This is where I spent most of my time." Calay slid open the door to the big red barn at the far end of the property.

"Wow." Jacob laughed. "It's, uh, rustic."

Calay laughed out loud without restraint for the first time in as long as she could remember. "Yes, it is."

The inside of the barn smelled like straw and lilacs. Sunlight streamed through small windows on the upper loft, pitchforks and shovels hung along the lower wall. In a corner, stacks of boxes with old CDs and photo albums cascaded onto the floor.

A time-capsule of her childhood. Days long gone. Another life.

"This is all yours?" He made his way over to the ephemera.

"Yeah, it was."

They fingered the items, sorting through memories and tugging on her heartstrings. It was more than a lifetime ago that Calay was this girl. The girl with mix tapes and band t-shirts. The girl whose eyes shone when she smiled. The girl with a mother and a father that loved her. The girl who believed in a future filled with love and family and kindness. And yet, something of her still existed deep inside Calay. Something small and real. She could almost grasp it. Everything had changed and yet, it had stayed the same. She was neither the woman she thought she was nor was she different. Now, she existed in two spaces at once and was all too aware of it. It was a very tenuous place to be. Was she human or alien? Should she stay or go? Could she accept this new reality, or should she reject it? Where did she belong?

Does it even matter?

Calay blinked up from a handful of old Polaroids and really saw Jacob for the first time as something other than a friend or foe; she saw him as she saw herself. Hope and despair. Same and Other. He was just like her, but in a very different way. She contemplated if it was time to really open up to him? To be with him in a way she'd only ever considered with Tess? Tess wasn't here, but he was. Waiting, with more patience than they had to give, for Calay to let him in.

Holy hell, is he ever here.

Jacob's t-shirt stretched taught against his chest, and his hair dangled into his eyes while he sorted through all of her old crap. He looked up, an amused smile danced in his eyes, his mouth strong and his face kind.

Calay stepped forward, rushing her lips onto his. He tasted like bacon and maple syrup. In the best possible way. She leaned into him as his body wrapped around hers. They kissed, his tongue searching her mouth, exploring her taste buds, licking her lips, grazing her teeth. His hips leaned into her body and she felt the hardness of him, pressed against her. There was no hesitation in his body. There was none in hers either.

She wanted him. Needed him. Now.

Unlike the way he took her in the cabin, this was less desperate, more careful. More precise, but just as passionate.

Jacob ran his fingers through Calay's hair, cupping the back of her head as he pulled her closer to him.

It was all that ever was. All that ever would be.

Her hands found the button on his jeans and slowly slid the zipper down, tooth by tooth. She savored that noise—it was the sound of his thick cock being released from its denim cage.

His lips found her neck and then he was on his knees. He pushed her shirt up over her waist and ran his tongue along her soft stomach. His hands reached up to find her nipples hard and without a bra.

In moments, he had her shorts off and was exploring her nether regions with his hands. His strong hands. Around every corner. Every inch. Every crevice. She was wet with need.

At his touch, Calay melted to the floor. She pulled him to her, their hot sweaty bodies pressed together, hay clinging to their hair. He was hard, pressed against her belly, and her back arched at his touch.

"Now, Jacob," she begged, the words a breath from alluding her, "make love to me. Please."

His hands wrapped around her ass. He scooped her up off the floor, carrying her to a bed of straw a few feet away. As he laid her down, she spread her legs, opening herself to him. She was ready.

"God, woman," he said as he indulged in the taste of her. Calay let out a moan. His tongue dipped deeper inside her. He was like a cat ravenously lapping up milk, unable to get enough.

"More," she pleaded.

He obliged.

Time stopped. Now, it was only them, alone in the universe. Together. In that moment. Only their bodies. Their hearts. Her body pulsed with pleasure as he went down on her. Her quivering legs wrapped around his head and she pushed his mouth against her as her entire body began to tingle with want. A rush of warmth flooded Calay before she felt the release she craved so badly. She loved every single moment. He rattled a groan into her.

"Yes!" she gasped.

"Yes," he growled as he crawled on top of her, thrusting inside her.

"We fit together," she gasped, feeling every inch of him slide in and out of her.

"We were made to fit together," he whispered back.

Jacob filled her up, breathing her in. They consumed each other. She rode that wave until he exploded inside her, sending Calay into orgasm aftershocks of her own. Her hips rose and fell with his until they both collapsed out of pure exhaustion, neither of them able to move.

"Now that was epic passionate fucking." She giggled, the weight of him still on top of her.

"Damn right it was."

His mouth met hers, their faces pressed together. They stayed that way, barely moving, for a long time.

"Calay," Jacob whispered as they were getting dressed.

"Yes, Jacob," she gently teased.

"I…I want you to come home with me."

"What?"

"I want you to come home with me. Back to 3C303. To Téras."

"You're ridiculous." She smiled and tossed his shirt in his face.

"No, I mean it. And not just because it's my job. But because I need you."

Calay stopped mid-dress.

"Jacob, you know I can't do that."

"Yes, you can. Our galaxy can be as much your home as it is mine. You're half of me, and all of my heart. You're a contradiction, Calay. A contradiction I can't resist. You're the most beautiful thing I've ever seen."

A knot wedged itself in Calay's throat. She tried to swallow but it persisted. She didn't know what to say. She pulled her gaze from his and coughed as she slid one leg into her jeans. Then, the other. Each movement felt like an eternity. And yet, not long enough.

"Jacob, I can't just leave Earth. My home. My father…Tess. Have you forgotten about Tess?"

"You've lived without your dad for the past five years. You said yourself just this morning, you weren't sure he was genuine. This isn't your home, Calay. And you don't even know if Tess is still alive! You've been searching for how long now? Days? Weeks? Months? For all you know she's dead."

"No. don't you say that. Don't you dare say that! How dare you?"

"You don't even know where she is!"

"I have an idea! And I'd be there by now if you hadn't gotten in the way."

"Gotten in the way? I'm pretty sure I saved your ass. More than once."

"Oh, so what do you want from me, then, Jacob? Do I owe you for that? Do you want a thank you? A shag? For me to travel light-years away from everything I've ever loved, needed, and wanted? Is that how I repay you for your never-ending generosity? What is it with men? They only do something nice for you because they want something in return! Right?"

"You know damn well…"

"Fuck you. Don't tell me what I know."

"Fuck me? Fuck you! I don't know if you've realized it or not, but Earth has kind of gone to shit recently and I…"

"You don't know if I've realized it or not? Are you serious? I'm living it. Every single day."

"Then you know what I'm doing for you…"

"Jacob, you don't get to do something nice for someone and then expect to be repaid for it. That's not how this works."

Jacob sighed and raised his hands in surrender. "Look, this is getting out of hand. You want a home? I'm offering you a home. With me. We're good together. We fit together. You said it yourself. Calay, you and me. We're the same."

"We are not the same! You're only saying that because you're trying to complete your mission." She knew what he was saying wasn't wrong. Hadn't she only thought the very same thing when she was justifying going to bed with him? Maybe that's why it stung so much—like what she knew about herself, half of what he was saying was true.

"How can you say that? Haven't I proven my loyalty to you by now? After everything we've been through together, haven't I shown you what you mean to me? I need you, Calay. Like you need me."

Her heartbeat rippled, sending shockwaves of heat through her body. His assumption, correct or not, made her want to run and escape from him. From all of it. She didn't want to admit she'd relied on him—even used him. She didn't need this. *Not now.* She couldn't need this. She couldn't need him. She wouldn't.

"I told you before and I'm going to tell you one last time. You don't get to tell me what I need," she said, pushing her vulnerability down below the surface, "what I need is for you to get dressed, and then get the fuck out of my way so I can get back to the woman I love."

Calay whipped Jacob's pants at him and turned. The look on his face was more than she could stomach. Especially when her stomach threatened to spill her breakfast contents all over the barn. This was too much. It was all too much.

"I was right to leave you at the cabin," she announced, hastily throwing on the rest of her clothes, "and I'm right to leave you now."

Calay stormed out of the barn. She strode across the field only to find herself at the edge of the farm. She looked out at the mountains and clouds that nestled amongst them. How could he ask her to leave Earth? Not only was the mere notion ridiculous, but she'd been clear all along —her mission was to find Tess and restart their life together. If he could so blatantly disregard her feelings and wishes, she couldn't possibly trust him now. Or ever. That was no life. No partnership. She didn't even know if she could trust herself when only three days ago, she didn't know who—or rather, what—she was. He couldn't understand that. He'd never had everything he loved shattered and taken from him. And he'd never have her.

No, she was doing the right thing. She had to stay the course. Tess was out there somewhere. Searching for her, too. Maybe struggling on her own. They needed to save each other. She hadn't lied to Jacob; she had a pretty good idea of where to find Tess. Or at least where they said they would meet up if they were ever separated. And that was where she was going now. Admittedly, she still had to figure out how. She knew one thing for sure though, she wasn't going to do it with Jacob hanging around. He was a good man and he meant well. But he would always be pushing her for what he wanted, asking her to give up her dreams for his.

No, that was too much of a risk. Too much of a distraction. *Just too damn much.* Calay pulled back her shoulders and chanced a glance back toward the farm. The sky was growing darker, clouding over. The breeze nipped at her skin. Despite the warmth in the air, a chill ran through her bones.

Jacob had to go.

CHAPTER TWENTY

It was near dark by the time Calay made her way back to the house. She'd spent the better part of the day stewing in her thoughts. Her fury. She knew she was being stubborn. Jacob was right—she wanted him, but not in the way he wanted her. His mission was not hers. It couldn't be. Not ever.

She felt angry and hurt. Or perhaps she felt angry because she was hurt. At Jacob for his demands of her. At her father for betraying her all those years before The Change, and then his expecting they could start over at the drop of a hat. At her mother for never telling her the truth and not being there now. At the aliens for invading Earth, at humanity for fucking it all up. And at herself, for all of it.

The only person she didn't feel anger toward was Tess. For her, Calay felt fear. Fear Calay wouldn't find her. Fear of what may have happened to her. And fear that after all this, their love wouldn't be the same.

While heartbroken about the challenges she faced with her family in the past, Calay still clung to the idea that somehow it could all be okay. But now, more than ever, she needed to get to Tess. And if that meant leaving her newly reconciled father, so be it. He would understand. He'd lost the love of his life, and she was sure he wouldn't want her to lose hers. Not now. *Once Tess and I are reunited, maybe we can come back. Start a new life on the farm. Together. As a family.* The idea danced in her mind and she entertained a feeling that resembled hope. She knew Jacob had to go. But if he really meant what he said about wanting her to be happy, he'd help her the best way he could, by staying out of her way. Then, maybe then they could all start to heal.

The house was empty. Dark. Peaceful. As Calay made her way through the rooms, the sound of Max's paws on the hardwood floor came to greet her. She bent down, nuzzled his face.

"Hey you." She smiled, scratching behind his ears. "Where is everybody?"

"Jacob?" Calay called, "Dad?"

Silence was the only thing that called back.

"Seriously, where is everyone?"

Calay made her way through the house. She checked the second floor, the basement. Nothing. No one. She was alone in the house. *Their trucks are parked in the driveway, though.* They had to be there, but where?

Maybe her father was still out doing chores. They often joked about the never-ending work on the farm, and the truth was it was a sun up to sun down kind of gig. She remembered it often went longer than both.

She looked out the kitchen window and saw a dull glow in the barn. *He's probably still smarting from earlier.* Or he was waiting for her to come back. Calay took a deep breath. If apologizing to Jacob was how she made this happen, she'd do it. She could explain her decision to him. Appeal to his reason and better nature. *He'll just have to accept it.* He would have to accept her. As is. Not as the alien explorer her mother was, or the partner he wanted her to be. But as she was. *Human flaws, needs, and all.*

Calay left the house, leaving Max inside, and padded across the yard to face Jacob. For better or for worse.

Inside the barn, Calay saw shadows moving back and forth. She was glad he was still there, though anxious at the thought of having to confront him after he waited around all day. Her stomach clenched, worrying he was afraid for her. Or worse, still upset with her. Maybe distraught over their argument. She didn't want to fight. Not with him. She just wanted her wishes to be respected. *Is that so much to ask?* She convinced herself, that it didn't matter how he was feeling, this was about what she needed. What she wanted. It was time she stood her ground. And while she didn't want him to feel bad about her decision, she had to be strong. This was the best thing for her. For Tess. And he would have to understand.

She opened the barn door. It took a moment for her brain to process what she saw. Then, she forgot all about her resolve.

Jacob was laying on the floor of the barn in front of her. Blood pooled around his head, leaking from the corner of his mouth and a gash on his temple. The one side of his face was bruised, his torso contorted at a strange angle. No human could bend like that and survive. *Could an alien?* At his feet, her father. Peter's dark eyes fixated on Jacob; his hair stood on end. In his hand he held a shovel, the end of which was coated in something wet and sticky. Jacob's blood.

Calay stepped through the door. It slammed behind her. Peter whipped out of his trance, his eyes glazed and frantic as they met hers. She couldn't tell if her father was angry or afraid. But something wasn't right. *He looks damn crazy. And Jacob looks dead.* Calay's heart lurched.

"Jacob!" She rushed to his side. Peter, in a dash of clarity, moved in front of her just as she reached Jacob's broken body.

"No Calay," he told her, blocking her path.

"Dad, what the fuck is going on? What have you done?" Upon closer examination, Calay noticed Peter was shaking with adrenaline. His lips, twisted to one side, mouthed words but no sounds came out. His shirt was torn on one side, hanging by the seam.

"It isn' safe," he explained, shaking his head back and forth harder than necessary, "it isn' safe."

"What's not safe? Jacob's hurt, Dad." Calay tried to push past Peter but he raised his arm to block her. He raised the shovel too. Calay gulped a mouthful of air and stepped back.

"It isn' safe," Peter insisted.

Calay looked from her father to Jacob and back again. Her mind was trying to make sense of what she was seeing but all she could see was red. So much red.

"What do you mean it isn't safe?" Calay forced herself to put her hands on Peter's shoulders. "Dad? Tell me what's going on."

Peter's eyes cleared a little, his breath slowed. He blinked at Calay and shuddered, as if just now realizing what he'd done. That his daughter was in front of him. And that he owed her an explanation.

"I don't understand, Dad."

"I'm gettin' rid of him," he told her, nodding, "makin' it safe."

"How is it..."

'He' too much like Elora."

"Like Mom?"

"Yeah...yes." Peter's shoulders turned inward, and he began to rock at the mention of his dead wife's name. "Exactly. He'll bring trouble. They took her from me. I won' let 'em take you too."

"They aren't taking me anywhere, Dad. I'm right here."

"No. They'll come fer him."

"The other aliens?" She shuffled to the side, turning Peter with her, hoping to clear the path between her and Jacob.

"The people. Or Them. Yes, the aliens. It doesn' matter. If they come, they'll take you too. Just like your mother. Don' you see' I'm solvin' our problem."

"Killing Jacob won't solve anything, Dad."

"It will. If he's gone, we can stay t'gether as a family...finally."

Calay swallowed hard. She'd wanted so much for them to be a family again. To be together. His words caught on her heart in all the ways she'd wished for the last five years. This could have been something good. But Peter missed something very important: the irony that she herself was as much an alien as Jacob. Self and Other. The same but different. Was it only a matter of time before he turned on her too? Or was this some kind of extreme acceptance, making up for years of rejection and loss? A way to atone for past regrets? She chose her next words carefully, not wanting to spook him into further harming Jacob. Or her.

"Jacob is leaving. I'm not going with him."

"Don' you get it, Calay? Can' you be grateful for what I'm doin' for you, for once in your God damn life?" His voice turned hostile; the shovel raised above his head. "Don' you see? I'm savin' you."

So much for not spooking him. This was not going to end well. She'd wanted Jacob to leave, he didn't need to die. She was desperate to save him but didn't know how. First, she needed to disarm her father. Then... what then? *It's going to be okay; we can come back from this.* She heard herself think the words, but they felt hollow.

"Dad, I need you to put the shovel down."

Peter's eyes focused on the shovel in his hands, surprised to see it in the air. He looked at Calay. His eyes grew wide, surprise flared behind them. Then, rage.

"I saw you, Calay," he said between clenched teeth, spittle flying from his mouth.

"Saw me what?" Calay wanted to turn from him, to rush to Jacob. Something in her dad's words didn't sit right.

"You two. Right here. Earlier. I heard you. Watched you."

"What?" Her stomach dropped. She stared at Peter in disbelief. He couldn't be talking about what she thought he was talking about. Could he?

"I watched what you did with him," Peter spat.

"What do you mean you watched us?" Calay already knew what he was getting at, but she couldn't bring herself to admit it. The grotesqueness of it. It seemed monstrous. Wrong. It was not his place. It was none of his business.

"I know what I saw. That was either love an' you're gonna leave me for him...or you're a whore."

Calay blanched. She stood, shaking. Her father had done a lot of shitty things in her life, but he'd never called her a name. Never anything like this. She shrunk under his gaze. She felt violated. Betrayed. "What happens between me and someone else is none of your business."

"You're my daughter."

"That's exactly my point. How dare you call me names!"

"Well? What are you Calay?" Peter challenged, stumbling forward. He lunged with the shovel but stopped short of skewering her with it. *A threat, only a threat. He doesn't know what he's doing.* Peter pressed tip of shovel pressed against Calay's collarbone. "Are you in love with him? Or are you a whore?"

"You don't get to call me that," she countered. She gathered her courage and raised her hand, batting the shovel away. "You don't get to judge me, Dad. You lost that privilege when you abandoned me four years ago! Do you have any idea what that did to me? What that felt like?"

"I'm makin' up fer it now, aren't I? I'm endin' it. Makin' it safe. So you can stay."

Calay steeled herself. This didn't make any sense. Jacob was bleeding out on the floor before her and there was no telling what her dad was capable of. What broke him. Where the kind man she'd known as a child had gone. Now was not the time to dive into the fucked-up intricacies of her relationship with her estranged father. Now was the time to get the shovel away from him. And save Jacob. "I'm right here, Dad. But you need to give me that. He can go back to where he came from. I'm here with you."

Her mind reeled. She needed to do something. Below them, Jacob still wasn't moving. *Please,* she prayed to the universe and all the beings in Galaxy 3C303, *don't let him be dead.*

Peter shook his head hard, smacked the handle of the shovel against his chest several times. "I can' lose you again, Calay." The glazed-over look had returned to his eyes. She watched his head turn, as if possessed by some unknown force, down at the crinkled mess on the floor that was Jacob's body.

"I need you to stop, Dad. Please." Calay's eyes ran with tears. "You don't have to do this!"

"It isn' safe," he repeated, "it isn' safe. It isn' safe. It isn' safe."

Peter slowly turned his full attention to face Jacob. He raised the shovel. Calay considered jumping Peter while his back was to her. She might be able to wrestle the shovel away from him. But even as the idea waded through her head, she knew she couldn't overpower her father. Peter was a much larger man. He had at least fifty pounds on her and several inches. And while she intended to take Jacob out of the picture, execution wasn't exactly what she had in mind. She couldn't let this happen. Not like this. Never like this.

Horror pulsed through Calay at the prospect of what she was considering. Her body turned cold and stiff. Her arms clung heavy at her sides. Her mind shut down. *Not. Like. This.*

A wheezing breath escaped Jacob's mouth. *He's still alive! He's not dead! Not yet.* There was still enough of him left intact to come out of this. She just had to stop what was happening. Now. Before Jacob sustained too much damage to come back. To regenerate. To go back to his home planet where he belonged.

"Jacob!" Calay called from behind Peter, "Jacob, I'm here!"

A flash of rage flashed through Calay's veins. Five years ago, Peter put her in the difficult position of choosing between her family and someone she loved. And it was happening all over again. All she wanted was to make her own choices. To be her own person. Her own woman. She didn't need protecting, she needed respect. It wasn't fair. She loved Peter. He was her father. She felt the agony of his abandonment bloom somewhere deep inside her body. His affront made her want to puke. Nausea and regret flooded her core. He'd violated her privacy. And now he was assaulting her friend. It was sick. *He was sick.* She knew this man, and yet, he was a stranger. She barely recognized him under the glare of the barn lights and in his rage. With a shovel raised high above his head.

He had no right. He'd given up his rights.

Years ago, when he'd forced her to choose between her family and the truth about who she was. Between them and Tess.

She wanted to tell him this. Her body screamed to tell her truth. But he wouldn't— couldn't—hear her. She didn't know who this man was. All she knew was he was dangerous.

Could she do what needed to be done? Could she disable her father? What if she accidently killed him? What if she killed him on purpose? What if she killed them both? Or what if she just ran far, far away, and let the universe decide who lived or died? The options snaked through her mind; her eyes narrowed. 'he'd made a similar decision only a few days before and it had almost killed her. Just like at the compound, she was staring down the barrel of an unthinkable choice. The memory filled her vision. Blood seeping out of the holes in Jacob's chest, the mist that had been Guy's brain, and the terror she'd felt as she fled that night. She'd done what needed to be done in that moment, before realizing she'd even made the decision. Instinct had decided for her. She'd be damned if she was going to let that happen again. She promised herself she wouldn't make the same mistakes twice.

She was in charge of her decisions.

Her body. Her future. Herself.

Calay realized her history was hers to make, whether she wanted it or not. She didn't get to watch it happen. She had to make it happen. And she had to live with the consequences.

Peter hovered over Jacob, his full attention turned to Jacob's slumped and bleeding body.

"Makin" it safe..." Peter repeated as he raised the shovel higher above his head. His eyes were almost white, the pupils rolled back in his head. He didn't see Calay slowly, almost mechanically, reach for a pitchfork on the wall. She held it in her hands, heavy and cold. It weighed a ton and yet, it weighed nothing at all. She had to do something or she'd live with the decision that she hadn't done anything at all. Her heart shattered into a billion pieces. Any visage of their happily ever after—the one thing she wanted more than anything else in the world—ruptured violently. Calay swung the fork from the wall and embedded the end of a prong into her father's skull.

Unceremoniously, Peter silently crumpled to the floor.

Calay's body went numb. Her mind too. Her eyes peeled wide; her jaw hung slack. She stared at him.

Peter. Father. Daddy.

He was dead. No screams. No pleas for mercy. No struggle. It was almost like he was so far gone already; he was never really there. Not since she'd returned. She thought of her childhood. How happy it was early on. The camping trips they had taken. Her mother's laughter flowing through the farm. And then how they'd abandoned her when she needed them most, ripping apart her dreams of their happy family. Only two days ago, he'd promised to give it all back to her. In Peter's asinine hell-bent way, maybe he was trying to make good on that promise tonight.

But it wasn't enough. Not then. Not now. Not ever.

She should have known better.

I was foolish, believing in fairy tales.

Calay wailed. It started deep within her core and escaped through a breathless chest. It was as if her soul had been ripped from her body, the remains scattered in the wind along with her voice. They floated away in the evening sky like ash. Her legs gave way and she folded onto the barn floor. She had no life left in her and yet, she existed. Despite herself. Despite everything. But what was she to do now? She wanted to reach for Jacob. To check on him. To heal him. She knew this wasn't over. Not yet. *It can't be.* But he reached for her first.

He pulled her into him and wrapped his broken body around hers, swaddling her in a mass of bruises, broken bones, and shredded rags.

There, on the cold ground of the barn she'd grew up in, a place she knew that after tonight she'd never return to, she allowed herself to be enveloped by Jacob. A man she both wanted to run from and run to. And she wept.

Her father may have been a man she didn't recognize anymore, but the little girl inside her only wanted her daddy back.

CHAPTER TWENTY-ONE

With dried blood and straw in her hair and dirt on her knees, Calay sat with the knowledge that her father was in fact, dead. And by her hand no less.

Just like that.

She'd sat atop the barn where he died all the next day. As she watched the sun set over a field of near-ripe corn, its silk dancing in the gentle wind, the breeze chased clouds across the fading sky and her broken heart.

She thought she'd felt sad before, but it was nothing compared to the despair overwhelming her now. It was in every cell of her body. Both her parents were gone. And, she was, on some level, at fault for both of them. Her mother because they were the same, and Calay wasn't there to save her. And her father because…Calay gagged on a sob. She couldn't bring herself to think about the vibrations the pitchfork made up her arm as it connected with Peter's skull. The sound of his body slumping to the floor. Like her mother, Calay did nothing to save him either. Instead, she'd rushed to Jacob's broken body. Grief didn't begin to describe the trauma seeping through her limbs. Not only was she no closer to finding Tess, but in the span of forty-eight hours she'd lost her mother, her father, and granted by choice, her only friend. Jacob didn't know it yet, but Calay knew in her heart of hearts, their friendship couldn't continue. Not like this. He wanted her to do things she couldn't do; he wanted her to be a person she couldn't be. If it weren't for him and his kind—her kind—none of this would have happened. *I really am alone now.* She wondered if she would be forever. In only a few days, everything had changed.

It was the same day; it was a different day.

Tears stained her cheeks and her clothes were a rumpled mess. Hours before she had peeled herself off the floor and climbed up there. She stared into whatever was before her. Into the abyss of her future. Unsure if she wanted to see.

She and Tess should be living somewhere, happily, blissfully even. Unaware of the dangers that lurked in the galaxy, or the existence of aliens. She'd still be human, in her mind if not her body. Enjoying the pleasures of humanity, rather than drowning in their malevolence. Drinking. Fucking. Loving. Laughing. Exploring. That was her life before everything went down and now...now, what?

When she looked at Jacob, Calay saw all the things that had gone wrong in her world. She saw the only thing that kept her tethered to this life now, too. He was a miasma of everything horrible and all that was beautiful, all wrapped up together in one alien package.

Despite her father's death, or maybe because of it, Calay's mission only became clearer. The thing that concerned her now was getting back to Tess. Tess was the love of her life, last part of her old life, and the last thing that mattered.

Tess.

Calay heard the sound of footsteps on the ladder behind her. Jacob poked his head up, all but healed from his injuries. It took the better part of the day but he'd regenerated. It would appear he'd been telling the truth. Again. Peter gave him a concussion, several broken ribs, and more bruises than she could count. Not to mention a firm resolve.

"Hey," he said.

"Hey."

Calay wasn't sure she was ready for this conversation, but she kept that to herself.

Jacob pulled himself onto the roof and sat down beside her, folding his long legs underneath him. She knew what was coming before he said a word.

"We have to go somewhere," he began.

"Where?"

"I don't know. Somewhere. Anywhere," he sighed, raising a hand to her knee. Calay tensed, her muscles contracting from his touch. He cringed, obviously pained by her reaction. He pulled his hand back to his lap. "Does it matter? Anywhere but here."

Calay sat back, her feet hanging over the red wooden slats. She considered her decision to leave him behind, before the scene played out inside the barn, and struggled for words. How could she tell him, after all this, she was going on alone? How could she admit it to herself? They'd been through so much together. They'd survived. They're made love. And he'd almost died for her. Several times. The word traitor echoed through her mind. She'd failed him in more ways than she could count.

"Calay."

She pulled the necklace out of her bag. Fingered it as she watched the last sliver of sunlight dance in its reflection. She held it firm, the metal sharp against her palm before she clasped it around her neck.

"Jacob..." she said.

"Hear me out."

"No, you hear me out," Calay insisted, "I heard everything I needed to hear earlier."

Jacob's strong hands fumbled in his lap; his head hung low. He looked like a child, scorned. Her heart ached to hold him. And to push him away.

"You have to understand, Jacob. I love her. She's literally the only one who has ever loved me the way I need to be loved."

"She's not the only one, Calay."

"I can't...Jesus. I can't love you. Not like that, Jacob." Calay felt the lump rise in her throat again and the tears sting her eyes. She blinked them back, surprised she had any tears left at all. "I can't love you like I love her."

Jacob's face fell.

"I needed her before I knew I needed her. I loved her before I knew I loved her. When they kicked me out, she took me in. She and I have gone through everything together. The arrival. The Change. Everything after. She's my soulmate, Jacob. The other half of my heart. Of me. She's my home. But you…you showed up. You confused me. But I'm not confused anymore."

"Trust me, Calay."

"I feel like a fraud, Jacob. Don't you get it? I've risked everything I have with Tess by being with you. By trusting you. I've lost my mother. I just killed my father. All I have left is Tess."

"You have me, too, Calay. There's something here. Something important. Something real."

"That doesn't matter. It can't. Not now. I don't know if it ever did. Don't you see? I'm trying to find Tess. She's out there, somewhere. In danger, possibly. Hurt, maybe. And there's no reason she wouldn't be trying to find me too. She needs me. And I need her.

"I have to go get her. Now more than ever."

Calay pulled a map out of her bag and unfolded it in their laps.

"Here," she said pointing, "this mountain of caves. We used to go camping and spend time here together when we first started seeing each other. It was kind of our own little sanctuary. When we were there, we were…free."

Calay looked up from the map. The pain in Jacob's face nearly split her in two. She turned her gaze to the horizon.

"If you look really hard, you can see them in the distance there." She pointed.

"I see them," he said solemnly.

"That's where I'm going. When the war began, we agreed if we ever got separated, that's where we would meet. A backup plan just in case things went wrong. And since waking up in that warehouse, I've been heading that way, combing every town and city en route, until I make it there.

"I couldn't chance missing her, Jacob. I wouldn't. It's taken me far longer to get there than it should have. I don't know what happened to her. When I woke up in that warehouse, alone…I could only hope she'd made it herself. That she was safe. Is safe. But I can't delay any longer. Not now. Not when I've lost so much. When she could be injured. Or alone. Or…" Calay stopped herself from saying the unthinkable. "I have to get there as soon as possible."

Calay couldn't believe she'd just come clean and laid out her entire plan to Jacob. She'd kept her cards close to her chest in case he turned out to be one of the bad ones. But now, she had nothing left to lose. So she shared everything with him. An alien. A lover. A friend. A stranger. A man. The man she'd murdered her father for. The man she'd ultimately leave behind.

Because she had to.

"I'll go with you," he acquiesced, trying to catch her gaze, "I'll help you as long as I can. Until I can't."

"No, Jacob." Calay directed her attention to folding the map and putting it back in her bag.

"Yes. Look, I know you don't need me. I get that, okay? You're tough. You're fucking nails. You're a badass bitch." Jacob smiled. "But I'm not. I need you, Calay. I need you more than anything."

She saw the emotion in his eyes, his fists clenched on his thighs. She could see he wanted so badly to reach for her. To kiss her. To consume her. But Tess was the thing she wanted to reach for. To kiss. To consume. Calay couldn't deny that to him—or herself—any longer.

"Jacob, I don…"

"Let me help you," Jacob begged.

She didn't want to hurt him, especially now. In the wake of so much sadness and loss. After all they'd been through. But she couldn't live without Tess. Tess was where she was meant to be—her home. She had to do this without him. Still, if she could give him a flake of what he needed right now, she'd do it. Anything to take some of the pain away for either of them. Even if she couldn't hold true to her word.

"Fine. That's fine, Jacob," she agreed, fully intending not to keep the promise. Even though somewhere inside her she truly wanted to.

Later that night, careful not to wake Jacob or Max, Calay slipped the truck into neutral, rolled out of the drive, and made her way west to the mountains.

※

THE RIFLE SHE'D TAKEN FROM THE WOODSHED BOUNCED precariously against the seat beside her as she drove down the dark, winding mountain road. The trees extended far into the sky, obscuring the moonlight and creating a canopy of black—plenty of places for the boogieman hide. All the towns were behind her now. It was just her, the thoughts she was trying to ignore, and the dense forest ahead.

Despite getting closer to finding Tess, none of those things were all that comforting. Instead, Calay felt impending unease. Almost dread. Whatever lay ahead, she'd have to handle, just like she handled everything else. But as she let the thoughts in one by one, mile by mile, she knew this wasn't like everything else. This was...something new. She was on her way. She was moving. She was getting closer. And that was what mattered.

As she rounded a bend halfway up the mountain, Calay noticed lights dancing in the darkness. She pulled off to the shoulder and turned off the engine. Mindful not to slam the door, she got out. She kept to the treeline and snaked along the highway, creeping in for a better look. As she scanned the area, a chill swept through her limbs.

"Fuck." She breathed into the cool night air.

Flashlights. The flashlights were held by men. Men wearing the same uniforms she'd seen at the compound. The kind of men that intended to do damage. The last thing she wanted to do was come across Smith and his goons. She knew what they'd do to her if they caught her again. She didn't know who had survived the flurry of gunfire after Max's attack and she didn't want to. As far as Calay was concerned, they could all rot in hell.

As she crouched in the shadows, a car sped past and approached the blockage. Slowing to a stop, she saw a uniformed man lean through the front window. He pulled the driver out while several others searched the vehicle, methodically sifting through the backseat and trunk. Several blankets lay discarded on the side of the road, along with a few boxes that clinked as they set them on the pavement. *Bottles.* She'd recognize that sound anywhere. *What I wouldn't give for a drink now.* The uniformed men handed a slip of paper to the driver and ushered him back into the car. They kept one box for themselves. As the car drove off, Calay realized it was a checkpoint.

They were searching for something.

She wondered if they were looking for her? Or if they were looking for something—or someone—else? Tess? Jacob? Someone that had nothing at all to do with anyone she knew or loved? She could only hope. She watched one of the men bend down and pull a bottle of hooch out of the box. It hissed as he cracked the top and took a swig of the clear liquid. There was no label, no telling what was inside. Moonshine was almost as valuable as water these days. Whatever they were doing there, she wanted no part in it. She decided it was an unnecessary risk to try to drive through the blockade. Especially when she was so close to her destination.

Calay dashed back to the truck and grabbed her bag. Before The Change, she'd spent enough time on this mountain she could recall the hiking trails in her sleep. Not that she'd use them now. If it was easy for her to travel up the mountain, then it was easy for The Resistance too. She'd have to go off-road and scale the side. She'd use the trails as markers rather than follow them directly. If she could just harness those old memories. *If I can't drive up the mountain, I'll fucking walk it.* A perimeter fence blocked her path just beyond the trees, but it was nothing compared to the one at the compound. No razor barbed wire, no bright lights, no foreboding moat.

It was just a fence. She could hop it.

She was so close.

What was left of the scrapes on her ribs and arms ached with effort as she scaled the thing. It rattled under her weight. She froze and chanced a glance back the way she came. It was silent save for the sound of a gentle breeze in the treetops and the echoes of frogs from a nearby pond. No uniformed men came running after her. No one shot her down. If she was quick enough, they'd never know was there. She kept climbing and then dropped down easily to the other side. Twigs and old leaves dug into her palms as she caught herself on the other side. She waited. It was silent. *Now is as good a time as any.* Calay started making her way up the mountain.

As she fought fatigue and despair through the forest, her feet slipped in the wet leaves and underbrush. She second guessed her ability to find her way. The light from the stars was hard to see through the tree canopy, and a mass of dark clouds had gathered, making it difficult to know which direction she was headed. That seemed to be a recurring theme in recent days. Based on the burning sensation in her thighs and the sweat pooling on her lower back, she knew she was climbing. *Fantastic.* It had been so long since she'd last been there. Since it had was their own little Garden of Eden. It smelled the same—lush greenery and damp earth. But it felt different. It was different. Nothing was the same now and it never would be again. A sob rattled through her chest. *Focus, keep moving.*

"One foot in front of the other," she whispered, out of breath.

Occasionally she scaled the fence again, crossed the road, and climbed the fucking fence once more. She knew there was one road that led all the way to the top of mountain. She hoped this was it.

She just had to trust herself. *Easier said.* She hiked for close to two hours when the first drops of rain reached her on the forest floor. It turned the dirt into mud and made her climb much more treacherous. She clawed at branches and fallen tree trunks to pull herself up cliff faces, careful not to push off too hard and lose her footing. It quickly became evident as things got more wet; the terrain was only going to get more slippery. She was in real danger of falling to her death.

Calay had to find cover and wait out the storm.

She continued upward until she came to a jagged cliff, ceilinged by serrated granite. Trees grew almost horizontally out of the face, their roots and limbs twisting before jutting straight up as if to defy gravity. It seemed like an exposed place to wait out the storm, but the overhang kept the platform dry. Chances were, if she wasn't moving through this weather, neither was anyone else. She heaved herself onto the rock and tucked herself back against the rocks and dirt, and most importantly, out of the rain.

Dawn would break soon. And with that, a new day. *With new risks.* She considered her options. Though she wanted—yearned—to get to the top as quickly as possible, she knew she needed to stay put until the following evening. Her body needed rest. Exhaustion was setting in, and the throbbing in her unhealed wounds was threatening to overwhelm her. Months of city grazing had weakened her outdoor muscles. Nearer to Seattle, it was agility one wanted to cultivate—quick legs, nimble turns, deft decision making. Not brute force. Here though on the mountain, she definitely would have benefited from more body strength. Waiting until nightfall would also reduce her risk of being found. She figured if it was tough for her to see where she was going, it would be difficult for someone to spot her. Plus, with the thick brush it was unlikely The Others would come for her here. She still didn't know if they were searching for her as Jacob promised they would be or if The Resistance found the truck and was following her tracks as she rested. Either way, she didn't want to be discovered and she had to be smart about that now. If waiting until dusk was the smarter move, then that's what she'd do. She'd do anything she had to, if it meant she and Tess would be reunited. Finally.

Calay let her eyes get heavy. Her breathing slowed. Then, she slept.

It was twilight again when she woke. She'd been out cold a full twelve hours. With sleep, her mind was sharper. She calculated the time she had driven, along with the distance she guessed she'd already traveled by foot. If all went according to plan, she figured she'd reach the top of the mountain by morning. The weather had cleared, too. The stars twinkled above as if calling her higher. It was promising to be a good night.

She splashed some of the rainwater pooled at the edge of the cliff on her face and rubbed the dried mud from her arms and hands. She wasn't exactly clean but she felt more refreshed. *More human.* Though that wasn't possible anymore. It never would be again. Her body panged for food, but the ache to get to Tess was stronger.

It was time to go.

She slung the pack on her back and stepped out from under the cover of the overhang and onto the shelf. And came face to face with a uniformed and very heavily armed Resistance soldier.

With nowhere to go, Calay gasped and braced herself to be shot.

But he didn't shoot her. Or raise his gun. In fact, he didn't do anything at all. The man wasn't moving. He wasn't even looking at her. Instead, he stood stark still and stared over her shoulder into the forest. His face ashen as a corpse. Further back amongst the trees she saw what she thought was movement. Another soldier? Whoever they were, they were moving far in the opposite direction. And fast.

Maybe this this soldier wasn't after her. Or at least he wasn't right now. She peered closer. The pupils of his eyes were dilated, his breathing shallow. The gun shook loosely from his fingers against his leg. This man was terrified.

Then, Calay realized why.

Slowly, she turned and hovering not five feet above them was an alien pod. Quiet and still, no whirring or grinding or humming. It was right there. In mid-air. Close enough she could spit on it. She could almost reach out and touch its smooth, white, glossy surface.

But then the engines kicked in and the whirring and clicking began. That horrible whirring and clicking that destroyed her apartment building. That chased her across Seattle. Through the forest. That haunted her dreams. And if Jacob was to be believed, that wanted to take her away to a far-off galaxy. It trained a beam of blue light on the soldier. His wide eyes turned to Calay. His mouth slackened. He knew what was coming. They both did. And there was nothing he or Calay could do about it.

Red Mist enveloped her vision.

As it cleared, Calay saw the man was gone. Of course. There was nothing left of him. She watched the pod turn to face her.

She backed against the cliff, unable to run and nowhere to hide. The pod glided closer. Sharp rocks poked into the backs of her legs as she tried to increase the distance between herself and the alien ship. She stifled a sob. She'd come so close. And yet, she'd failed. Failed Tess. Failed Jacob. Failed her family. Failed herself. The pod whirred louder as the blue light creeped onto Calay's toes and up her legs, coming to rest firmly on her belly.

CHAPTER TWENTY-TWO

THIS IS IT; *I'm fucked.*

She stared at the gleaming white pod hovering before her. Her mouth ran dry and her eyes watered. The ship was blocking any route of escape, and there was no way around.

Her life flashed before her eyes. Or at least, the last several days. Waking up in that warehouse. Finding Jacob by the fire. Returning to the family farm. And then leaving it again. She questioned every decision she had made. Jumping from the building. Making love to Jacob—twice. Leaving him behind. Killing her father. Refusing to give up on Tess. Which one had led to this exact moment—to her end? Could she had done anything different to avoid this mess? Probably everything. All of it—every damn thing that had stolen a piece of her—could have been done differently. Especially this moment. Right here, right now.

Don't panic.

As the ship hovered before her, Calay realized it hadn't vaporized her like it did the soldier. *Why not?* Why was she still standing there, gaping like a fish out of water? She couldn't help herself. She gulped on a mouthful of air, assessing her next best move. If there was a next best move.

Then, like an item on a grocery list she'd forgotten, she remembered:

I'm half alien.

She didn't know if they knew that, but Jacob said they recognized their own kind. Were able to track them. *Heat signatures, right?* And they all had stars behind their eyes. She found the idea infinitely romantic. And terrifying.

"What do you want?" she called to the ship.

The pod whirred, stationary, seemingly equally intent to stare at her, as much as she was at it. Were they evaluating her humanness? Deciding on whether to blast her into a billion tiny particles? Abduct her and perform experiments on her pale 'alien' body? Or were they reading her heat signature as one of their own? Calay wanted to give voice to these questions but didn't know how. Instead, she swallowed the scream that so desperately wanted to escape her throat. Now was not the time for dramatics. She had to finesse this. Gently.

Being the victim of an alien abduction was not high on the bucket list Calay had for this trip. But if that really was one of Smith's men she saw running away, it was only a matter of time until The Resistance caught up with her. She needed to get out of there. Assuming after this she was still in fact around to get out of there. She didn't want to die now, after she'd come so far. But it was a risk she was willing to take. She'd have to move this close encounter along herself.

"Hello," she said, her voice shaky.

She willed herself to step away from the wall and closer to the pod. The orb bounced on the air, light as a feather. She saw no apparent doors or windows—no way in or out. Just a smooth white surface, hovering before her. She couldn't help but wonder if there was someone just like Jacob in there. Someone just like her mother.

Just like her.

Small cracks of light on the underside of the ship reflected jewel-colored tones not unlike sun shining through stained glass. They were the same lights that chased her through the city and the forest. The same lights she'd seen in her dreams since The Change. And her nightmares. The same lights that terrorized the planet for the last four years. She shuddered and instinctively stepped back.

No, if I want to get out of this alive, I have to do something.

She resisted the urge to curl into a ball and instead, leaned closer and raised her hand. It trembled. She took a deep breath, held it, and reached further. Her fingertips touched the pod.

Nothing happened.

No violent pain down her arm. No frying or disassembling of her internal organs. No portal to another dimension. She pressed the weight of her palm down flush with its surface.

There must be a way in.

"Um...hello?"

No response. Calay was at a loss. There was just, nothing.

Then, there was something.

She clenched her eyes in a rush of warm air. When she opened them, she found herself wobbling in a white swirling vacuum. Shades of gray wrapped around her like a tornado. She braced herself for another gust of wind, but it never came. In fact, the air was calm and pleasant. Shadows lingered just outside her vision. Just outside her skin. She tried to catch them but when she turned her head, they were gone. It was a desolate place, but she felt the presence of someone—or something—all around her. It was not unpleasant. In fact, it felt...free.

A sudden wave of emotion—a wholeness she'd never experienced before—consumed her. She felt connected and separate at the same time. Loss ached through her and as one wave crested, she was overcome with joy too. The burning need to be with someone and yet, her own independence roared in her heart. She felt fear and love in the same breath. She felt human and alien. It was the entirety of both, together but separate.

Is this Heaven?

As if in response to her thoughts, she heard a whisper of a voice coming from nowhere, yet it was everywhere.

It was kind.

"No Calay, but it is a space of Gods."

Calay couldn't tell if the voice was male or female, real or imagined. So she tried again.

What do you mean a space of Gods?

And the ambiguous voice answered, "you are home."

Calay was filled with dread and hope; they existed together. Her fear rose and as it did, love bubbled beneath the surface. It was as if one emotion was tied to its exact and equal opposite. She tried to pull on her anger as a test, on the off chance she might escape the pain she felt. That maybe on the other side she'd find joy.

"You cannot fool the universe, Calay." The voice chastised in an amused tone.

"What?" She responded.

"You will only feel truly happy if you feel truly angry. If you force it, it will not come. That is the way."

Calay considered this. "Where am I?"

"You are here. You are not here."

"Clearly," Calay huffed, thrust her arms across her chest, "what does that mean?"

"You are in memoriam."

What the hell does that mean?

"We want you to come home Calay. Come back to us."

Her spine straightened. A flash of anger sliced through her body. And a flash of joy. *Ha!* She tried to grasp onto it but it was gone before she exhaled.

"No," she refuted, blinking, "I belong here. On Earth." If she was being honest with herself, she wasn't sure if she was on Earth at the moment. But that's exactly where she intended to return to.

"Accept what you are. Come home. Leave this world behind for a better one."

"I will not."

Gray shadows whipped around Calay's body, caressing her skin. It felt seductive and good, despite her apprehension. And her equanimity. As she became more uncomfortable with the conversation and dichotomous space, the more the shadows played with her. They created a euphoric pleasure throughout her body. The sensations teased the edges of her consciousness. She thought back to the conversation with Jacob about what sex supposedly felt like where they were from. She was tempted to succumb to their request. And her desire.

Sensing this, the voice encouraged her.

"There is life ahead of you, Calay. With us. A place. True happiness. A home. A family."

The pain of losing hers clamored through Calay. As she felt it, she was met in that same moment with elation.

"Stop that."

"We cannot, Calay." The voice echoed through the empty, swirling space. "We cannot stop what is. You are what is. In your entirety. In one emotion lives another. This is something humans have not understood. This is why they attack us. They cannot see it. They cannot feel it."

"We can't be it!" Calay wailed, grasping the ends of her dark hair, "you're asking us to be something we aren't. And when we couldn't, you attacked us. You destroyed our world because of it."

"This is not your world, Calay. You are not human." The calm demeanour of the voice did not change, despite Calay's outburst of frustration. Fear. Despair. "We did only what was necessary to protect our own kind against the violence of humanity. You do not belong there. You belong with us. Let us protect you. Come home."

"I belong..." she began, but she didn't have the words. She was at a loss. She didn't belong to the world she grew up in. She was not human. The voice was right. Its whispers conjured the same yearning and familiarity she experienced in Jacob's arms. It was soothing and calm. Again, she felt a deep urge to lean into what The Others were asking of her. But Calay knew she belonged with them as much as she belonged on Earth. She fit into neither world. She never would. But there was one place she did fit. With Tess.

Her love. Her other half. Her life. She loved Tess. And Tess loved her. Accepted her. Needed her.

"We will accept you," the voice started again as if hearing her innermost thoughts, "they will not."

"No, let me go."

"Calay..."

"No!"

"There is only death here now."

"Let! Me! Go!"

Calay was free falling through negative space, the tether connecting her and the pod, severed. She saw herself sail through a billion lightyears of stars, down past the cliff she'd rested on and into the deep dark below. Boulders and razor-edged shards of granite quickly rose to meet her. She could see the gray color variants in the rock face as she plummeted toward them. She folded her arms over her head and curled her legs into a ball. There was no stopping it now. The best she could do was make herself as small as possible and hope she'd miss the worst of it. Her mind swam and her vision grew cloudy. Calay screamed until her throat was raw.

Then, everything went dark.

When she came to, Calay felt completely and unequivocally shattered.

She felt it. Everywhere. Deep within her heart. Her mind. Her soul.

That multidimensional connectedness was gone, and she missed it with every ounce in her being.

With each movement, she felt raw grinding. Enough pain to make her wince long enough to contemplate...nothing. Nothing at all. It hurt —everywhere.

She didn't think she'd be here.

On the cliff.

Alive.

In the corners of her vision, she saw shadows. Had The Others followed her back? Calay groaned, grinding her teeth as she tried to roll over. She rubbed her eyes, turned her head.

It wasn't The Others.

It wasn't human.

It was all animal. A bear and a big one at that. With two cubs playing just beyond the ledge in the blackberry thickets below.

A large heavy paw pressed down on her back. The sharp claws dug through her shirt; the tips clipped her skin. Calay sealed her eyes shut, tried to remain calm. To slow her heartbeat and ration her breath. She tried to remember—was she supposed to play dead or fight back?

Fuck.

The bear shifted her side to side, examining her body. Its breath short and gruff, it was hot on the back of her neck. Its cold nose traced her ribs and landed in her hair, it pushed dark, damp strands into her face. She resisted the urge to sneeze as the ends tickled her nose. She tried to keep her body still despite every impulse telling her to run or fight back. Hadn't she read that at some point? If you played dead, you had a better chance of survival. The beast's ears appeared in the corners of her eyes. Its face closed in on hers. She sealed her eye lids, held her breath.

Be. Still.

Slow. Wide. Turns.

Do. Not. Panic.

The moment lasted an eternity; the universe had nothing on her.

And then the beast, tired or disappointed with its find, gave up. Calay felt the pressure release on her backside as the bear let her go. She opened her eyes to find it laboring toward its cubs. Together, the family disappeared into the dense forest.

It was gone.

Calay was alone once more.

Shaking, she peeled herself off the rock and dragged her calloused hands over her body. She was bruised and a little scratched up, but amazingly, nothing horrible had come to her. She was in one piece. Breathing. Alive.

She was here.

After everything, it was clear to her that the aliens—and her Otherness—were too. They were real. As real as Tess. After the experience she just had, there was no denying that.

Calay reminded herself she had no loyalty to Them. No place with Them. Her place and loyalty were here. Even if that meant betraying a part of herself. The dark and cold of night chased away any lingering thoughts of leaving Earth and the warmth she'd felt in that alien space—whatever it was. It was time to go.

It's always time to go.

Calay pushed away the thought. She was almost there.

She saddled up her pack, secured the pockets. It was dark, and time was of the essence. She shook off any lingering feelings of confusion and by the cover of night, broke trail for the top of the mountain.

CHAPTER TWENTY-THREE

It was dawn when Calay found herself scurrying down an avalanche of loose rock. She'd reached the summit. Stones slid beneath her feet, threatening to shake her footing and send her into an epic display of how *not* to ascend a mountain. It would have been comical if it weren't for what was at stake.

Her life. Tess's safety. The extinction of humanity. *Not to put too fine a point on it.*

"Whoa!" Calay caught herself on a tree, her fingernails dug into the bark. Her feet skidded beneath her as she crouched low. She surveyed what lay ahead.

A beautiful meadow sprawled across the mountain top. Against the backdrop of the rising sun, wildflowers swayed in the gentle breeze. They reminded her of her mother—she'd loved flowers. Before Calay left home the first time, she'd watched Elora dedicate hours tending to them. The yard was a haven for flora, bees, and honeysuckle. Her mother regularly smelled like sunshine and blossoms—as much a part of the Earth as Calay was Other. The vivid memory was almost too much for Calay, and she felt her knees weaken beneath her.

"Mom." She breathed in the memory. She let the warm sun kiss her skin and exhaled. "For Mom."

Calay redirected her attention. She had to focus on what she had to do now. On what was in front of her.

It was all so serene. A calm before the storm. The air was damp and fresh. The birds were starting to wake. As night retreated for another day, dark clouds gathered in the distance. Even now, she could see the winds were starting to pick up. It might have been a beautiful morning, but it was going to be an unforgiving day.

In every way possible.

Calay and Tess used to go to the mountain as a respite from the oppressive heat and relentless scrutiny they couldn't escape in town. It had been exhilarating and refreshing to get back to nature. There was always an adventure to enjoy. To just be together, away from judgemental eyes and a community more concerned with gossip than growth.

The locals preferred things stayed just the way they were. Day after day. Year after year. Change was something they avoided at all costs, while tradition was upheld. That's why Calay was compelled to leave. Why her mother was murdered. Why she was in the position she found herself now. Her hometown was just a parable for the collective called the human race. When things got uncomfortable—when they changed—people lost their shit. They turned on each other. Just as her parents turned on her. Rejected her. And broke her heart.

After all that had happened, the landscape now felt less enticing than she remembered. The fond memories of her time here with Tess, a fading dream. Now, it was foreboding. If Tess was alive, she was here somewhere. *And I'll be damned to hell if I'm going to let the last one good thing in my life be swallowed by this place.*

Calay spied crouching behind a tree, for a sign of Smith's men and saw no one.

The caves loomed far and wide across the pasture, beckoning her to continue her quest. To complete it. Calay inched away from the relative safety of the treeline and into the field in front of her. With the crunch of small rocks and twigs underfoot, her fingers grazed the tall grass. It was stiff and sharp against her fingers.

The birds stopped chirping. The breeze stopped blowing. The

expansive space grew eerily quiet. Calay halted where she stood, halfway between the forest and the caves. A shudder ran down her back, landing at the base of her spine. The place seemed desolate, despite the array of fauna. Almost dead.

"This can't be," she murmured as her gaze combed the field. She remembered the warning she'd received from the pod: 'there is only death here now.' She wondered if she should turn back. If Tess were here, surely there would be a sign of some kind. Some indication of life other than her own. She considered calling out for Tess, but couldn't risk someone finding her. Not yet. Calay started to second guess her decision to come to this place. Her nerves tightened and her heart raced. A barrage of questions flooded her mind. What if Tess hadn't come? What if she was dead or abducted or had simply moved on, unable to wait for Calay any longer? What if this was all for nothing? What if she should have stayed with Jacob? Where was he now? What if she'd made all the wrong choices? What if she was truly and irretrievably alone? Then what?

She stood in the field, unable to move. She was paralyzed by indecision. What she wouldn't give for a drink right now. A hit off a pipe. A palm of pills. Anything to take the edge off. To make this easier. To mute the fear coursing through her body.

The silence was broken by the sound of a dog barking.

Several, actually.

Followed by the distinct echo of gun shots.

"Shit," she inhaled; the cool mountain air sharp in her lungs.

If booze, weed, or Alprazolam couldn't help get her moving, the threat of Smith's men close on her heels would. Calay made her first difficult decision of the day and took off, sprinting forward across the field toward her goal. The wind picked up as she ran, whipping her hair around her face and pulling her clothes, as if the mountain itself was trying to hold her back. She fought against it and against anything that had ever held her back. The distance between her and the caves closed. As she reached their entrance, Calay collapsed.

Gasping for breath, she pulled herself to sit up and surveyed the field behind her. She saw nothing to give away the presence of her pursuers.

Maybe they weren't after her at all. Maybe they had a different target in their sights. She hoped it wasn't Tess. *I'll just have to find her first. Now, focus.* Despite herself, she had the nagging feeling Smith was gaining on her. That something wasn't quite right. She stood and wiped at the cold sweat on the back of her neck. She didn't know if it was from physical exertion or nerves, but it didn't matter. Calay was going to find Tess and get them the hell out of there as fast as possible. She had to get up and keep moving.

The caverns looked both familiar and foreign. It felt like a lifetime ago that she was here last. As the mouth of the cave opened up it led in two distinct directions. Left, or right? Calay couldn't remember which cave they'd agreed to meet in. What she *did* remember was the tunnels were a labyrinth of twists and turns. If she chose wrong, it could be the last choice she'd ever make.

"Which one...?" she whispered, still catching her breath. Calay's head swivelled in both directions. She wiped her palms on her pants. Then, pressed them together.

To the left, the opening was smaller. The cave looked dry, more closed off. To the right, the rock was definitely wet, which meant it would be slippery as hell, but the path was more open. How much time did she have before The Resistance found her?

"Royally and totally fucked. That's what this is. The whole lot of it," she mumbled.

There was no way to know for sure how close they were. She shook off the indecision, closed her eyes, and let her gut make the decision for her.

She was right; the more open, wet tunnel was a death trap with slick algae and moss.

Glacial water ran down the sides of the rock, gathering in small cold pools that splashed beneath her feet. It was the more dangerous route. If she slipped and was injured, it was possible no one would ever find her and she'd die alone in the darkness. She gauged the risk. She knew it would be impossible for The Others to follow her through the water. There wasn't much she could do if Smith came after her, but she knew she could reduce the danger of being found if she halved the number of threats. Besides, humans needed water to survive. If Tess was here, waiting for Calay, this is where she'd be.

Hard, wet, cold rock dug into Calay's palms as she steadied herself on the uneven ground. It grew darker as she made her way deeper into the cave. The rising light from outside gathered in small spotlights through fissures and cracks in the cave wall, but she was basically going in blind.

Calay walked for what felt like hours. Her stomach churned at the stale stench of organic decay. She knew she was unable to turn back and yet, was fearful she wouldn't make it through alive. Her legs propelled her further, as fast as the terrain would allow. Tess was close; she could feel it.

"Tess!" she called, uncaring if someone heard her now. Her desperation was running away with her pulse. Her heart beat like a drum, thumping against her chest. Darkness charged toward her with each step. She called a second time and then a third. But was answered only with silence.

Calay whimpered, found her next handhold, and pressed on.

As she rounded a corner, the tunnel suddenly grew brighter. Before she had a chance to prepare herself, light flooded the space through a massive crater in the roof. Blinded by gold and blue, it took a moment for Calay's vision to adjust. She snatched her eyes closed to give them a chance to catch up. When they cleared, she squinted, awe struck at what lay before her.

"Thank God!" She staggered back against the cave wall.

She remembered this place. Almost like it was yesterday, knowing it was a lifetime ago. A life she'd never get back.

She found herself in a capacious underground room. The walls shone with water and sparkled with small minerals. Sunlight streamed into an emerald pool, the shore dotted with cascading ferns and freckled boulders. The sound of a trickling stream echoed through the space. Through the opening above, Calay saw the roots of evergreens and pine trees, intertwining and disappearing into the rock. It was magnificent. Across from her, a table was stowed against the far wall.

A table.

Calay rushed to it. It was littered with maps, reports, and folders, not unlike the ones she'd discovered at the compound. Plans and memos from The Leader. Much of it the same information she already knew, but other details, too. Calay set one folder aside and picked up another. It detailed the experiments done on the aliens, just like Jacob had described. The methods of how they strategically took down ships and captured whoever—whatever—was inside. The way they took them apart and tried to put them back together again. And what they'd done with the remains so the press—or what was left of the press—wouldn't find out. They'd actively covered it all up.

It was all true. All of it. Everything Jacob said. Calay's hand flew to her mouth. She couldn't believe could she was part of a race that did this to another. A civilization who disregarded life because someone was Other; that was nearly extinct. *Maybe it's for the best I found out where I came from. If this is what it means to be human, maybe I don't want to be.*

Calay blinked, pulling her attention back to the cave. She glanced around the space, narrowed her eyes. There was no sound other than that of the stream and her labored breathing. What had she just stumbled into? She called out. No answer. Her heart ached; her stomach dropped.

Tess wasn't here.

Calay smashed her fists into the table and swallowed a scream. Instead, she cried a silent wail for all she had lost and all she would never get back. Papers, binders, and folders fell to the hard floor and she sunk down to meet them.

She was woozy with regret. Despair. Longing.

"What have I done?" She mourned.

Her greatest fear was realized: she was alone. Truly alone. It was all that ever was...

As she looked around at the carnage of information strewn on the floor, she noticed something reflecting the sunlight. It was buried amongst the papers. Something small. Something gold. She crawled over to it. The hard ground bit into her knees. She grasped it with both hands.

It was a pendant in the shape of a crescent moon.

She pulled the necklace Tess gave her from her throat. She held it up to the one she'd just found. She compared them side by side, though she already knew: they matched.

"Tess!" Calay screamed, her voice hoarse and frantic. Her lover's name was out of her mouth before she could stop the words. It rushed forward, up the back of her throat, sprinting across her tongue, and past her lips. "TESS! I'm here!"

A voice rose from behind her. "We have to stop meeting like this."

CHAPTER TWENTY-FOUR

Guy towered formidably in the entrance to the tunnel.

"What the fuck are you doing here?" Calay stared at him. She was still kneeling on the floor, her jaw hung slack. She was holding both necklaces between her fingers, but barely. Her hands trembled at the sight of him. He was close. Too close. *This is very, very bad.*

"Surprised to see me, yeah?" He sneered. The side of his head was swaddled in bandages. A lot of bandages. And he looked pissed.

"I-I shot you."

"You're God damn right you shot me, you bitch!" Guy hissed, "took the better part of my face off. Next time you might want to, I don't know, actually look and aim where you're shooting. But no, there's not going to be a next time now is there?"

Calay had no words. She couldn't believe she'd shot both Guy and Jacob and neither bullet did what it was supposed to. It was ineffectual. Her decision was ineffectual. *She* was ineffectual.

"Pretty ballsy of you to be yelling like that, you dumb cunt. Anyone could have heard you."

Calay braced herself for what was to come. She was terrified, but she wasn't going to let him know that.

"I have bigger balls than you'll ever have," she spit back. She clung to the gold chains with one hand for courage, the edge of the table with the other. "At least I have the guts to go after what I want. You don't have the grit to face anyone. You sneak up on them from behind. Why is that, Guy? What did your mother do to you?"

His thin lips pressed together.

"Or not do? Huh? Did mommy not love you enough, you prick? What?" Calay taunted, unable to stop herself. She wanted Guy to suffer. To make him feel horrible for what he'd done to her. She wanted him to feel small. *Have a taste of your own medicine.* "You're too weak. Too limp. Too powerless to attack a little girl from the front, where she can see you coming."

"Oh, I'll show you power, yeah. I'll take you from behind, bitch!" Guy thundered, suddenly storming toward her, "I'll shove my giant balls so far down your throat that yeah, you shit them out the next day."

Calay scrambled back. She pulled on the edge of the table but was unable to get her feet beneath her. She didn't want Guy to know she was afraid of him, but she couldn't stop the fear from cascading across her face as he loomed closer. She panicked. He advanced closer, his footsteps falling like boulders. Boulders that would crush her. His hand struck out and enclosed around her throat. She gasped for air, struggling under the strength of his grip. She felt her body rise. Her feet leaving the ground. And then the unforgiving firmness of the table on her back as he slammed her down onto it. The table—and Calay—groaned under the impact.

"This is my world now. And you're going to wish you hadn't been born into it, whore." Calay couldn't tear her gaze away from Guy's. His eyes were mad with hate, his face twisted in rage.

She had to redirect this; it was going horribly wrong. She hadn't meant to provoke him. She'd only intended to show her strength. To hide her fear. Admittedly, she'd gone overboard, as she was prone to do. That was a mistake. A glaring one, for which she was afraid she was about to suffer the consequences. She knew what men like Guy were capable of. She wanted no part of it. *I have to get out of here.* The pendants dangled from her clenched fist as she dangled off the table. They glinted in the reflection of the water. *There has to be a way out of here.* She couldn't very well escape with his weight against her. She'd have to get loose. To do that, she needed him to talk.

"Where'd you get the necklace?" She diverted her eyes and adjusted her tone to sound less threatening.

Guy paused; his head cocked.

"Where did you get it?" she pleaded, sounding more desperate than she meant to. *Another mistake.*

"What necklace?" He smirked.

"Where is Tess? What have you done with her you monster?" Calay forced herself to meet Guy's eyes. The anger grew in her belly, the panic rose in her throat. She couldn't help it. She didn't want to give him her emotions. Any of them. But she was human, for better or for worse.

Guy squeezed her neck harder. His other traced her collarbone and grabbed one of her breasts, holding it firm.

"I'm going to pop these like bubble gum. Yeah, just like I did to your..."

"My dog?" She spurred; her voice hoarse from the pressure of his hand. She coughed, took a breath. "I know you didn't kill him. He's alive, you sick bastard. And he saved me!"

"Maybe. It doesn't matter. Because you're going to be a lot less alive than that mutt in a few minutes."

"You know what I think? I think you wanted me to *think* he was dead, but you didn't have the guts to actually do it. So you chopped up...no, you got someone *else* to chop up some poor animal that was already dead and leave it on my doorstep. Because you're a coward!"

"Shut up."

"But he was fine, and he came back! And he attacked your men. They chased me down in that field but they didn't get away with what they wanted to do. And neither will you."

Guy spit in Calay's face. His grip tightened around her. She grasped for something— anything—to get free. He wasn't going to take her down without a fight. Tess would have fought. She would have made him work to kill her. So she'd do what Tess would have wanted.

Calay's fingers wrapped around a stapler on the table. With all the force she could muster, she brought it down onto the bandaged area of

Guy's face. A spray of phlegm flew from his mouth. He didn't let go, but his hold lessened. He blanched and stared at her.

Progress.

Guy roared and pulled a gun from the back of his pants. He smashed the butt of it into Calay's nose. Everything spun, her vision a haze of tears.

Not great progress.

"I'm going to fuck you up," he whispered as he pushed the gun between her legs, against the seam of her pants, "I'm going to destroy every hole you have, yeah, with every object in this room, and when I'm done, I'm going to cut your twat into tiny pieces and feed it to you."

"Fuck you!" Calay struggled beneath his weight. She couldn't get her feet firmly on the ground. *If I could just get some leverage.* She winced, feeling the anger and hatred ooze out of Guy as he held her there against her will, drooling over the prospect of hurting her. In that way. She wouldn't say the word. Wouldn't even think it. She wouldn't give him the satisfaction.

She had nothing left to lose.

Her hands strained for the gun.

Guy, in his power and arrogance, hadn't been expecting that. The weapon fumbled in his hand. He released Calay's throat to regain control. She struggled, crushed against the table under the weight of him, his wrists bent at an awkward angle. Calay pressed down on one and she felt it crunch. She may not have leverage to push him off of her, but she did have the element of surprise.

Guy released a scream. He drove his knee up into Calay's stomach, knocking the wind out of her. He shoved the muzzle of the gun into her abdomen with all his weight behind it. It felt like he was going to press it right through her. This was what it had come to—a wrestling match with a psychopath, partially underground, in the middle of nowhere. This was civilization at its worst. It was her at her best. And yet, she'd completely failed Tess. Her father. Her mother. Jacob. Herself. Everything that had ever mattered, she'd let slip away. And for what? What was this? What was any of it? Calay's gaze met his. Yet again, and perhaps for the last time, she felt the anger simmering in her belly, the panic rising in her throat, and she braved asking what she desperately didn't want to know, "what have you done with Tess?"

The deafening sound of a gun shot rang through the cave.

Calay and Guy blanched at each other, their eyes mirroring surprise. She waited for what was to come. To bleed out. For everything to fade to black. But she felt no pain. No bullet burning its way through her body. The realization dawned on Calay that she wasn't the one that was shot. But neither was Guy; the gun was still trained on her stomach.

"Stop!" a voice commanded from across the room.

Calay would know that voice anywhere.

Tess.

Tess crossed the cave, looking feral. Her long dark hair twisted in every direction. Her blue eyes wide and unblinking. Her clothes were soiled with mud and debris. She looked like she'd just dug her way up from the grave.

"Get the fuck off her." Tess surged forward.

She trained the gun on the back of Guy's head.

"Or I'll blow your fucking head off here and now."

Calay watched fear sweep over Guy's face. *For once he's going to get what's coming to him.* He twisted her breast as he stood up, kneeing her in the ribs as he pushed himself off her.

"Give me the gun."

"Do you know what she's done?"

"Give. Me. The. Gun."

Guy let the pistol hang at his side, but his arm looked like a tightly wound ball of rubber bands, ready to snap back at any moment. He just needed the excuse. Calay grimaced, hoping Tess didn't give him one. She watched Tess push the barrel of hers into the back of his head. Guy pulled his shoulders back, his eyes narrowed. He lifted the butt end of the gun to Tess and stepped a foot back. His gaze didn't leave Calay's as his head hung between his shoulders like a petulant child. Tess lifted the back of her shirt, tucked her weapon in the waistband of her pants. Calay exhaled. *Thank God.* She endeavoured to sit up, every inch of her body ached from the struggle.

"I can't believe you're here." Tess beamed at Calay. "I didn't think you'd ever come."

Calay swiped at the blood on her face and limped to Tess's side. She showered Tess with kisses, her hands flittering around the debris in Tess's hair. Tess ran her hands over Calay's arms and checked her for injuries. They both seemed whole. Physically banged up, but unbroken. And very much alive. If not in need of a good, long hot shower. Together.

They wrapped their arms around each other. Tess was alright, Calay thought, she was alright.

"Thank God," Calay whispered into Tess's hair.

Tess smiled through the embrace and pulled back to look at Calay. Their eyes met.

Tess looked deep into Calay's eyes. With total acceptance. Total love. *Everything is going to work out. Finally.* Tess brought her hands to Calay's face and traced the scratches and bruises Guy had given her. Her brow furrowed.

"You poor thing," Tess said, affection oozing out of her voice, "what you've gone through. What he's done to you."

"It doesn't matter," Calay wept, "not now. We're together. Thank Christ! I need you."

"Well, you found me."

"It was all for you, Tess. It's always been for you." Tears of joy and relief streamed down Calay's face. She'd done it. She'd found her. And now, they'd never be apart again. She was home.

"I know it has, honey." Tess kissed away the tears on Calay's cheeks.

"I've missed you." Calay closed her eyes, breathed in the warmth of Tess.

"I've missed you too, my love. Every single day I've missed you. Every moment."

"I'm sorry it took me so long to get here."

Tess smiled.

"I'm sorry you've had to endure so much for me," she said, "but I'm even sorrier I have to kill you twice."

CHAPTER TWENTY-FIVE

Tess turned from Calay and shot Guy square in the kneecap. He screamed and fell to one leg. The gun clattered to the floor, skidding out of his reach on the slick surface.

"What the fuck, Tess?" he screamed.

Calay blanched, confused.

Tess looked at him and cocked her head before she cocked the gun. She snapped the hammer back and shot him again. Right between the legs.

The sound that escaped Guy's mouth was not human. Nor was it alien. It was pure animal. He doubled over and frantically grasped at his nether regions.

Tess walked across the room and stood over his writhing body. His breathing short and shallow.

"It's not so fun. Is it, Guy?" she paused, her head tilting to one side, "when someone puts a gun between your legs?"

He pawed at himself; strange sounds escaped his mouth. Calay stared, unable to move. To think. To breathe.

"And it's really not fun when someone does it to the woman I love."

Blood was quickly pouring out of the two wounds, the majority of it from the second one.

"Hey, look at me when I'm talking to you." Tess squatted, lifting Guy's head with the barrel of the gun. "Did you forget the rules? Do you need to be taught?"

"I'm fucking bleeding to death, yeah?"

"I see that." Tess nodded.

"I need help, Tess! I'm going to die."

"Maybe that was something you should have thought about before you attacked Calay."

"You shot my cock off, you bitch!"

"Little boys who can't play nice with their toys don't get to have them, do they?" Tess straightened her legs, stretched. Then, kicked him in the ribs. "I said, look at me."

Guy furiously looked up at Tess from the ground, the color draining from his face and onto the cold floor below.

"You were going to rape her. That's not allowed. You know better. That's why I shot you in that pathetic appendage you call a dick. But more importantly, you didn't report you'd captured her and brought her back to The Society."

Calay watched Guy shudder. Then, she shuddered herself at the truth she didn't want to acknowledge. A cold sweat broke out across her lower back. Her legs trembled. Tess knew they captured Calay days ago. And Tess had left her there, alone, with those men—for days. She knew Calay was looking for her. And she hadn't come. Calay's heart sank and her mind reeled.

"Tess," Calay pleaded, desperate for something to make sense, "what do you mean you have to kill me twice? You knew The Resistance had me? What are you talking about right now?"

"In a moment, my love. He doesn't have much time." Tess's gaze was trained on Guy. "Now Guy, you know the penalty for treason."

"No, that's not it," Guy stuttered through gasping breaths. He writhed along the floor. Tess lifted her foot, pressed down on his wrist with the sole of her military-issue boot. Guy twisted, straining to look up at Tess. "We were going to report it, but…"

"I don't want your excuses," Tess said through clenched teeth, "I want your obedience and compliance. Without hesitation. I had to hear about your botched attempt to capture, and then conceal her, from Adam. He was cleaning up the records room my darling girlfriend destroyed, when he realized you hadn't filed the proper paperwork. You tried to sneak it past me, didn't you? Do you know what that does to my authority, you piece of shit? To my ability to lead us through chaos to bring order? It undermines me, Guy. I can't have my officers second guessing me. If we're going to win this war—if we're going to lead humanity to become a pure race again—I need total and complete loyalty. It's your moral duty. Do you understand me, soldier?"

Guy nodded, his energy fading quickly as the last of his life drained out of his crotch.

Calay's arms hung at her sides. She couldn't move them, she couldn't think. She couldn't believe what was unfolding in front of her. Everything Tess said was word for word what she'd read in the pamphlets. But Tess wasn't just spouting information. The conviction in her voice was unadulterated. Undeterred. Unhinged. Calay knew this woman, intimately. Yet she was beginning to realize she didn't know her at all. And now that she listened to Tess speak out loud what Calay had only read, she heard it—the undeniable tone and turns of phrase. Why didn't she see it before? How could she have been so blind? She'd heard Tess speaking, day in and day out, but had failed to understand her words and the meaning behind them.

"And now because of your insolence, she's here. Do you think I want to kill her again?"

Calay swayed as her mind spun.

What was she talking about, kill her twice? Kill her again? She wanted to ask, to fight, to flee. But she couldn't make her limbs do as she told them. She stared at Guy, groaning on the ground, making incoherent noises that sounded like pleas for help, but Calay couldn't be sure.

This doesn't make any sense.

"Crazy bitch!" Guy shouted, flinging spit and blood in Tess's direction, "you don't get it, yeah? You're untouchable! But her, she was all mine. A way I could get back at you for everything you've done to us."

"Done to you?" Tess smirked.

"We have needs. You keep us locked up in that fortress. All men. Do you know how unnatu…" Guy started.

"Ugh, useless."

The gun went off again and with it, the unbandaged portion of Guy's head. Brain matter coated the cave floor around them, his body went limp.

Calay was pretty sure this time, he wasn't coming back.

Tess sighed. She turned to Calay who stood ghost white in the morning light. Calay blinked, disbelievingly, at Tess.

"I'll make it quick," Tess promised, the pistol still in her hand.

"What?"

Tess walked towards Calay, raising the weapon as she got closer. The realization of what was about to happen hit Calay like a crate of whiskey. She swooned at the horror of it.

"Oh my God. No Tess, stop!"

Tess stopped.

Calay wracked her mind for answers. For any possible explanation other than the one she knew to be true. She couldn't believe it. Didn't want to believe it. She had to figure out a way through this. There had to be a reasonable explanation.

"Tess…" Calay choked out.

"Cay."

"You're…you're The Leader, aren't you? Of The Resistance."

"I am."

"What…" Calay searched Tess's face for the woman she thought she knew. In her place, there was someone else. "What happened? How? Why are you doing this?"

"Do we really need to go through all this, Cay? I love you. I don't want to do this. But I have to. I'd really much rather get it over with."

"I need to know, Tess."

"But darling, wouldn't you rather just be done with it? End the suffering? It won't make either of us feel better to draw it out. It isn't healthy."

"Healthy?" Calay balked.

The civility of their words was both appalling and intriguing to Calay. It almost felt like they were having just another conversation about their relationship. An evaluation of boundaries. A negotiation. Compromise was what Tess had always emphasized—a good relationship was built on compromise. Calay never felt more confused than she did in that moment.

"Please."

"Fine." Tess pulled the gun up and aimed it at Calay's chest. "Just to be safe."

"Safe? Interesting choice of words." Calay was the most unsafe she'd ever felt in her entire life.

"This has been a long time coming," Tess began, pushing her weight to one foot, "our separation, I mean. I noticed it happening months ago. A shift in the way we were living. You wanted to hole up and hide out, and I wanted to fight back."

"Truthfully, I wanted to fight back the moment they destroyed our apartment. Our life. They had no right. The trips I took into the city to find food and resources gave me a lot of time to think about this, Calay. About how we were going different directions. And about how I wanted to take back what they'd taken from us. I met some people."

"You met some people?"

"Yes, others like me who wanted to do something; take action."

"You never told me about any people," Calay said. Her heart broke for the billionth time that day. She knew it wasn't her place to judge dishonesty. The things she'd done with Jacob made it not her place. But she couldn't help but feel a little jealous, if not betrayed.

"How could I, Calay? How could I tell you what I was going to do? You were so against it. You rejected any idea of retaliation. You practically rejected me."

"I'd never reject you. Ever. You are…were my…you're everything, Tess. Every-fucking-thing."

"Oh yeah? Then why didn't you want us to win? Why wouldn't you fight with me? For me?"

"I have fought for you! Why do you think I came here? I fought the world to save you! There was no way to fight back against the aliens, Tess. It wasn't about winning. I wanted us to survive."

"Exactly! It wasn't about winning—for you. For me, it was. Those people I met, they showed me they could disable pods. That we could reclaim our world. Our planet. When I started making up reasons to go on longer runs…"

"When you said the cities started running out of food and supplies…"

"They hadn't, not entirely," Tess admitted. For the first time her gaze fell from Calay's. She stared at the floor for a long minute. Her eyes glazed over. She seemed to go somewhere else. Then, she came back. She refocused her attention on Calay and continued. "You weren't supposed to find out. You never left the camp. I figured what you didn't know wouldn't hurt you. I wanted to learn more and I could, if I spent more time with them—do more. And you were safe where you were. They were so organized, Calay. It was mind-blowing. They had plans—real plans. And evidence to back them up. Including tests, scientific exams you could do. To check."

Calay's blood ran cold. She gasped. The realization of what Tess had done formed fully in her mind. She shook with the truth of it.

"You tested me."

Tess nodded.

"One morning you had a mirror. You were checking a bruise on your face."

"And you shone that flashlight in my eyes."

"You thought I was just horsing around with you. Calay…"

"You checked," Calay finished her sentence.

"I saw the stars."

"Why didn't you just tell me? We could have talked about it!"

"Talked about what? That I knew you were a God damn alien and I was going to have to kill you? Are you insane?"

"Are you?" Calay countered, her body vibrating with resentment, "you said we could get through anything together, Tess! Talk about anything. You and me, till the end. You promised!"

"This is the end, Calay. Don't you get it? It's the end of the fucking world. And sadly, the end for you."

Calay glanced at Guy, his blood a massive black stain on the floor. He was very dead.

"You're crazy," she said, unable to tear her gaze from Guy. Unable to turn back to Tess.

"I'm not crazy. What I'm doing makes perfect sense, don't you see? Use the logical side of your brain, Calay. Think! A species only wants to survive. It's human nature. I'm doing what comes naturally. When I realized what you were, I aligned myself even more wholly with the movement. I spent more time at the compound, where it was actually safe and not just a fort in the forest. We aren't kids for fucks sake. This is life and death. And I worked my ass off there to get ahead—to thrive; to get where I am today. There was a major battle not far from where we were stationed. The Leader before me was killed. And I claimed his spot."

"How very admirable of you," Calay spit, raising her face to meet Tess's.

"I did some real good there, Calay. During your stay at The Society, I'm sure you saw it wasn't exactly a female friendly place. And I saw an opportunity to take control of my own destiny. Of our destiny as women! I could lead us to victory. And I have! We've grown in numbers, we're seeing more success, learning The Other's weaknesses. We could actually win this thing! And when society rebuilds, it will be women who lead the way."

Calay cringed. She found Tess's enthusiasm repulsive. Horrifying, even. Did she really expect her to feel excited about all this? She was talking about satiating her desire to kill Calay's kind. *To kill me.* She felt her stomach heave. She pushed down the urge to vomit and pressed on.

"So what happened before? You said you killed me once already. Tell me about that."

"Do we really have to rehash the past?"

"The past? I'd say it's pretty here and now Tess. You do have a gun pointed at me."

"Ugh, fine." Tess rolled her eyes, shifted her weight to the other foot.

"It wasn't something I *wanted* to do, okay? That morning we left you in the warehouse should have been the end of it. While you were sleeping one night, I met a small group of people belonging to The Resistance, and we came for you. You stirred when we entered the tent, so we knocked you unconscious. After that, it was just a question of causing enough injury to your body to make sure you couldn't repair yourself."

Tess's words scorched Calay through to her bones. The pain burned through every inch of her being. The one person she'd loved more than anyone—the one person she'd trusted more than anything—outsourced a team of hitmen to murder her. She had no words, just a deep ache within her chest and the relentless swooshing of her heart in her ears.

"Why didn't you just shoot me or something?" Calay breathed.

"I didn't really have a choice. We needed to know how little we had to do to your bodies to kill you. An experiment of sorts. So we knew how much energy we had to expend. Besides, with limited resources, guns and ammo won't last forever. So we broke every bone in your body, my love. We worked from toes to skull. And then stashed you in the warehouse to monitor what happened. It took some time to get it just right. We thought we had. Evidently, we didn't."

The bile rose in Calay's stomach. She doubled over and retched on the floor.

Every. Bone. In. My. Body.

Methodically broken.

Tess hadn't just murdered Calay. She'd tortured and dismembered her and left her to rot.

Tess waited for Calay to finish vacating the contents of her stomach, tapping her foot on the floor.

When Calay finally stood upright again, she was unable to look Tess in the eye. She felt destroyed. She had been. Literally. But...as Jacob had promised, she'd regenerated.

"You're lying."

"I'm not." Tess lifted her chin. "I wish I was, my darling. I wish we wanted the same things. I wish you were human."

"What happened after that?"

"What do you mean? You healed and then ran away and disappeared off the edge of a building."

"No, I mean for you. How could you live with yourself after you had your girlfriend assaulted and murdered?"

"I can imagine how you're feeling right now, sweetheart, I really can, and I…"

"Can you, Tess? Can you really? Do you realize what you've done? And how this sounds? You've got it all wrong. Humans fucked everything up. They—we—attacked the aliens first. They were just defending themselves."

"That's ridiculous." Tess smirked. "Did we attack anyone from our shitty little apartment? I sure didn't. Did you?"

"No of course not, but it's the truth. We're our own worst enemy. We're killing each other and our planet, and all The Others want is to go home. We're the primitive ones. The violent ones. I can prove it."

"That's the alien in you talking, honey. Don't listen to it. It's trying to trick you."

"It's not Tess. I've seen it!"

"You're wrong and I'm right. The aliens took everything from us. They're impure. Disloyal. Hungry for our blood. The cause is what matters now. We must bring chaos to bring order. We must bring about a pure, moral society."

"No, you've got it all wrong."

"The aliens have to die. Even you, my love." Tess nodded. She stood taller, raised the gun higher. "We always hurt the ones closest to us."

Everything in Calay's body raged in agony. Her spirit was broken, her body battered and bruised. Her heart might as well have been a gaping, seeping hole in her chest. She'd given up everything for Tess. Her parents. Jacob. The possibility of a new start in a new galaxy, far far away from all the butchery and slaughter on Earth. She'd literally climbed every mountain, crossed every desert, braved hell and high water to get to her. Only to find out Tess hadn't loved her at all. Not really. Not in the end.

It had all been for nothing.

Calay knew there was no way out this time. She realized their relationship had never been a compromise of mutual respect and acceptance. It had been a perfect illusion. Right up until Tess murdered her in cold blood for what she was. For who she was.

Calay cried as Tess lifted the gun to meet her face. She wasn't going to beg for her life. Or lack thereof. But she was going to mourn the remnants of it. Of the idea of home. Of love. Of belonging.

"It's going to kill me to do this—again." Tess had the audacity to sound sympathetic. Pained, even.

"No, Tess. It's killing me! You're killing me!"

Tears rolled down Calay's cheeks. Ruined and lost, she stared down the barrel of the gun, and waited for everything to fade to black.

CHAPTER TWENTY-SIX

"No. It's killing her." Jacob peeled himself from the shadows of the entrance to the cavern.

Calay could barely believe her eyes. Despite her best efforts, Jacob had found her. As was becoming the norm. The ever loyal Max stood alert next to him, his black tail erect and his sharp ears pointed. There wasn't a moment she regretted sharing her meager finds with that beast; there wasn't a second when she wasn't grateful he'd wandered into her camp. Now they were inseparable. Woman's best friend—she meant the dog, of course.

"Who the fuck is this?" Tess challenged.

"The person who's going to put a stop to all this—a stop to you—is who the fuck this is," Jacob answered. The sharp blade of a hunting knife gleamed in his hand. He took a step forward. His gaze measured Tess. Hers measured him back. Calay gulped, her head swinging between the two.

Prepared—but not ready—to die at the hand of the woman she once loved so fiercely, Calay was both relieved Jacob appeared and frustrated as all get out. This guy was more difficult to shake than a bad hangover. Whether or not she actually wanted to shake him, was now unclear in her mind. She'd just begun to accept she was about to die. To leave this place. To become nothing. And yet here was...*something*.

"What are you doing here?" Calay teetered precariously on emotions.

"I'm here to save you, isn't it obvious?" Jacob smirked that delicious grin.

"I don't need saving!" She stomped her foot. "I've told you that, I don't even know how many times!"

"Um, darling, I think you just might this time."

Calay swallowed his words. She swallowed her pride. He was probably right. It was infuriating.

Tess narrowed her eyes as she gazed at Calay. Then, Jacob. Calay watched the moment of recognition washed over her face, recognizing the tension between them. She watched Tess's face shift from regret to rage.

"What's going on here?" Tess's voice was brimming with hate. It tore Calay apart. She knew Tess was angry. She just never knew how angry. How spiteful. How...inhumane.

Jacob grinned broadly at Calay; his eyes lit up. She could feel her resistance against him fading. She let go of something as the warmth of his smile hovered between them. She was happy he was there for her when she needed him most. Despite her attempts to push him away, he was still there. She wasn't sure what that meant, and right now, she didn't care. Needing him didn't mean she was weak, it just meant she needed help. And everybody needed somebody, sometimes.

"What's going on here," he said, shifting his eyes from Calay to Tess, "is I'm going to take Calay away from this place—away from you. And all the damage you've caused her. She's better than that. Better than you. Fuck, she's better than I'll ever be. But first...first I'm going to take my time killing you, Tess. After all you've taken away from us, it's the least I can do for my kind."

"Us? Who's Us?" Tess stared at him; her lips puckered.

"T, it didn't have to be this way," Calay offered. She almost took Tess's hand before she stopped herself. She folded her arms across her chest to keep from reaching for her. "Humans and aliens. We could have all gotten along."

Tess's eyes grew dark. Her body became stiff. The knuckles on her hand holding the gun turned white.

"He's one of them."

"Yes." Calay nodded.

"You...you slept with him, didn't you?" Tess gaped between the two of them. "You've been with him. I can feel it. That's disgusting!"

"That's none of your business. You left me. You killed me. You thought I was dead. And you were about to kill me again! What do you care about who I choose to be with?"

"You promised we were together until the end."

"So did you."

"But I betrayed you for a good reason."

"The road to hell is paved..." Jacob chimed in from the far end of the cave.

Tess didn't even blink in his direction. Her focus entirely on Calay. Calay felt like a mouse caught under a cat's paw.

"You're part human! He's an alien. An Other. That's sick!"

"No, I think that's you sweetheart," Jacob added.

"Shut the fuck up." Tess turned the gun on him, her eyes never leaving Calay's face. "You were with him—physically."

Calay turned her chin up, unapologetic, though her eyes gleamed with remorse. Everything had gone so sideways. She didn't know what was right or wrong anymore.

"Do you think you're in love with him?" Tess pressed on.

Calay remained silent. She realized there was no reasoning with this woman. The woman she thought she'd spend the rest of her life with. The woman she'd tortured herself over betraying, by being with Jacob. Not once, but twice. The woman who had a gun trained on the *one* last thing Calay could possibly hold on to. This woman was not her woman any longer.

"You do! You think you love him!" Tess squinted, examining Calay and Jacob, Jacob and Calay. As if she there would be some evidence of what had transpired between them. "I see it in your stupid eyes you think you love each other. No, this is wrong. This is so very, very wrong."

"He's my kind, Tess."

"You're mine!" Tess shrieked. Calay stepped back as if she'd been slapped.

"That's what this is really about, isn't it, Tess? You think you own me."

"We belonged to each other."

"You never belonged to me. That's why you made your trips into town. Why you hid them from me. Why you left me for dead. You were never really mine. I don't know, maybe on some level I knew it all along. Maybe that's why Jacob and I connected so quickly. He gets me. He sees me for who I really am. Can you blame me for finding comfort in his arms?"

"He's an entirely different species. You can't do that!"

"Not entirely different." It was the first time Calay had said it out loud to anyone other than Jacob or her father. She was part alien. Always would be. It was time she started to accept it.

"Yes, you're right. That's why you had to die. Now you're starting to understand."

"I'll never understand how you could do what you did Tess."

Tess began to pace, her face turned downward. She mumbled something to herself, broken fragments of sentences. Calay knew Tess felt betrayed. She would have, too. The damage done to their relationship was inconceivable. Irreparable. Calay kept her attention on Tess, but out of the corner of her eye she saw Jacob inch his way closer.

"Tess." Calay knew what Tess might do to Jacob. She had to keep Tess's attention on her. So she started talking. "I chose you. I came for you. I gave up everything—everyone—for you. You fucked it up when you decided to murder me. Do you hear how insane that sounds? You tried to murder me! And then that dumbass Guy followed me here, and he messed up our reunion. Our chance to be together again. Because we do have a chance, Tess. Just you and me. Forever."

Calay chanced glanced at Jacob. That was a mistake. The look on his face nearly tore her apart. She knew how he felt about her. While she imagined he understood she was only distracting Tess—he wasn't slow—her words clearly still pained him; it was written all over his face.

Calay felt the moment Tess's gaze tore from her and fell upon Jacob. He seemed to be frozen where he stood. Calay's words caught in her throat. She saw Tess register the pain on his face as clearly as Calay did. A twisted smile wound itself across Tess's lips.

Tess moved to Calay, pulled her against her body, and devoured her mouth with her own. Their arms intertwined and their breasts pressed together. The kiss was familiar to Calay, and yet, foreign. Welcome, yet not at all. Part of Calay wanted to push her away, but she couldn't help herself. She took the kiss, greedily. If this was to be their last one, she was desperate to lap up every moment of it.

The anguish in Jacob's face as they pulled apart was unlike anything Calay had ever seen before. It was worse than when she'd left him tied up her camp. Or alone at the cabin. Or at the farm, when she'd told him she couldn't be with him. *God, I've been terrible to him.* But she had to be, for Tess. Calay never wanted to hurt Jacob. She'd never meant to lead him on. Her purpose was clear—she was meant to be with Tess. She'd been honest from the beginning, hadn't she? At least she thought she had. She tore her eyes from Jacob, unable to shoulder the pain she'd caused. It was then that Calay saw Tess wasn't focused on her. Tess was glaring at Jacob, that insane smile spreading from her mouth to her eyes. Calay's stomach dropped as she realized the kiss wasn't a final goodbye. The kiss was a weapon. A knife to Jacob's heart. Tess had Jacob right where she wanted him. And they all knew it.

A whimper escaped Calay's lips, it echoed across the cave. None of this was about her. This was about Jacob. And Tess was making sure he suffered.

"See? Isn't this a happy little love triangle?" Tess pushed Calay off her and raised the gun.

Calay fought to keep her legs under her. *Everything's gone so wrong.* She mouthed 'I'm sorry' to Jacob, but no sound came out.

"No, darling. I'm sorry," Tess said as her arm waved toward Jacob. She fired several shots. Each one found their home in one of his internal organs.

Jacob collapsed to the floor.

"Noooooooooo!" A scream ripped from Calay's throat. Her arms reached for Jacob, but he was too far away. She couldn't save him. Her heart ached at the realization she never would. She collapsed to one knee. Paralyzed halfway between standing and falling. Love and hate. Life and death. She shuddered; her shoulders trembled.

It was now or never. She'd botched the decision of who lived or died at The Resistance compound. *I won't make that mistake again.* She chose right in the barn, even if it took every ounce of her heart. *Daddy.* And now, she was forced to choose again, to either kill or be killed. But this was Tess. *How did we get here?* Before this moment Calay thought she'd lost everything. But now, having a choice—an opportunity—to turn on the woman who was the love of her life, she realized she still had so much left to lose.

Everything Calay had done leading up to this moment grew from her love for Tess. For their relationship. It defined her. It was all that ever was. All that ever would be. Now, she stood to lose not just her life, but the very essence of who she was.

The last four years flashed before Calay's eyes. All the decisions she'd made. All the places, things, and people she'd given up to be the person Tess needed her to be. She'd sculpted herself to fit Tess's mold. And the one time she'd stood her ground, Tess abandoned her. Betrayed her. In every possible sense of the word. Tess failed Calay in ways beyond her wildest imagination. Her worst nightmares. Calay knew she could stay the person Tess claimed to have loved and let the knowledge of that fact destroy her. Or she could burn that person down and rise out of the ashes. She could become someone who took real control of her destiny.

Someone real. Someone whole.

She could fight. Fight for everything that was still right in this world. For herself. For Jacob. For their salvation. For their species.

Calay saw now she was much more than the person she was when she was with Tess. She was both herself and Other. The same but different. And if she remembered correctly, a lot stronger than her girlfriend.

A gravelly noise ripped from Calay's throat as her body twisted, and her fist landed square on Tess's mouth. Both of them sprawled onto the hard, damp ground. The gun skittered across the granite floor.

Calay managed to get a few hits in before Tess kicked her off. Calay's back arched before it came down hard on the ground with a sickening crack. Still, she scrambled to her feet. Tess was on her in seconds. She came at Calay with a large rock, but Calay managed to slip sideways as Tess bludgeoned it into the wall of the cave. Tess lifted it again, winding back for another attempt. Calay grabbed hold of Tess's wrist. Her long nails bit into Tess's skin, sinking to the fingertips. Tess screamed. Calay wrangled the rock away from her. Her victory was short-lived. Tess sucker punched Calay in the stomach. The wind was forced out of Calay's lungs, her chest ached. Calay gasped for air as Tess drove her shoulder into Calay's stomach. The two women stumbled backward onto a boulder by the water's edge.

They were both bleeding. Calay winced, the weight of Tess on her sending a sharp pain through her chest. Calay figured a few of her ribs were broken. *Are we really going to fight to the death?* Calay tensed. She wasn't sure she could go through with it.

Tess's fist landed across Calay's temple. Calay's head swam with memories of their apartment together. The morning of The Change. The taste of Tess on her mouth and the feel of their limbs entwined. The look of love in Tess's eyes. The promises. The visions faded to stars as Calay began to blackout, but they weren't as beautiful as the ones behind her eyes. Her roadmap home. Unlike the latter, she was pretty sure the only place these ones led to was darkness.

Forever.

The two lovers tumbled into the emerald pool. Brilliant green water splashed all around them as they struggled. Between waves, Calay caught glimpses of Jacob's fallen body, bleeding out by the entrance to the cave. Even if he wanted to help her, he couldn't now. The water would kill him if the bullets hadn't already. It was up to her to get herself out of this. Or give in.

Tess straddled Calay in the shallows and wrapped her hands around her throat. Max clamped his jaws around Tess's calf. She screamed, releasing the hold on Calay as she threw her fists toward the animal. *Do something.* Calay struggled to regain her strength. She pushed herself to sit up, gasping for air. She heard a yelp and cleared the water from her eyes in time to see the poor dog's body flung against a rock. Calay went rigid as she stared at Tess, her eyes wide. A chunk of Tess's calf was missing, threads of flesh and sinew waved in the water, plumes of blood pulsing out of the hole with every thunderous heartbeat. *That's arterial.* Max had bitten Tess's leg almost in half. The color drained out of Tess's face. Then, her hands were traveling across Calay's collar bones, over her shoulders, and back around her neck. Almost as quickly as the respite appeared, it vanished. *Seriously?* Calay's head bounced in and out of the water as she gasped for breath. Water filled her lungs, only to be coughed back out again. She could feel the life slipping from her as she grew weaker trying to fight Tess off.

It was ironic. Calay looked up at her girlfriend from beneath the surface. Being as she was half human; she could survive water. Yet she'd die the very way her other half would perish.

The aliens were right. Earth was a dangerous, violent place.

The aliens. The Others. Jacob said they were good. That their society was a place of peace, love, and acceptance. A kind place that she could call home.

A place far away from this one.

"Shh my love," Tess growled, her eyes growing distant, "go easy."

Calay's body resisted. Her spirit, even. She couldn't let Tess win. She couldn't let hatred be her undoing. She couldn't give up now. There was too much at stake.

Calay closed her eyes and summoned all her strength. In a last-ditch effort, she heaved her entire body forward. Tess flew back and splashed into deeper water. Calay lunged for Tess. Her teeth rattled as their bodies collided. Calay straddled Tess, using her momentum to thrust Tess further into the water. She steeled herself, closed her hands over Tess's shoulders, pressed down, and waited.

Calay loved Tess. She hated her. She watched the love of her life fight against the closing darkness; it was as if one emotion was tied to its equal and exact opposite. She felt guilt and joy. Shame and pride. Remorse and justice. For a moment, Calay caught a fragment of what The Others had been trying to show her. And then it was gone, like a whisper on the wind. Like love.

With it, the last breath from Tess's lungs.

And any remaining ties to her old life—her old self.

Calay fell off her girlfriend's lifeless body. She let the warm water wash over her. Tears streamed down her face as waves lapped her skin, rinsing the blood off her knuckles and away from her nose. But not the pain from her heart. Nothing would take that away—not now, not ever. Tess was dead. Dead. The word echoed through her mind. Through her body. Tess was her home. And now, the home she'd known was gone. Forever. In its place, a foreign and inhospitable nothingness. A void. Memories of their life together dangled like dreams. Or nightmares.

It was all gone.

Calay began to cry.

CHAPTER TWENTY-SEVEN

A RING of sunlight streaming through the opening above illuminated Tess's body as it floated deeper into the water. Almost as if Heaven was beckoning her—if there was such a place. Calay wasn't so sure.

It should have been beautiful in that cave. The clear emerald water. The glittering walls. The lush foliage. And it had been, once. When they were younger. Before The Change. Before everything. Now Calay saw nothing but ugliness. A life without love. A world without humanity. A planet not worth saving.

A casualty of war.

She was shivering as she pulled herself out of the lagoon despite the warm water. Goosepimples raised hard and frigid on her skin. She fell against the cave floor as she choked back tears and coughed on sobs. The water dried from her clothes as the rising sun broached the precipice of the shore, shining down on her exhausted body. Small bugs danced in the crisp morning air. She laid there for a long time. For what felt like as long as the universe had been in existence. For all intents and purposes, she may as well have; time ceased to exist.

Finally, out of breath, stiff, and emotionally shattered, she crawled to Jacob. Max limped to her, nuzzled her neck. He whimpered as she pulled him close to her.

"Jacob," Calay's voice croaked. She reached for him.

Jacob groaned in reply, holding his stomach. The metallic stench of blood was thick in the air. His. Hers. Tess's. Calay's heart lurched, her eyes grew heavy. There wasn't anything she could do to save Tess. Maybe there never was. But there was still a possibility she could help Jacob.

She remembered she'd seen a first aid kit on the table when she initially arrived. Shaking and dizzy, she pressed herself to stand. She braced herself and made her way to the table—or what was left of it—and retrieved the box.

"Jacob," she pleaded as she kneeled and then collapsed at his side, "I need to get at the wound."

He didn't respond.

"Jacob, move your fucking hands."

He moved his hands.

Calay worked to patch up the area as best she could, knowing he'd heal in due time. It was the way he was built—who he was, what he was. If he was human, he would have been long since dead. A tingle made its way down her spine as she realized it was the first time that she was glad he wasn't.

He rolled over and gazed up at her. His blue eyes clear and full of affection. And unconditional love. He smiled. Behind the darkness that lingered, he looked almost childlike. Almost.

"I have to tell you something," Calay started.

"No, you don't," he whispered, raising his fingers to tuck a handful of wet strands behind her ear, "you don't have to tell me anything. You don't have to do anything you don't want to Calay. I won't push you anymore."

She took a deep breath, relieved. Then, she told him anyway.

"I need you, Jacob."

It was the first time she'd admitted that to him. It was the first time she'd admitted it to herself. She didn't dare allow herself to love him. At least, she didn't think she did. But she knew one thing for certain: she couldn't do this alone. She needed somewhere to belong. A home. Maybe he could be that place for her, maybe not. She wasn't ready to explore that. She didn't know if she ever would be. But she knew if she didn't keep that door open, she'd never walk through it.

"I need you too," he murmured between labored breaths. An uneven exhale escaped his lips. His hand grasped the back of her hair and held strong. Jacob nodded. Calay knew he loved her in a way he didn't know how to express or make her understand. She couldn't. Not yet.

Calay curled into Jacob's chest and he wrapped her in his arms, pulling her tight against him.

It was the first time they'd been completely honest with each other. All the cards were on the table. No lies. No deception. No secrets.

This was real.

CALAY, JACOB, AND MAX LABORED OUT OF THE CAVE SLOWLY. They made their way into the bright sunshine.

On one side, the meadow she'd crossed to get to Tess. It felt bigger before. An expansive ocean of wildflowers and dark skies. It seemed small now. A gentle breath of fresh air amongst giants. The forest loomed before them, full of both danger and respite. On the other side, the ocean glittered far below.

The three of them walked to the cliff's edge and looked at the waves.

"When did it go so wrong?" Calay pulled the gold chains out of her pocket. The metal seemed duller, the clasp on one was broken.

"When did what go so wrong?"

"All of it."

Calay felt Jacob's hand rest on her shoulder. She knew he didn't have an answer for her. That he couldn't possibly tell her when humans chose fear over love. When—if—they would ever choose something else. Something better.

The Resistance had things backwards and they were slowly killing what was left of humanity.

"We can't be the only ones, Jacob."

"We can't."

"I can't be the only one…"

"I'm sure you're not."

"The Resistance—and The Society, whatever it is—needs to be stopped."

"How do you suppose we do that?"

"I don't know," Calay admitted, her gaze falling to the rocks below, "but the aliens are here. And if there's more like me, coexistence is the only reasonable way forward. The only way we survive."

Calay and Jacob blinked at each other. *Can we survive?* Calay wasn't ready to find out the answer. She let the words hang unsaid.

"How did you find us Jacob?"

"How do I always find you?" He grinned down at her.

She kicked some loose shale over the edge as she thought about her answer.

"Heat signatures?"

He smiled and nodded.

"But how did you get through the tunnel? There was water…everywhere."

"I told you we have our ways."

Calay wondered if she could ever find true comfort in their ways. In his arms. Or if she'd ever find a home to belong to. On Earth, or in a new galaxy. A planet far from this one.

"I don't know what to do next."

"Do we ever really know what to do?"

She nodded; it was true. Hindsight was twenty-twenty and the future was…unreliable. Calay stood there, on the edge of the cliff, silent. All she knew was that she didn't know who they were anymore. *Do we really ever really know anyone? Human, alien, or otherwise?* One thing she'd learned, was that the Other is Us. In the same moment we were both alone and not. Dichotomies were everywhere. And so was life. Here on Earth and in galaxies far, far away.

A chill unfolded down Calay's spine. She reached for Jacob's hand. Whatever storm was brewing in the skies earlier that morning was gone. The sun sparkled across an endless sea, the shadows that chased her up the mountain and to this place, laid to rest for another day.

"Now what?" she wondered.

It was all that ever was. All that ever would be.

※

Thank you for reading! Did you enjoy? Please add your review because nothing helps an author more and encourages readers to take a chance on a book than a review.

And don't miss more in the *The Broken Stars* series coming soon! Until then read ADRIFT IN STARLIGHT by City Owl Author, Mindi Briar. Turn the page for a sneak peek!

Also be sure to sign up for the City Owl Press newsletter to receive notice of all book releases!

SNEAK PEEK OF ADRIFT IN STARLIGHT
BY MINDI BRIAR

There's less than an hour left until the courtesan house opens for business. It's mid-afternoon in Hepburn, one of the wealthiest cities on the glamorous, celebrity-studded planet of Monroe. Half of my colleagues are still in pajamas, fogging up the dozens of mirrors that line every wall in the gilded underground boarding house we call home. I'm dusting powder across my cheeks as I sit on the floor, leaning back against my friend Perry's knees as he braids my hair. He's telling me all about the date his boyfriend took him on last weekend, but he has to whisper because our matchmaker, Nita, doesn't like it when "the talent" dates people for free.

"And then it turned out the spot he picked for dinner was right on the lookout point above this gorgeous waterfall! It was so romantic, Tai, you wouldn't *believe*." Perry sighs happily.

"Oh, I believe." I've heard every detail of their last three outings. Either Perry is stealing date stories from romantic comedies, or he's managed to find the only person on this planet who's as disgustingly mushy as he is.

"You're just jealous," Perry teases, poking my cheek.

"You caught me. Darling, I love you. Tell Henrik I'll fight him to the death for the honor of your hand." We both descend into giggles, drawing annoyed looks from our colleagues.

Perry ruffles my hair. "I do wish you wouldn't be so cynical, Tai. Love is nice. You should try it sometime."

"It's messy," I say, tilting my head back to frown at him. "You know I don't do romance unless—"

"—they're paying you double, yeah, yeah." He rolls his eyes. "You're missing out. Right, Eliana?"

The red-haired courtesan wrinkles her nose. "Still not telling you anything about my girlfriend, Per."

"Oh, come on! I need details—"

Nita sweeps into the room, curly-toed slippers silent on the plush, pink carpet. Perry snaps his mouth shut mid-sentence, and we all sit up a little straighter. We're not bound by slave contracts like the employees of less reputable pleasure-houses; Nita doesn't own us. But without her our paychecks would be a lot smaller. She's the one who advertises our services under the name "Lovelace's Lovelies." She background-checks each client, making sure they've got no history of violent abuse or transmittable diseases, and then she facilitates "introductions." If we're in her good graces, she sends us the pretty ones first.

"Titan Valentino," she calls.

I accidentally drop my makeup brush, scattering pale-pink powder across the carpet. Luckily, it matches.

Perry nudges my shoulder with his knee, reminding me to answer. I clear my throat. "Yes?"

"Your presence has been requested in my office."

Nita doesn't normally let clients in here before open hours. If she's made an exception, that means I've been singled out by someone extremely wealthy, extremely famous, or both. I climb to my feet, running my fingers through my long, blond hair to undo Perry's braiding.

I turn around to raise my eyebrows at him, and he mouths, *Good luck*, grinning.

Nita's office is positioned right by the lobby so that every client entering the building has to pass in front of her watchful gaze. In addition to several screens displaying the security cambot footage, the office contains two soft-cushioned armchairs and a magenta loveseat shaped like a lipsticked mouth.

One armchair is occupied. As Nita ushers me in, the client turns around, and I have to work to keep my expression neutral.

Xander Bose. The actor's face is instantly recognizable even though I haven't watched any of the trashy action holos he tends to star in. I believe his last role was in *Hovercycle Gang III*. Perry saw it without me, and he said, quote, "I'd like two hours, fifteen credits, and half my brain cells back."

Xander has the confident, careless presence of a man who's accustomed to everyone adoring him. His shoulders are almost broader than Nita's armchair. His arms bulge with muscle, but his face—clean of the blood, sweat, and dirt they smear onto him during fight scenes—looks surprisingly young. Maybe it's the chin dimple.

I turn my manners up to full blast. "Welcome to Lovelace's, Mas Bose. It's a pleasure to meet you. To what do I owe the honor?"

Xander looks me over, from the curling ends of my golden hair, to the feminine sweep of my overrobe, to the heeled slippers on my feet. There's a flash of lust—so predictable, these clients—but mostly his gaze is calculating. As if he's comparing me to something.

"She's more femme than I expected, but that might be good," he says, ignoring me to address Nina. "She can find out if my fiancée secretly likes women."

I open my mouth to protest, but Nita beats me to it. "Mx. Valentino is gender-neutral. They use the pronoun *they*, not *she*."

"Oh." Xander looks me over again. "Sorry."

"Have a seat, Titan," Nita says, indicating the other armchair. I sit, arranging my robe in a delicate fall of silk around me.

The current fashion is for both men and women to wear loose, open-front robes over their regular garments. Men's robes tend to be darker colors, with boxy sleeves and a hem that stops at the ankle, while women's robes are bright and extensively decorated, with long, draping sleeves. Formal styles allow the hem to drag behind in a sort of light, fluttering train.

It's the feminine style that I've been drawn to for as long as I can remember, though I was assigned male at birth. Xander's confusion is a common mistake. Although gender-fluid and gender-neutral people are widely accepted as normal, we are still a minority. People are trained by society and language to auto-assign strangers a binary gender based on their clothes or their hairstyles or their jewelry. Most folks don't intend to be cruel when they misgender me, but I hate having to correct them regardless.

"Mas Bose approached me this morning with an interesting proposal," Nita says, folding her hands on her desk. She nods at Xander, waiting for him to fill me in.

Xander seems a little flustered. "Er, so, I'm engaged."

"Congratulations," I murmur. The courtesan house is no stranger to clients who are otherwise partnered. People have all sorts of needs that their marriages can't fulfill. Maybe Xander is here to hire companionship for an engagement party?

"My fiancée is...ah...different," Xander says.

I wait for him to elaborate.

"She's...well, I didn't really pick her, to be honest," he blurts. "It was an arrangement with her father. He's a patron of the arts, big fan of my work. Wants grandkids to carry on the family legacy and all that. He said I've got the right genetics."

I suppress the urge to wince. Some people are way too into genetic purity, keeping their bloodline "Earth Classic" with no gen-mods or cross-species marriages. Those people tend to be the sort I'd rather not spend time with. Particularly because my parents were gen-modded.

"He's a lord, and he's massively rich, so I agreed to marry his daughter," Xander goes on. "But that was before I met her. She's a thirty-year-old virgin, if you can believe it. Never dated before at all. Won't kiss me, won't hug me, won't even let me touch her. Stars know how I'm s'posed to make babies with this glitch, if she won't come near me with a three-meter stick."

Now I'm really struggling to keep a straight face. Has Xander come to ask a courtesan for tips on how to romance his bride-to-be? With those holo-star cheekbones, I'll bet he's never had to put in any effort to get a woman to like him. *Oh, this is hilarious. Wait 'til I tell Perry.*

"I'm sure we can help—" I start to say.

But Xander keeps going. "So I figured, why not get a professional to soften her up for me a bit? Y'know. Seduce her. Show her how to have fun."

Oh. Hmm. That's not where I expected him to go with this.

"Are you sure you don't want us to…just…give you some advice on how to approach her?" I ask.

"Oh, yeah, that'll help too!" Xander says eagerly. "You can report back and tell me how she likes it. What gets her hot. That sort of stuff."

Stars. This man has to be the laziest lover I've ever encountered—and I've seen some bad ones in my time. I feel sorry for his future wife.

His future wife, whom *I'm* supposed to seduce.

"Why me?" I ask. I assume Nita gave Xander her full catalog of courtesan profiles to look through. I would have thought Xander would want to choose someone who resembled himself. Kellan and Breck are both muscular, dark-haired, male courtesans. Why choose me, a femme-presenting, tall, slim blonde?

Xander looks at Nita. Nita looks at Xander, then back at me. "I told him," she admits.

"You told him what?" I usually take care to pitch my voice at a soft tenor, but the words come out as more of a growl.

"She told me about your special ability," says Xander, tapping a finger to his temple. "You've got a computer in your *brain*. Never heard of that before! I thought they banned brain implants a long time ago 'cause it was too dangerous."

He's right. Cybernetic brain enhancements were banned in the tenth century D.E. Most modern cyborgs wear a headset to transmit brain signals to their tech parts rather than having the hardware implanted straight into their brain.

I'm the exception. The lucky, cursed exception.

"She said you have some kind of, like, body language translator that helps you know how to approach difficult people. I thought, *yeah, that'd be great*, 'cause my fiancée is totally difficult."

"*Nita.*" Anger roughens my throat. She and Perry are the only two people in this house who know the truth about my condition. I swore them to absolute secrecy, but it seems Nita chose to disregard that. She tends to view my tech-brain as an asset, assigning me to ultra-picky clients who don't know what they want. And yeah, all right, my body language reader *does* make me good at my job. But it's not as though I became a cyborg for the career opportunities.

"Oh, but it wasn't just that," Xander babbles on. "She said you're one of the most popular courtesans in this house. She said *everyone* loves you."

Not untrue. I've had seven marriage proposals in the last five years. But I wish Nita had stuck with *that* pitch and glossed over the part where I'm a cyborg with semi-illegal brain augmentation.

Nita murmurs to Xander that he should mention the reward.

"Oh yeah!" he says. "Almost forgot about that." And he names a number that's so high, I almost weep. That many credits could change my life. I could finally pay off my medical debt—maybe even have a little left over.

"I'm in," I say. There's no room for misgivings in my mercenary heart. I can't even stay angry at Nita for her loose tongue—I need those credits too badly.

Nita smirks. "Thought so."

We chat for a while longer, working out the details of the job. Xander's "plan" is woefully weak, but easy enough to follow. I'll pretend to be one of his actor friends and introduce myself to his fiancée at a party. From there, Xander says, "You can do whatever you want. Take her on dates, romance her, bang her brains out for all I care. But you can't make her fall for you, obviously. Just, like, get her juiced up for me, right?"

I know how the heart works, and I don't think this is going to play out as easy as Xander thinks it will. But the promise of that reward is enough to keep me from asking too many questions. For that number of credits, I'd do just about anything.

※

The following evening, Xander sends a hovercar to pick me up. I'm not a car person, but Perry is, and he gasps when he sees it: a sleek, luxurious model painted with reddish-blue multichrome. "That's a celebrity car if I ever saw one," he says.

Eliana pokes her head out of her room as I ascend the staircase. "What's going on? Has some big-time actor hired you as their date to an awards gala? You're going to need to wear something much prettier than that old rag."

"That old rag" is my best robe—ivy-green, embroidered with swirls and starbursts in glittering gold. I flash her a rude hand gesture and check my makeup one more time in the hall mirror. It's flawless, of course. Perry is one of the best makeup artists in Hepburn.

It's a longer drive than I expected, far outside the city limits. The hovercar purrs along on autopilot, so I crane my neck to look out the window, watching the city lights fade in our wake. Monroe's landmasses are covered in jagged mountain ranges with cities clustered in the valleys. It begins to snow as we ascend farther up the slope, gravity pushing me back into my seat as the incline steepens.

At last, the hovercar pulls up to a huge gate. As it swings open, the headlights catch a glint of gold.

Xander said the place was a mansion belonging to his fiancée's father, Lord Malik. But as I step out of the hovercar, I'm thinking it looks more like a *palace*. It's a good thing I dressed to impress, because the "party" appears to be a ball worthy of the Imperial Court. I lift the hem of my robe as I climb the steps to the wide-open front doors, wincing at the thump of the bass. I'm a "quiet piano music" person, not…whatever this is. *Ugh.*

A guardbot stops me before I can enter. It's a newer model, a domed torso on wheels with a scan-screen embedded in its chest. All down its side, blasters are mounted on swiveling arms. I count ten of them—enough to riddle me with more holes than a box of doughnuts—before the guardbot drones, "Identification, please."

I hold out my wrist so the bot can scan my keycuff—the identity bracelet that carries my credit balance, my friends' call codes, and the files that prove I'm a legal citizen of Monroe. Mine also has, among other apps, a bio-monitoring program that's supposed to warn me in advance of a seizure. That's one downside of having tech installed in my brain: when it glitches, so do I.

"Mx. Titan Valentino," the bot drones. "You are cleared to enter."

But I don't go directly into the ballroom. I walk the length of the hallway, admiring the opulence all around me. Bluish ambient lights glow from the walls, and there are several luminescent paintings, which I recognize as the work of a famous artist. They sell for millions of credits, and this house just casually has a whole hallway lined with them.

This is deep water I've jumped into. I hope I don't end up regretting this.

Accessing the uniweb with my tech-brain, I do a quick search on the fiancée's name. *Aisha Malik.* There are plenty of society pages mentioning her father, Lord Laban Malik. He's friends with Monroe's governing council. He spends millions at charity art auctions. The Emperor just granted him governorship of *another* mining colony.

But Aisha seems to stay largely out of the spotlight. The only pics I can find are professional headshots posted on some museum's "meet our staff" page. If she has a social profile, it's set to max privacy, because there's not a single candid pic of Aisha Malik floating around the uniweb.

In her most recent pic, her curly, black hair is tied in a low ponytail. She wears minimal makeup, highlighting her lack of cosmetic gene modifications. There's no symmetrical perfection in her features: nose a little too big, eyes round, brows unruly, full lips unsmiling. She looks as though she had to be coerced into taking this portrait.

Still, I wouldn't say she's unattractive. There's a bright intelligence in those wide, dark eyes. A spark of fighting spirit in the tight set of her mouth. She looks…interesting. Someone I might be friends with.

I dive a little deeper into the uniweb search and discover that she's a curator for the Imperial Museum of Galactic History. Her name has been in the newsies recently because she's putting together an exhibit on some alien civilization. The exhibit opens to the public in two days. *Ooh. Date idea?*

I suppose I can't put this off any longer. I steel my ears against the grating music and step inside the ballroom.

The scene is colorful chaos. Each guest has tried to outdo the next one with ostentatious fashion displays. Beads, gems, and glittery makeup catch the multicolored lights, refracting rainbows across my vision. In the center of the dance floor, there's an active antigrav field, allowing dancers to float up to the vaulted ceiling as they twirl and gyrate. Expensive perfumes war for dominance over the sweet smell of cake wafting from the snack buffet off to my left.

I scan the room for Xander and spot his broad shoulders encased in a chestnut-brown robe bedazzled with garnets. He's striding purposefully toward the snack table. I follow his trajectory, and that's when I notice Aisha Malik, looking regal in a sweeping purple robe. Her eye-catching fashion makes her hard to miss—as does the fact that she's resolutely skulking against the wall, refusing to join in the merriment.

I activate my body language reader and stand in the doorway of the ballroom, watching her. She's content to stay in the shadows, barely condescending to speak to anyone. It's not that she's shy; her stance shows plenty of self-confidence. It's that she thinks all these people are boring as blazes. She's not wrong. They're far enough up their own asses to see the light when they speak.

Xander sees me and swerves, coming to stand next to me instead of intercepting Aisha. "Good. You came," he says. "Let's go introduce you to her."

"Not yet." I turn to him; the app reads impatience and nervousness in his stance. "You go talk to her first. I want to see how she reacts to you."

✳

Don't stop now. Keep reading with your copy of <u>ADRIFT IN STARLIGHT</u>, by City Owl Author, Mindi Briar!

And sign up for the latest news, giveaways, and more from Kristy Gardner at here.

Don't miss more of *The Broken Stars* series, coming soon, and find more from Kristy Gardner at kristygardner.com

Until then, discover ADRIFT IN STARLIGHT, by City Owl Author, Mindi Briar!

✺

When set adrift in the universe, some things are worth holding onto.

Titan Valentino has been offered a job they can't refuse.
Tai, a gender-neutral courtesan, receives a scandalous proposition: seduce an actor's virgin fiancée. The money is enough to pay off Tai's crushing medical debt, a tantalizing prospect.

Too bad Aisha Malik isn't the easy target they expect.
A standoffish historian who hates to be touched, she's laser-focused on her career, and completely unaware that her marriage has been arranged behind her back. This could be the one instance where Tai's charm and charisma fail them.

Then an accidental heist throws them together as partners in crime.
Fleeing from the Authorities, they're dragged into one adventure after another: alien planets, pirate duels, and narrow escapes from the law. As Tai and Aisha open up to each other, deeper feelings kindle between them. But that reward money still hangs over Tai's head. Telling Aisha the truth could ruin everything...

Their freedom, their career, and their blossoming love all hang in the balance. To save one might mean sacrificing the rest.

✺

Please sign up for the City Owl Press newsletter for chances to win special subscriber-only contests and giveaways as well as receiving information on upcoming releases and special excerpts.

All reviews are **welcome** and **appreciated**. Please consider leaving one on your favorite social media and book buying sites.

For books in the world of romance and speculative fiction that embody Innovation, Creativity, and Affordability, check out City Owl Press at www.cityowlpress.com.

ACKNOWLEDGMENTS

This book has lived inside me a long time. I am grateful for the many people who have supported me in getting it into your hands. I'll never be able to thank them enough, but I'll try.

I am immeasurably grateful to my agent, Julie Gwinn, and the team at The Seymour Agency. Thank you for making my dreams come true and for believing in my book from the very beginning. I am honoured to have you by my side.

To my talented editors, I'm not worthy. Thank you. To Michelle Martis, for suffering through my never-ending Canadianisms. To Danielle DeVor, for challenging me to take this book deeper. Dirtier. Darker. To the fiercely talented Tina, Yelena, and the whole team at City Owl Press and MiblArt, for bringing this book to the world and making it something more than the sum of its parts. It's indefinitely better because of all of you.

To my beta readers who were willing to brave reading my first novel before I knew what the hell I was doing: Alina, Emily, Andrew, other Andrew, and Adriaan.

To my rideordie, my husband, and my best friend, Tyrone. You graciously give me the space, time, and kind support to emotionally process not only the writing journey, but life. Thank you for believing in me when I don't, being my partner, our ally, and never being afraid to be the first on the dance floor.

To my Momma, thank you for the endless supply of various writing instruments, notebooks, support, and courage. You make me feel brave(r).

To Sweeney, thank you for letting me squat on your patio day after day and giving me a safe space to write the hardest parts of this book.

To my friends and family, both IRL and online, who have offered support, enthusiasm, and encouragement. I love you.

To my writing community, you give me light when there is only darkness.

To anyone who recommends this book to friends, who posts it on social media, or leaves a rating and review, you have my eternal gratitude. It really does make a difference for writers, like me, whose dream it is to sell enough books to write more.

To you: writing makes my aching soul feel alive. It's my excruciating hope you enjoyed this story and the future ones to come. I write the stories I want to read, but truthfully, they're all for you. If the stars should align and we're fortunate enough to find ourselves in the same room, please say hello.

ABOUT THE AUTHOR

KRISTY GARDNER is a queer sci-fi fantasy writer, author of the award-winning cookbook, *Cooking with Cocktails*, and coffee addict. Furnished with degrees in Gender Studies & Sociology, she crafts complex female characters who adventure through space, time, and emotional maelstroms questioning what identity – and home – really mean.

When she's not jet-setting words on her laptop, she's chasing stars, mountain adventures, belly laughs, curating playlists for her books, and packing her carry-on for another escape to SE Asia. She resides in Vancouver, BC with her partner and 90 pound rescued American Bulldog.

The Stars in Their Eyes is her first novel.

kristygardner.com

twitter.com/kristygauthor
instagram.com/kristy_gardner
tiktok.com/@kristy_gardner

ABOUT THE PUBLISHER

City Owl Press is a cutting edge indie publishing company, bringing the world of romance and speculative fiction to discerning readers.

Escape Your World. Get Lost in Ours!

www.cityowlpress.com

facebook.com/YourCityOwlPress
twitter.com/cityowlpress
instagram.com/cityowlbooks
pinterest.com/cityowlpress